Good Girl

Christina Frank

iUniverse

GOOD GIRL

Copyright © 2016 Christina Frank.

All rights reserved. No part of this book may be used or reproduced by any means, graphic, electronic, or mechanical, including photocopying, recording, taping or by any information storage retrieval system without the written permission of the author except in the case of brief quotations embodied in critical articles and reviews.

iUniverse books may be ordered through booksellers or by contacting:

iUniverse
1663 Liberty Drive
Bloomington, IN 47403
www.iuniverse.com
1-800-Authors (1-800-288-4677)

Because of the dynamic nature of the Internet, any web addresses or links contained in this book may have changed since publication and may no longer be valid. The views expressed in this work are solely those of the author and do not necessarily reflect the views of the publisher, and the publisher hereby disclaims any responsibility for them.

Any people depicted in stock imagery provided by Thinkstock are models, and such images are being used for illustrative purposes only. Certain stock imagery © Thinkstock.

ISBN: 978-1-4917-9772-3 (sc)
ISBN: 978-1-4917-9773-0 (e)

Library of Congress Control Number: 2016909580

Print information available on the last page.

iUniverse rev. date: 6/16/2016

*For my parents, my husband, and my children.
You are my everything.*

Chapter 1

The shiny black limousine wobbles its way along the curb in front of our pizza shop. My five sisters and I laugh hysterically from our hiding place behind the faded For Sale sign propped up in the window. The car and its pancake-flat tire bump one last time before coming to a thudding halt.

To say a limousine driving down the streets of our New Jersey town is rare would be an understatement. Occasionally, one comes through on its way to a wedding or a funeral, but that is all.

Somehow, the sight of this one unexpectedly stranded here has us in stitches. Nothing ever happens in this worn-out town, so this is entertainment.

The red-and-green neon sign announcing Rossi's Pizza blinks above our heads. Along with our father, my sisters and I work twelve-hour days trying to keep the shop alive. But we are failing, and we know it. The bills are piling up, and Poppy's health is failing. Each day, I worry, watching him struggle to do the little he can. For the sake of us all, we have no choice but to sell.

"Oh my God, someone's getting out!" my sister Mia screams.

The windows of the car are tinted, so we are anxious to see who will appear. The uniformed driver—a clean-cut blond gentleman in his mid-thirties—exits from his side of the car and comes around to open the back passenger door. We watch expectantly. After a moment, a man also in his mid-thirties gracefully climbs out of the backseat. He wears a black suit, white shirt, and red tie. His black aviator sunglasses make his eyes a mystery I can't help but want to solve. He has short black hair that falls perfectly on top of his head. With movie-star looks and perfect features, he is lean yet muscular, and he is tall, about six foot three or four, but not overbearing. He has a perfect tan. Absolutely gorgeous, he is the kind of guy one would stare at and naturally wonder who he might be. People who look like him usually are somebody.

My sisters gasp collectively.

The stranger squints up into the bright sunlight and then reaches up to his tie to yank the knot free.

More gasping ensues. There is something hot about a man undoing his tie.

Once the tie is free, he tosses it carelessly into the backseat before pushing the car door shut. As he unbuttons his collar with one hand, he takes off his sunglasses with the other.

Suddenly, he glances toward the window.

My five sisters scream and jump before scattering like little girls. When he sees this, a small, amused smile crosses his lips. Only I remain standing, and in that moment, we make eye contact. His smile fades, replaced by a look of intrigue. I blush, hold my breath, and look away.

※

The next afternoon, the door chimes jingle with the sound of approaching footsteps.

"Can I help you?" I don't bother to look up from the magazine I'm leafing through.

Finding out the latest on William and Kate is far more interesting than whatever—or whoever—has just wandered through the shop door. After all, it's difficult to get excited over another slice of pizza.

"I'd like a Coke, please."

I look up, and standing right in front of me is the man from the day before. My throat closes, and I have to keep from appearing too startled. He is even more gorgeous close up. This time, he's dressed in a casual white button-down shirt and jeans. Again, his aviators are hanging from his collar. His eyes—no longer a mystery—are baby blue, and the way they contrast his jet-black hair and tan skin is breathtaking. Over his shoulder, I can see a sleek red convertible Mercedes parked illegally on the curb outside. There is no limo this time.

Speechless, I turn to retrieve his drink. I can feel his eyes on me and my face flushing.

When I turn back with his Coke, he slides two dollars across the counter toward me. I take the money and fumble with the register—which I have been working since I was six years old—and make his change. I drop the random coins into his hand without making contact.

"Thank you," I mutter.

"You're welcome." He nods and then pauses and stares at me for just a second, as if he can see right through me. "Noah," he says, offering his hand with only the slightest of smiles. "Noah Bentley."

I gulp and let his hand hang there for a moment before realizing that I should shake it. "Gabby," I manage as I apprehensively offer two fingers to shake. Then I add clumsily, "Rossi."

This makes him grin, which instantly makes me blush. He turns away, and I think he might leave, but instead, he begins to walk the perimeter of the shop, looking at the photographs that line the walls: family photos of my parents, my grandparents, and my five sisters and me in all stages of growing up. He is halfway around the room, when he pauses. "I like this one," he announces. He has stopped at the only photo of me by myself. I am about seven, my hair is in pigtails, and I'm wearing a pink dress and Mary Janes.

Thankfully, he doesn't look up to see my reddening cheeks. What is it about this guy that makes me blush?

Noah moves on, continuing to view the photos. I'm mesmerized watching him. He is incredibly comfortable in his own skin; he moves with grace and, every once in a while, takes a sip of his Coke.

"I see the place is for sale," he says when he stops by a photo of my grandparents on their wedding day.

"Yes," I manage. "My father is selling it." The obvious sounds dumb coming out of my mouth.

He nods. "I might be looking for some property on this street."

My eyes widen. I cannot believe my ears. We haven't had so much as a looker in four years. My heart begins to beat wildly. "Would you like me to get my father?" I ask urgently.

"No, not yet," he says.

I frown.

"What I'd like to do," he says before slowly taking the last sip of his drink, "is see what else is on this block."

"That matters?" I ask.

"From a business standpoint, it does."

I suddenly feel embarrassed that I've even asked.

"Would you be free to show me around?" He faces me now. His expression is impossible to read. Surely, he can walk himself down the street. My mind races. No matter how soft his words are, he is intimidating me. But the opportunity to sell the shop would mean the world to my family. Selling for the right price would not only enable us to get out from under but also give us the chance to start new lives.

"I guess I could." I shrug casually, trying to hide my hesitancy. After all, it is just a walk down the street. "Give me a second."

He looks directly at me, and his unreadable expression becomes a smile. "Good girl," he says.

I blink, unable to take my eyes from his. He makes me feel like a child yet not like a child at all. I go into the back to grab my sweater and tell my sisters to watch the front. I wish I had worn my good jeans.

Back up front, I meet him around the counter. He holds the door open for me. The door chimes obnoxiously, and I look back just long enough to see Teresa, Mia, Gina, Maria, and Angela gaping at us as we walk out the door.

Noah and I walk along the sidewalk. There isn't much to see. My heart sinks as I show him the struggling family-owned businesses that lie between the boarded-up storefronts. I tell him what is and what has been. He listens attentively and nods. He acts interested, but I am not sure how he can be. I can't help but pray that I am a good-enough saleswoman to pull this off. We've almost reached the end of the block, when he pauses outside of Luciano's Ice Cream.

"My treat," he says, and he opens the door for me. Oddly, he says this as a statement. We go inside, and without asking what I want, Noah orders us two vanilla cones. He pays and leaves a generous tip.

Lisa, who owns the shop, leans forward as she hands me my cone and whispers, though not softly enough, "I approve." I glance sideways. He pretends not to hear, but I know he does. I make a mental note to smack Lisa later.

We walk slowly back up to the pizza shop in silence, enjoying the ice cream. Everyone who passes stares at him. He has that kind of magnetism. When we reach the door, he smiles down at me. "Thank you for the tour, Gabriella," he says.

I blink. I'm surprised that he uses my given name. "Thank you for the ice cream," I say.

"I'll need to come back tomorrow for one last look," he says.

I nod.

"I'll be back about four," he says. Again, he is telling, not asking. I watch as he gracefully climbs into his shiny red sports car. I continue to watch as he disappears.

༄

"Ice cream!" I insist. "It was just ice cream. Nothing more." I all but yell this at my sisters, who surround me mere moments after his car pulls away. "We will probably never even see him again."

Part of me wonders if this is true. Maybe I will see him again. Maybe I won't. Either way, I decide I'll keep the fact that we might have a buyer for the shop to myself and see where it goes before I get everyone's hopes up.

Chapter 2

"He's back!" Mia screeches from the front of the shop.

I am in the back, stirring spaghetti sauce. I glance up at the clock. It is exactly 4:00 p.m. *Punctual.*

"Your Knightly's back," she squeals.

Knightly is what my sisters and I call boyfriends, dates, and cute guys who come into the shop—our knights in shining armor.

"He's not my Knightly," I tell her.

"He just might be. Who knows? Think positive for once in your life, Gabby," she scolds.

Mia is now beside me, bouncing happily from one foot to the other.

"Mia, please." I sigh. "Get a grip."

"You get a grip. I can't believe this is happening to you," she gushes.

"Nothing is happening to me." I wipe my hands on a dish towel and straighten my skirt.

We both go out to the front. There he is, climbing

out of his limo as the driver holds the door dutifully. I wonder how he decides which car to bring. Noah's attire is formal again: a black suit, a white shirt, and the ever-present aviators. I study him and take in some air. He enters the shop and nods when he sees me, but he only offers the briefest smile. If I had blinked, I would have missed it. I decide smiling is a problem for him, something he only does when it's necessary. He doesn't approach the counter. Instead, I can tell he is waiting for me to go to him. His manner seems businesslike and, actually, a little unfriendly.

"Watch things," I tell Mia. I walk around to the other side of the counter. He makes no pretense about looking me up and down. I'm embarrassed, self-conscious about my pale blue skirt, white blouse, and sandals.

"Pretty," he says, referring to my outfit. I let out the breath that I don't realize I'm holding and wonder why I am glad to have pleased him.

༄

"Six months. One million dollars," Noah says without emotion. "That's my offer."

It is ten minutes later, and I am opposite him in the most secluded booth in our shop. My head is spinning. It is my turn to respond, but I am not sure I can.

"I will make your father richer than he has ever dreamed possible," he says. "One million dollars richer. He'll never have another worry in his life, Gabriella." Noah nods slightly toward Poppy, who is having one of his bad days. He struggles just to lift a pizza out from the top rack of the oven. My heart breaks at the sight.

"You'll buy the shop for one million dollars," I manage. My mouth is so dry it feels as if it is full of cotton. "And …" I'm unable to finish the thought.

"And I get you," he says like a man unfamiliar with patience. "For exactly six months, I get the pleasure of your company."

I gulp. "Why?" I ask.

He closes his eyes. "Why what?"

"Why me?"

"Too many reasons," he says. "And none of them are your concern."

I glance over at Poppy. Maria has now come to his aid.

"And he'll never know?"

"He'll never know a thing," Noah insists. "Only that he got a good deal on a failing business."

"What will you tell him?" I can't help but ask.

"Again, none of your concern," he says.

"Is this what you do?" I ask incredulously. "You take advantage of other people's misfortunes?" I don't try to hide the disdain in my voice. He raises an eyebrow as if in warning. I am trying to be brave, but his expression puts me in my place.

"Sometimes people make out quite well," he says. "Just like your father will."

If we don't run out of time.

Teresa has now brought Poppy a glass of water and is fanning him.

"You might not want to wait long to decide," Noah says, motioning toward Poppy.

"When does he get his money?"

"In exactly six months. After you fulfill your obligation."

"And what do I have to do?" I know now that I am making a deal with the devil. But then again, I wonder if he really is the devil. It seems as if he's the answer to my problem. Could he be both? "What is my obligation?"

"To please me," he says simply.

Not knowing why, I find myself intrigued as to what pleasing him means. The idea of finding out more about this man is appealing.

"If you leave before your time, he gets nothing."

A thought comes to me. "What if you tire of me?"

"A loophole." He laughs lightly. "You are a smart one—another attraction." He smirks. "I won't tire of you," he assures me.

I continue to look at him expectantly. He still hasn't answered my question.

He tilts his head to one side. "If, by chance, I tire of you, then he gets his money immediately," he answers curtly.

At least I have hatched my plan. I'll play along for a while, as long as it suits me. Then, when I've had enough, I'm sure I can push him far enough to realize that he's bargained with the wrong girl. I look over at Poppy. He is gray and trembling, holding his head in his hands.

"When? When do you need …" My mind is racing.

"You have exactly one week to decide," Noah says. "Then I retract my offer." He checks his watch; it is twenty-five after four. He slides a business card across the table to me. "I will hear from you by exactly four thirty next Friday, the eighteenth, or there's no deal."

I take the card. I nod. This can't be happening to me.

Noah rises from his seat and reaches out, tucking a fallen strand of hair behind my ear. He grazes my cheek with his hand as he pulls away. His touch makes me tingle. He replaces his aviators, turns, and walks out of the shop.

Chapter 3

The next week is excruciating. I have never been in a position like this before. I have no idea what to do and don't feel as if I can confide in anyone. I don't sleep or eat, and my mind races with endless scenarios. I feel as if I am a stranger in my own now-upside-down life. It's as if I'm sleepwalking.

My sisters constantly ask what is wrong, but I put them off, insisting that I am fine. I spend the rest of the week studying our situation. The mail arrives each day with yet another bill that we can barely pay. I watch Poppy's worried face as he opens each envelope. Physically, Poppy's condition is worsening. His heart is getting weaker, his color is grayer, and his gait is less steady. It makes me panic.

I study the faces of my sisters. We are all in this together. We always have been and always will be. We have made a vow that no one will leave, that we will stand by each other come what may—until there is literally no place left to stand.

But I know that we are nearing that time.

What will they think of me if I tell them that I have a job opportunity in New York City and am going to take it? How can I make them understand without explaining everything? This could change all of our lives for the better. I go back and forth all week: one day I am going, and the next, it's ridiculous. For an entire week, I walk around with Noah's business card tucked in my pocket. I reach into my pocket a million times a day, rub the card, and pray that the right decision somehow becomes clear to me.

My prayer is answered on Friday morning. Poppy falls while trying to lift a pizza from the top rack of the oven. Thankfully, we get him into a chair. It is a close call, but he is not badly hurt—not this time anyway. As my hysterical sisters surround him, my eyes fill with tears, and I go to the phone, unnoticed.

Trembling, I dial the number on the well-worn business card in my pocket. I keep one eye on the pathetic scene behind me. He answers the phone on the third ring.

"Yes?" he says simply.

"I'll do it."

"Say your good-byes," he tells me. "My driver, Liam, will collect you at exactly eight o'clock tomorrow evening."

The phone line goes dead as my heart skips a beat and falls into my stomach.

"I don't know," Poppy says. "It doesn't sound right."

"Oh, but it is," I say, willing my voice to sound calm and reassuring.

It is after eleven, and the shop is closed. I have waited until the end of the day to announce my news. My sisters have gathered and, for once, are quiet—speechless, actually. They are wide-eyed, happy for me, a little jealous—you name it.

"It's a secretarial job." I begin chattering frantically, making each word up as I go along. "With room for advancement. It's an opportunity."

I use this word intentionally—Poppy is big on opportunity. Ever since I was a little girl, he's talked endlessly about recognizing opportunity when we see it and making the most of it.

"You can do without me here," I point out. "Maybe I'll just try it for a while and see what happens."

"New York City is a big place," Poppy says, worried. "Where will you live?"

"I already have an apartment arranged," I lie. "I'll be safe. It's with a bunch of other girls," I say, adding to the pile of deception that I have already created.

"But so soon?"

"I don't want to miss this chance," I insist. We need to get off this subject. It is beginning to wear me down.

Finally, Poppy runs his hand over his balding head. He is worn out as well. "My first one to leave the nest," he muses, looking at me with sad eyes.

"I'll be fine," I whisper, and I kiss his cheek. I sigh

in relief. "And for sure, I'll be back." I say it as much for myself as for him.

I will be back in exactly 180 days—if not sooner, I think.

At the very least, I should be home by December.

※

We spend the entire next day at the shop saying goodbye. My sisters and I cry, hug, and kiss. Poppy looks on sadly.

"This is a good thing," I promise him.

At exactly 8:00 p.m., the shiny black limo pulls up to the curb in front of the pizza shop, and I turn white. I'm suddenly cold and clammy.

I watch as the driver, Liam, gets out of the car. He walks around the back of the car and enters the shop. He sees me behind the counter and nods. "Miss Rossi."

"I'll be just a minute," I say before turning to close my eyes and pray that I am somehow doing the right thing.

I go into the back. Thankfully, my sisters and father are all out of sight of Liam and the limo. Everyone is crying now. I give quick hugs to the girls and a long one to Poppy. I am doing this for him. Not knowing what else is left to do, I grab the small suitcase that holds my few possessions and walk out the door. Liam instantly takes the suitcase from me and deposits it into the trunk. He opens the back door of the car. Hurriedly, I climb in. We pull away.

Through the tinted glass, I watch as the world I know disappears behind me. My mind races as Liam drives. I am grateful that he attempts no small talk. I am also grateful for the tinted partition that separates us. This way, he can't see me shedding the tears I have been holding back all day.

I have no idea what I have gotten myself into, and I'm scared to death. I work on gathering what courage I have inside of me and concentrate on the only loophole I can see.

I must make Noah want to get rid of me.

I decide this will be my only goal—and I will start right away.

Chapter 4

Forty minutes later, we are in downtown Manhattan. The limo halts in front of an immense apartment building on Fifth Avenue. It is ultramodern, with silver tinted windows and sharp angles. The moonlight bounces off of it majestically, and I am mesmerized by the sight. Then I realize that Liam is speaking to me.

"Here we are, miss," he says again.

I am shaken from my fog and take a deep breath as he exits the car, retrieves my suitcase from the trunk, and opens the door for me. I gulp as my eyes well up a bit. This might be too much for me. I am a fish out of water.

When I was growing up in New Jersey, my time in Manhattan was limited to school fieldtrips. We never had the means to visit any other way. Cautiously, I step from the car. A doorman is already holding the immense glass door open for me and Liam. I look at Liam pleadingly. He smiles reassuringly but offers no words. Instead, he leads me to the elevator, and we step inside. I scan the buttons. There are fifty floors. The elevator operator swipes something like a credit card and presses the number fifty—it lights up. Apparently, you can't just get there by pressing the button. We zoom to the top, and my ears pop when I swallow. My stomach is in knots.

Everyone seems to know where we are going but me.

"Here we are," Liam says brightly when we stop. He nods to the other man, and then we step out into the most spectacular foyer I have ever seen. It is decorated in silver, gold, and mirrors. The floor is white marble with silver veins running through it. The walls are covered with paisley-print wallpaper and a gold mirror, under which a table sits. A huge, colorful floral arrangement stands on the table—next to house keys. My heart sinks.

He is home. I don't know what I expected, and I have to remind myself to breathe.

"There she is," a voice says lightly.

Suddenly, Noah is standing before me. He is breathtaking: barefoot and wearing worn blue jeans and a tight black T-shirt. I can't seem to look directly at him. Instead, for some reason, I study the veins in the marble tiles I am standing on.

Noah and Liam exchange nods, and I realize that Noah is dismissing Liam. Soundlessly, Liam backs out of the foyer, and then he is gone. I am unhappy to see him go and am feeling intimidated by being alone with Noah. Noah's extreme confidence somehow draws the insecurity out in me. I'm on my guard not to let this show.

"How was the ride in?" Noah asks. I only nod. "Are you hungry? Mrs. Middleton has dinner ready."

I don't know who Mrs. Middleton is, but I'm glad she's here, because that means we're not alone.

He is looking at me with a puzzled expression. "Follow," he commands before leading me out of the foyer.

I hate that he orders me, and I hate that I find myself doing as he says.

I follow him through a stunning great room. Plush white carpets, an equally plush white sectional couch, and a giant big-screen TV are the centerpieces of a room that boasts a gigantic fireplace and gold mantel. End tables with gold-and-crystal lamps and pretty paintings serve as accents everywhere. The room looks as if it belongs in a decorating magazine. I look both ways while crossing the room and see other elegant rooms, including one that looks like a library and another that might be a kitchen. The apartment seems to go on forever, and I suspect I have only seen a small part of it. I can't imagine anyone living in such luxury—not even in the movies.

Noah leads me to a glass doorway that opens onto a large balcony. I step out and look up to find a clear black sky dotted with stars. I look down at the bustling city below. On the balcony, a table for two has been set with white china and gold utensils. I wonder if this is normal for him.

"Sit," Noah orders.

Annoyed at being commanded, I hesitate long enough to show a touch of defiance. He watches me skeptically. Our eyes meet for just a moment. Disappointed in myself, I look away first. Then, with nothing else to do, I sit at my place at the table. He takes the seat across from me. I can feel his eyes on me but am unable to look up. Then, remembering that I have a plan, I gather my courage and meet his gaze with angry eyes. If I am uncooperative enough, I might be out of there by the end of the month. By the end of July, I could be home.

"I won't tire of you, so don't bother trying," he says.

The fact that he has read my mind scares me a bit. His new manners surprise me as well. I am so startled that without meaning to, I sit up a little straighter. "You will," I say.

He raises an eyebrow. "We disagree."

"We do."

"Then game on." He winks, expressionless.

Suddenly, a graceful woman appears with our dinner. She appears to be in her fifties, and she is blonde, fit, and immaculate. She is dressed smartly in a pale green skirt, white blouse, and low tan pumps.

"Mrs. Middleton," Noah announces.

She certainly doesn't dress like household help.

"This is Miss Gabriella Rossi. Gabriella, this is Mrs. Helen Middleton."

She smiles warmly at me, and I smile back. After all, she's not the one from whom I need to escape.

"Mrs. Middleton will tend to any needs of yours that I cannot," he says.

Mrs. Middleton nods, confirming this, and for some reason, I nod too, as if this is somehow okay. She sets plates of grilled salmon, baby carrots, and mashed potatoes in front of us; pours water from a bottle into our glasses; and then retreats back into the apartment.

"Gabriella," Noah says firmly, "I will not tire of you. You will be here for six months. I strongly advise you to settle in and cooperate."

"We'll see," I say, feigning a boldness that I don't feel. "If you tire of me before then, I get my money."

His eyes narrow, and he studies me. "I was hoping that we could do this the easy way, but it seems that you are determined to be difficult." He leans across the table and, with one finger, raises my chin so that our eyes are locked. "You do as you feel you need to for now," he says, "but in time, you will obey as you should."

His words make my blood boil. I hate the way he says the word *obey*. My face reddens, but this time, I am not blushing. "I don't obey," I announce.

"You will."

"I don't heel, sit, or speak on command either," I add. I don't know what has come over me. I've never spoken this way before in my life. But inside, I am panicking. The feeling of being trapped makes me strike out.

A small, condescending smile crosses his lips. He seems almost amused—which infuriates me. "Gabriella," he says so calmly that it makes me want to scream, "you will learn—hopefully sooner versus later—to do as you are told. I assure you of this."

I glare at him. His intense calm is somehow disarming. He is good at this war of words; I am not. I repeat the only words I can think of: "You'll tire of me."

"Well, I am not tired yet," he says. "So let's try to have a nice dinner on your first evening home."

"Home?" I ask incredulously. "This is not and never will be my home," I insist. He has crossed some sort of line that I didn't even know existed. New Jersey is my home. New York is not. Somehow, just hearing the word *home* makes my heart ache in my chest.

This time, he looks at me almost understandingly. "I can see how you might think that, and I understand that you feel that way now, but this is another thing I am certain of," he says coolly. "In time, you will come to realize that you are home and that there is no going back."

"You're a freak!" I whisper. His words frighten me, and out of panic, I've said the meanest thing I can think of. I am becoming unhinged. "What kind of man makes a deal like this? Are you too defective to get a girl on your own? A willing girl? One who wants to be with you instead of someone who has to?" I scowl with tears of anger dripping down my cheeks.

His face is impassive, but I must have touched a chord. "I think for you, Miss Rossi, dinner is over." His words are even and measured; as always, he is in complete control. "I don't believe you are in the correct frame of mind to share a meal right now. You are excused—and for future reference, you may not leave the table until you have been excused.

"Because tonight is your first night, I will overlook your smart mouth and poor behavior, and you will simply be sent to bed without your dinner. But don't expect me to be as understanding next time. A bath and bed are what you need," he says. "Mrs. Middleton will tend to you."

Seemingly from nowhere, Mrs. Middleton appears by my side, waiting for me to get up. I am at a loss. My anger consumes me. I find no words. Inside, I am screaming, but on the outside, I am paralyzed. However, as always, he is perfectly in control, his eyes like blue ice. My own eyes betray me as tears pool within them. Rising from the table, I refuse to let them fall. Like a child who is being punished, I follow Mrs. Middleton from the balcony. She leads me to a guest bedroom.

It is a beautiful room, large and spacious and decorated in all shades of pink. A white canopy bed is in the center, with night tables and ornate lamps on either side. The room has a separate sitting area with a lounge chair, and a lighted mirrored dressing table is in the corner. I just stand there, staring at the elegance.

"I'll draw you a bath," Mrs. Middleton says.

This is beyond odd for me. No one has ever drawn a bath for me. I sit on the edge of the bed, trying to calm my heart as it races in my chest. I look around the room, searching for my suitcase, but I can't find it. Mrs. Middleton reappears from the bathroom.

"Where is my bag?" I confront her a little more strongly than I intend. After all, she hasn't done anything to me.

She purses her lips and frowns sympathetically. "Let's just use new things for now," she suggests, trying to sound bright.

"Where is my bag?" I repeat, my words now biting. I am almost starting to panic, realizing that my purse and cell phone are gone as well.

"You will find plenty to wear in the walk-in behind you," another voice says. It is his voice. He is in the doorway.

"I want my own things," I insist.

"The clothes in the closet are yours now," he says curtly. Then, ignoring me, he turns to Mrs. Middleton. "If there are any problems, just let me know." I take this as a warning to me. Without looking at me again, he turns and walks from the doorway.

I open my mouth to protest, but he is gone. I am becoming weary. I rise from the bed and enter the bathroom. Mrs. Middleton leaves me to myself. The bathroom is nothing short of opulent, with gold fixtures and sparkling mirrors. The wallpaper is a burgundy floral print, and small, ornate photos dot the walls. Even here in the bathroom, a chandelier hangs overhead. The tub, which is now filled with bubbles, is huge.

I undress, leaving my clothes in a pile on the floor. I climb into the tub, sinking into the warm, sudsy water, and try to process what has happened so far. I wash myself slowly.

I am not sure I can handle this. Maybe I have made a terrible mistake. But I feel trapped. How can I go home now? I think of Poppy and the girls. If I can somehow pull this off, it will all be worth it. I console myself with the fact that I am sure I will wear Noah down and make him get rid of me before the six months are up. *He hasn't seen anything yet*, I promise myself.

I climb out of the tub and dry myself with the softest, most luxurious towel I have ever felt. Still wrapped in it, I go into the bedroom. Laid out on the bed is a pale pink baby doll nightie, a tiny top with matching panties. It is silk with satin trim. Mrs. Middleton appears. I frown.

"Those aren't my clothes."

Again, she is sympathetic. "They are now," she answers quietly. Again, my eyes fill with tears of frustration, anger, and embarrassment.

"I'll give you some privacy," she says. "If you need anything, I am close by."

Before she leaves, she turns and puts a plastic container in my hands. I open it up and know immediately that it contains birth control pills. I feel as if I am going to be sick.

"One a day." She nods sympathetically, reading my reaction. "I'll help you to remember," she promises. Then she turns and walks toward the door. Once there, she turns back to face me. "Gabriella," she says softly with a small, gentle smile that I am not sure she means, "it will all be okay."

I want to throw myself into her motherly arms and

ask her how she knows that, but she turns from the doorway and is gone.

Left alone, I put on the nightie. I walk to the full-length mirror that stands in the corner and study myself. I frown, feeling self-conscious in such a thing. I have never worn anything like this before. I find myself thin and gangly looking. I've always been the skinny one, except for my breasts, which have always been ampler and larger than those of most other girls. My black hair falls in messy ringlets past my shoulders and down my back.

What could a man who looks like him ever want with a plain Jane like me?

I sigh. Being alone has allowed me to somewhat collect myself, and I feel suddenly exhausted. Feeling like Goldilocks, I crawl into the bed, which Mrs. Middleton has already turned down. I snuggle into the plush comforter and satin sheets and fall soundly asleep.

Chapter 5

The next morning, I wake with a start. It takes me a moment to process where I am. I lie back down and try to calm my racing heart. I still can't believe what I have agreed to. I shudder and pull the covers up to my neck.

Someone, probably Mrs. Middleton, has drawn the drapes, so only a sliver of sunlight peeks through. I have no idea what time it is. I hear no noise and wonder where Mrs. Middleton and Noah are. I hope she is here and pray he is at work already. Someone who can afford all of this has got to work long hours. That should be a plus.

I get out of bed and tiptoe to the door. The plush carpet feels soft on my feet. I open the door carefully so that it makes no sound and slowly make my way down the hallway to the living quarters. I pass what I think is Noah's room, but the door is closed. Is it possible he is in there and still asleep? I pass several other rooms with the doors ajar. They all seem to be guest rooms, each more beautifully decorated than the next.

I can smell the aromas of freshly brewed coffee and bacon and guess that both Noah and Mrs. Middleton are awake. I reach the kitchen and peek around the corner, hoping not to be caught, but I am.

"Good morning," Noah says.

He is sitting at the counter with a cup of coffee, an empty plate beside him, and an open newspaper. He looks startlingly handsome; he is dressed in a black suit and tie, but his hair still has a sexy, slightly messy look. All of a sudden, I realize I am still in the pale pink nightie, and I could kick myself for giving him the pleasure of seeing me this scantily dressed.

Mrs. Middleton whisks the empty plate away from him and smiles warmly at me. "Good morning," she says softly before tending to duties on the other side of the spacious kitchen.

"Sit, Gabriella," he says, motioning toward the seat at the counter across from him.

I toy with the idea of declining but decide I can always fight with him later. I make my way to the stool, my bare feet padding against the marble floor. I climb up and sit, facing him.

He wears half a smile. "You must be hungry. Mrs. Middleton will have your breakfast momentarily."

Yes, of course I am hungry, I think. *After all, I'm the one you sent to bed without dinner last night, remember?* But I resist voicing this out loud, because I am hungry. The kitchen smells like heaven, and I don't want to be sent back to my room without breakfast.

"Did you sleep well?"

I offer half a nod.

"I'll take that as a yes," he says, "but I require eye contact and complete answers to my questions. Eyes and words."

I look at him incredulously. Who does he think he is?

"And there will be no more such looks," he says.

In spite of myself, I blink and do make eye contact. I have never met anyone so arrogant.

Thank goodness Mrs. Middleton breaks the gaze between us and arrives with my breakfast. It is a healthy portion of scrambled eggs, crispy bacon, wheat toast, and fresh fruit. I realize I am famished.

How do people live like this? I wonder. *With people catering to their every need, making things appear and disappear from seemingly nowhere?*

"Well, although I would prefer to sit with you while you enjoy your breakfast," he says, refolding the newspaper and rising from the stool, "I am already late for a meeting, so I need to leave now. But I will be home at six."

Without meaning to, I have given him my full attention, because my eyes seem to be glued to his.

"Today you are confined to the apartment," he says, "but you may not wander. You may spend your time in the common areas. My bedroom and study are off limits to you. Do you understand?"

I am confined to the apartment? He didn't tell me I was going to be imprisoned. This is crazy. I don't even know how to begin to argue with him about this.

When I don't answer right away, he raises both eyebrows. He intimidates me. His cold and calculated manner disarms me and makes it difficult for me to respond. Unable to think of anything to say, I nod, but he waits for more. Betraying myself, I swallow and say, "Yes. I understand."

It is a victory for him. He takes a step closer to me. He reaches out, tucks a loose strand of hair behind my ear, and then leans in and chastely kisses me on the forehead. "Good," he says before turning and walking from the apartment.

Unable to take my eyes off of him, I don't stop watching until he closes the door behind him. I have lost my appetite. I'm beginning to move off of the stool, when Mrs. Middleton says, "Gabriella, try to eat something."

I forgot she was there. I sigh. "I'm not hungry," I say. I am embarrassed that my eyes are once again filling. I don't like what this man is able to do to me.

"Please sit," she says before taking the stool across from me, where Noah once sat.

I sigh and sit. Again, I remind myself that I have nothing against her. Actually, I think I might like her.

"You're too thin as is," she says with a warm smile. "We don't want you getting any thinner."

I smile at her. She has a kind, motherly way about her.

"Let me reheat this for you," she says, reaching for the plate.

"No," I say, picking up the fork. "It's fine. Just sit with me."

"I will," she says, and we begin to talk.

I tell her about myself, my sisters, and Poppy. I tell her that my mother passed away four years ago. I tell her about working in the pizza shop and how it is struggling.

She tells me that she has worked for Mr. Bentley, as she calls him, for twelve years. She is widowed and has two successful grown sons. Their names are Adam and Andrew. I tell her I like those names, which makes her smile. She is proud of them. I ask her why she works, and she tells me that she likes to make a house a home. I tell her that this place looks more like a museum. She tells me to give it time.

The only thing we don't talk about is the elephant in the room: what in the world I'm doing here.

After a few minutes, I look down and realize that I have cleaned my plate. "I guess I was hungry," I admit sheepishly.

"I'm glad you ate."

With nothing else to say, I get up from the stool and head for the door. I stop in the doorway. "Mrs. Middleton?"

She turns.

"Thanks for breakfast and the talk," I say. "I'm glad you're here." When I am almost out the door, she stops me.

"Gabriella?"

I turn to face her.

"He's a good man."

I furrow my brow a bit, confused. From what I've

seen, I don't know how she believes this. I'm just about to ask her why, when she turns back to the sink and the dishes. I wait a moment, but she doesn't turn around, so I take her statement for what it's worth and walk away back down the hall to my room.

I go into the bathroom and wash up. I am only gone for minutes, but by the time I come back, the room is completely straightened up—the bed is remade, and clothing is laid out on it. Mrs. Middleton seems to be choosing my outfits.

Curiously, I go over to the walk-in closet in the corner of the room. It is larger than my entire bedroom at home, which I share with two of my sisters. I switch on the light and find racks and racks of brand-new clothes—all with the tags still on. There is an entire wall just for shoes. The clothes are organized according to occasion, from the most formal ball gowns I have ever seen to jeans and T-shirts. They are all my size. On a separate wall is sexy nightwear in every color. I roll my eyes at this. The sight of the nightwear screams a presumptuousness and an audacity that unsettle me. Having seen enough, I switch off the light and return to the main room.

Mrs. Middleton has chosen a tan sundress and ballerina flats. *Good for doing nothing around the apartment,* I decide.

I dress and go out into the hallway. I can tell where Mrs. Middleton is, because I can hear the whirring sound of the vacuum at the other end of the spacious apartment. If I can keep track of her, maybe I can do a little bit of snooping around.

I begin my exploration in the bedrooms. Just like the bedroom that I sleep in, the first is decorated in all pink tones. Down the hall is another bedroom; this one is just as pretty but is decorated in yellows. The next one has green tones done in plaids and is more masculine. It is a five-bedroom apartment. Each bedroom has a spectacular connecting bath and a unique view of the city.

The room farthest from mine is Noah's room. It is the only closed door. I pause when I reach it. The vacuum is still on and far away. Carefully, I turn the knob. Surprisingly, the door is unlocked and opens for me. I only glance in at first but then decide to enter. I'm nervous, but the urge to know everything about this mystery man wins.

It is the most spacious bedroom I have ever seen. Decorated in grays and blacks, it is ultramodern, with shiny mirrors and silver accents everywhere. Mirrored closets cover one entire wall. The wall opposite is made entirely of windows, which offer a spectacular view of New York City. It is the only bedroom with a skylight, and sunlight pours in from above.

I don't know Noah well, but the space seems to suit him perfectly.

The room sports a king-sized bed with silver bedding, two night tables, and a lounge chair. In the center of the room is an oversized gray velvet ottoman. Curious, I walk over to one of the night tables and carefully open the drawer. I find several sets of handcuffs tossed carelessly inside. At first, I am confused, but I gasp when I realize what they might be for. I gulp and kind of wish I had never snooped in here. I make a vow to avoid this room at all costs. I exit and carefully close the door behind me.

The vacuum is off, and I seem to have gotten out just in time, because I pass Mrs. Middleton in the hallway. She smiles sweetly at me. She seems to be done with the other end of the apartment, and she is beginning to clean the bedrooms now. The place is already spotless, but I bet he insists on it being immaculate.

"I think I'll go out on the balcony for a bit," I say as we pass. She nods and carries on.

Once out of her sight, I linger and wait for the whir of the vacuum to resume. When it does, I go in search of his study, the other place I am forbidden from.

I want to find out as much as I can about this man, although I feel as if I have already found out more than I bargained for. They say that by knowing your enemies, you will then know their weaknesses. Once I discover those, I can put my plan into place.

The study is magnificent. Decorated boldly and filled with rich wooden paneling, it is by far the most masculine room in the apartment. A huge cherry desk and leather chair are its centerpieces. The walls are lined with framed awards from dozens of organizations. He's been thanked by every civic group in the city. I'm not sure how I feel about this. Considering what he's doing to me, it seems incongruous that he spends so much time engaging in activities that benefit others instead of himself. I shrug and move on.

On top of the desk, I find the usual items. The only thing that catches my eyes is a small jewelry box set off to one side. My curiosity gets the best of me, and carefully, I open it. Inside is a spectacular oval-shaped pendant made of black onyx and diamonds. It is the most stunning pendant I have ever seen. With one finger, I touch the stone. It must have cost a fortune, yet he has it carelessly laid out on his desk. I know that in my lifetime, I will never own such a piece of jewelry, and I wonder what it might be like to wear one just once.

I carefully lift it out of its box. The silky chain straightens itself, and the pendant spins perfectly in place. I manipulate the delicate clasp and clip it around my neck. I look down at it and am taken aback by its beauty. The vacuum continues in the distance. I will snoop for a few minutes more and then replace the pendant and be done.

I eye the desk again. There must be something else of interest. I open the middle drawer and find Post-it notes, paperclips, and a staple remover. I close it, open the drawer to the left, and find a simple manila file folder. "Gabriella Rossi" is written on the tab in simple black ink. I grow a little cold at the sight of my own name scrawled in what looks to be his handwriting. Inside are dozens of photos of me, all taken from a distance at the pizza shop. They don't show anything in particular, but knowing that they were taken without my knowledge and that someone was watching me is unsettling. Aside from the photos, the folder is empty.

As I go to replace the folder in the drawer, a faded crayon drawing catches my eye. It was obviously created by a child—Lucey, the scrawled signature indicates. The drawing shows two stick figures. One looks to be a little girl with long red hair and a triangle-shaped body that makes her look as if she is wearing a dress. She is holding hands with the other figure—obviously a male, based on his rectangular body and short hair. I almost laugh at the way the child drew the hair on the taller male figure: a mess of black ringlets atop his head. The taller figure is obviously Noah, and I can only assume the little girl is Lucey. Both figures wear huge smiles, and hearts dance above their heads. I think of his sternness and wonder if there is another side to him, but I can't imagine it. Still, whoever Lucey is, she thinks the world of him.

Suddenly, I realize that the vacuum is off, and I can hear the sound of Mrs. Middleton's feet coming closer. I replace the drawing and the folder and close the drawer before scurrying out of the room.

Mrs. Middleton and I pass again in the hallway, exchanging polite smiles. I head to my room, and she enters the study to clean. My heart nearly pounds out of my chest.

About noon, Mrs. Middleton fixes me a tuna fish sandwich and some fruit. I sit at the counter, eating by myself. She continues her cleaning. I truly am in a different world. I wonder what my sisters and Poppy are doing now and feel pangs of homesickness. Six months is a long time.

After lunch, Mrs. Middleton announces that she needs to run to the market a block away. She promises not to be gone long. I wish I could go with her, but we both know I'm not allowed.

While she is gone, I use the time to explore some more. There is only one room I haven't been in yet: a library just off of Noah's study, with double paneled doors adjoining it to the study. With oak shelves filled with books, it is breathtaking. A brick fireplace stands in the middle of the room, and various pieces of leather furniture are scattered about the room, inviting visitors to choose a book and make themselves at home.

Ever since I was little, I have had a deep love of books, devouring almost one daily, so this room speaks to me. I particularly love poetry and the classics. I walk around the room, slowly scanning the shelves. His collection is diverse but contains lots of classics and poetry. I could easily lose myself in this amazing room. I stumble upon a book that first makes me smile and then makes me gasp. It is an original 1756 version of *The Beauty and the Beast* by Madame Jeanne-Marie Leprince de Beaumont. I am sure it is priceless. At first, I'm afraid to touch it, merely caressing its binding with one finger to feel the indentations of the gold leafing. Unable to resist, I take the book from the shelf. I find a comfortable love seat and lose myself in the magical story. I savor every word and study the intricate details of the drawings.

A voice startles me out of a sound sleep. "I see you have found the library."

Noah is standing over me. After my restless night, I apparently fell asleep while reading.

I sit upright. "I thought it would be okay," I murmur, and then I am instantly angry for explaining myself to him.

"The library is open to you," he says. "Reading is a great pastime." As always, his voice is flat and even. He takes the book from my hands and looks at it. He smiles faintly. "What an appropriate choice," he says. "I know that you are a beauty, so I must be the beast," he adds with a raised eyebrow.

I want to tell him that he is right, but I don't.

"If you skip to the end, you'll find that she has a change of heart," he says. This comment makes my blood boil. He is beyond arrogant. Inside, I am screaming that I will never have any such change of heart, but again feeling intimidated and unable to put my defiance into words, I stay mute.

"Come," he says, walking to the door. I don't know what else to do but follow him. He leads me to his study. I take a tentative step inside and stand before him, fidgeting nervously. I have a sinking feeling in the pit of my stomach.

"I see that you have been places which were forbidden to you," he says evenly.

My heart skips a beat. I wonder how he knows. Then I think maybe he doesn't, so I try to keep my face from flushing and looking guilty. I am sure I have left everything looking untouched. "No, I haven't," I say, hoping my voice doesn't sound too defensive.

He cocks his head to one side and takes a sip of a drink that apparently Mrs. Middleton set out for him. He puts the glass down on the table and raises his eyebrows. He says nothing but reaches out and taps the pendant around my neck with one finger. In my rush, I forgot to take it off!

My throat closes, and my cheeks are burning. I have been caught. My eyes are glued to his, but his expression is even and calm. I have no idea what his next move will be. Embarrassed, I reach up and unclasp the latch on the pendant. I hand it to him. He takes it and slides it into his pocket.

"Gabriella, I have rules," he says. "Rules that you are expected to follow. When you fail to obey them"—*There's that word again,* I think—"there must be consequences in order for you to learn."

I don't know where he is going with this. I bite my lip and try not to act scared, but I can hear my own breathing and am staring at him with what are surely wide eyes.

"Now, what shall I do with you so that you will learn to follow the rules? What shall be done to make a disobedient girl obey?"

I know that this isn't really a question. He knows exactly what he plans to do with me, and I begin to panic as it becomes clear to me.

"Over the desk," he commands.

I freeze. I can't believe this is what he plans to do. "No."

"No?" He raises an eyebrow. "That's one word that will not come out of your mouth," he says. "No is not an option. Gabriella, you entered into an agreement. An agreement with me. A very big part of that agreement involves doing as you are told. Now, unless you wish to break the agreement and lose what you hoped to gain, you will bend over the desk and learn your lesson. Think of why—and for whom—you are here."

I fall into his trap and think of Poppy and the girls. There is no way out.

"I don't repeat myself," he says.

He waits. I know that only a few seconds have passed, but with my mind racing, time seems to stand still. Frantically, I weigh my options. If I don't do as he commands, I'll be home before dinner, watching my family suffer. If I can somehow endure this, I still have a chance. Finally, I don't know what else to do, so I turn and bend over the desk.

"Bare bottom will help you learn best," he says. Then he raises my dress and slowly pulls down my panties.

I am completely exposed now. The humiliation I feel is unbearable. I have never been spanked before—not even as a child and certainly not on my bare bottom.

"You will learn to obey my commands one way or another," he says.

I know that he is dragging this out because it is worse this way.

"The first few are for going where you were forbidden. The rest are for lying," he explains.

He puts his left hand on my back to hold me in place and then raises his right hand and administers the first smack on my bottom. His hands are as hard as steel. I never expected it to hurt so badly, and I scream out in pain. Slowly and methodically, Noah spanks me again and again. Just when I think it might be over, he applies another, and I cry out. My head swims from the pain. Somehow, he seems to know that I cannot take much more. With one final swat, it is over. I feel him pull up my panties and replace my dress. He turns me to face him, but I can't look at him. The humiliation I feel is unbearable.

"Look at me, Gabriella," he says. I refuse, but when he says, "Do you need more?" I force myself to make eye contact. "Now you may go to your room for the rest of the evening and think about what you have done," he says.

I have never hated anyone more in my life.

Chapter 6

I wake the next morning to a note left on my bedside table:

> Gabriella,
> Had to leave early for a meeting.
> Home at six.
> BEHAVE.
> N

I grimace at the word *behave*, but somehow, I still heed its warning. I won't be snooping today.

I eat breakfast alone at the counter. Mrs. Middleton keeps mostly to herself, offering gentle smiles when we do make eye contact. I wonder how much she knows. I want to ask her how she can work for such a monster.

I wander around the apartment all day long, trying to entertain myself, but it is futile. I watch game shows on television and read. There is only so much to do in captivity.

At precisely six o'clock, the phone rings. Mrs. Middleton answers it and has a brief conversation. I am out on the balcony, getting some air, when Mrs. Middleton hands the receiver to me. I am puzzled but take it.

"Gabriella," Noah says, "I won't be home this evening. I had to fly to Boston for a meeting and need to stay overnight."

"Okay," I say coldly.

"You may not leave the apartment," he reminds me. "Be good, and we'll do something special when I get home."

A long silence ensues. I refuse to be the one who speaks next.

"Do you understand?" he asks.

I let the dead air hang there. Then, finally, I say, "Yes. I understand."

For the next two nights, I receive exactly the same phone call, and we have the same conversation. I am trapped for three days. Mrs. Middleton watches me like a hawk—per his instruction, I'm sure. Furthermore, just in case, Liam is posted at the front door.

I spend a lot of time out on the balcony, where I can feel just the slightest bit of freedom. I look down at the bustling city and wish to be a part of it. I look out over the skyline and wonder in which direction New Jersey and home are. I wonder how Poppy and my sisters are and what they are doing. My homesickness feels like a rock deep inside my stomach. It aches.

Mostly, I wonder what in the world I have done.

My emotions are scrambled. I am glad Noah is gone, but at the same time, I am somehow waiting for him. I need to get on with my plan. I have never met anyone like him, but I feel sure that everyone has a breaking point. If I can bring him to his, he will surely let me go.

I am on the balcony, as usual, when Mrs. Middleton finds me. "Mr. Bentley will be picking you up promptly at six for dinner," she tells me. All I can do is nod that I understand.

I bathe, and as usual, when I return from the bathroom, clothes have been laid out for me. A short, silky black dress and black sandals are on the bed. Matching jewelry—a string of pearls and a bracelet—is there as well. I sigh and put it all on. When I look in the mirror, I don't recognize myself.

I don't like the feeling.

⑤

"How many have there been?" I ask during the car ride to dinner.

I am in a combative mood. Being cooped up in the apartment for three days has taken its toll on me. What kind of man practically kidnaps a girl, holds her hostage in his penthouse apartment, and then disappears for three days?

"First, I do not appreciate your tone," he says. "Second, I'm not sure that I understand the question."

"How many have there been?" I repeat. "How many girls have you had?"

He nods and smiles faintly.

Good God, I hope I haven't flattered him.

"Let's be clear. I answer to no one, including you," he says seriously. "But since it is a fair question, I will tell you that there are no other women in my life. Only you. You are one of a kind. I do not have a girl in every port, so to speak," he assures me.

For some reason, I kind of believe him, but I act as if I don't. "Why not?"

"Why not what?"

"Why don't you have a girl in every port?" I sneer. "You're a millionaire. So why not? Plenty of girls would line up for that."

He smiles as if he isn't entirely disliking this conversation, which annoys me.

"I am not a millionaire," he says. "I am a billionaire, and I don't want a girl in every port. I prefer my women one at a time. And right now, I have you."

I almost say, "No, you don't," but I stop myself because in truth, he does have me. This fact eats at me every second of the day. I can say that I am unwilling, but still, I stay. I'm not sure why, but he doesn't press this issue, one that he could easily win. Maybe it's obvious to both of us that he has kind of won already.

"You want what you want, and I want what I want," he says simply.

"I have a feeling neither of us are going to get anything," I say. Getting out of this arrangement with both my pride and the money seems unlikely.

"And I predict," he says coolly, "that we are both

going to get exactly what we want. You just don't know that you want it yet."

☾

At the restaurant, Noah places a guiding hand on my back and leads me through the crowd to an intimate table for two. I resent his hand on me and try slightly to wiggle away, but he only places it more firmly. We reach the table. The maître d' pulls out my chair, and I slide in, grimacing. My bottom is still sore.

Noah courteously waits until I'm seated before taking the seat across from me. We are handed our menus, and he deftly palms the host a folded bill. The man nearly curtsies and scurries away. I want to roll my eyes. I sigh, refusing to look at Noah. I can feel his eyes on me.

In the car, he attempted to explain that his business had taken him away and would again from time to time. He stopped short of apologizing. I bet he never apologizes for anything. He told me that until I was adjusted, he would try to keep his absences to a minimum. I pretended not to hear him.

Now he is running his fingers through his hair in either frustration or annoyance. I can't tell which but am satisfied with either.

"Gabriella," he says. His voice is commanding.

I don't look up.

"Look at me," he hisses.

My heart skips. His eyes are blazing, and his fingers have mussed up his hair. I have made him mad, and it scares me. I'm afraid not to look up, so I do. I attempt my most impassive look. He licks his lips and stares at me.

"We are here to have a pleasant dinner," he says softly. "So we will."

I work hard to keep my face bored. We open our menus. I am not hungry.

"I don't know what you like to eat," he says, being uncharacteristically friendly.

"Pizza," I say squarely. He closes his eyes. If we were not in this crowded restaurant right now, I would surely be over his knee. "I like to eat pizza."

The water boy appears and fills our glasses. As if in a synchronized dance, he trades places with the waiter, who appears seemingly from nowhere. Seeing Noah, the waiter apologizes for not being more attentive. I wonder how he could have been more attentive. We have only been in the restaurant for three minutes. I try not to make it my business. I try to remember that I am bored and resentful.

"This is Miss Rossi." Noah's voice breaks my thoughts.

I look up and find the waiter smiling down at me. "Eduardo," he says politely.

"Call me Gabby," I say. I can tell that this annoys Noah, who looks at me sternly. It is a small victory for me.

Noah is ready for Eduardo to leave. He is back to a businesslike, curt tone. "We will both have a filet, medium, with béarnaise; the green beans amandine;

and the roasted redskins, along with a bottle of my usual."

"Very good, Mr. Bentley." He nods and bows at the hips. He disappears momentarily and returns with the requested wine. Then he is gone, and we are alone at the table again.

"Don't," Noah says biting at the word and staring me straight in the eyes, "correct me again." His manner startles me and has me sitting up straight. "The staff will address you as I instruct."

I don't respond.

He pauses for a moment to collect himself and then takes a sip of his wine. "I ordered this because I thought you might like it. Try a sip."

Like everything else he says, this statement is a command. I don't move, not out of defiance this time but out of fear. His strong words have stopped me short. He waits. It's not that I don't want to move—I think a sip of wine might actually do me good—but his tone paralyzes me. I am afraid of him. He bites his lip, outwaiting me. Finally, I pick up the glass and take a sip.

"You are a defiant one," he muses. "A little more so than I expected."

"Then let me go," I say, my voice small and hoarse from having not used it in a while.

"Never," he says.

My blood runs cold. I involuntarily shudder. My mouth is suddenly dry, and I can't swallow. He means it.

"Six months," he says. "Then if you choose to leave, I will let you."

My heart sinks, and my throat closes.

Our meals arrive. I take in a breath of air. There is no way I can eat. I feel as if I might gag. Noah begins to eat, deftly cutting through his steak. He looks up and eyes me narrowly. "Eat," he orders.

"I can't."

"You can and will." He is dismissive. When I don't move, he looks at me with surprising calm. "Gabriella," he says, "remember the rules. Now remember the consequences. As much as you despise the rules, you surely dislike the consequences more."

I think of the punishment I received, and my eyes fill with tears of anger and frustration. I pick up my utensils and begin to play with the food.

It is a warm night, and we are on the way home. I've calmed down a bit. The wine has relaxed me. We are in Noah's Mercedes. He puts the top down. He has some sort of classical music playing on the radio, and although I am not a fan, somehow, I don't mind it. I love the feeling of the night air rushing through my hair. I love watching the city and all of its lights fly by me.

He looks over at me, and I cannot read his expression. He reaches down, takes my hand in his, raises it to his lips, and kisses it. I am glad that it is dark so that he cannot see me blushing. Why do I like his attention? I take my hand back, and he lets me.

"In time," he says softly.

We drive for miles, not saying a word. Finally, I break the silence. "Why did you pick me?"

"What do you mean?"

"That first day at the pizza shop, there were six of us standing there."

He nods. "There were."

"So why me?" I ask.

Without hesitation, he answers, "Ask me again another time."

When we arrive back at the apartment, someone is waiting to take the car. Noah comes around and opens the car door for me. We go upstairs and walk through the apartment. He leads me to the door of the guest bedroom. We stand there for a moment as if we are at the end of a date. He raises my chin and leans in to me.

"Open your mouth," he whispers, and he gently kisses me. He is patient, holding my head with his hand and entwining his fingers in my hair. When I am hesitant, he persists, forcing me until his tongue is inside, exploring. He knows he is teaching me. I have never been kissed this way before. My head spins in spite of myself, and my eyes close. I'm suddenly aching down below.

Satisfied for the moment, Noah releases me and looks hard into my eyes. For a second, our eyes lock. I look away first. He caresses my cheek and walks away.

Chapter 7

The next morning, I sleep late. When I wake, Noah is gone already, and Mrs. Middleton has laid out my clothes. I bathe and dress. When I appear in the kitchen, Mrs. Middleton explains that we have an appointment. I skip breakfast, and by ten, we are standing outside of a fancy salon a few blocks from the apartment. Mrs. Middleton has been oddly quiet—my first clue that something is up.

On the sidewalk, I ask, "Why are we here?"

Looking apprehensive, she says, "Mr. Bentley thought you might enjoy a bit of pampering." But her words don't ring true.

"I don't want a haircut or anything else," I say.

She frowns. "Let's just go in and see."

In the lobby, Mrs. Middleton is greeted by an attractive and immaculately groomed woman somewhere in her fifties. They whisper to one another before Mrs. Middleton nervously faces me. "Why don't you go with Cynthia?"

I realize that I am trapped, and with a look, I let Mrs. Middleton know that she has betrayed me. Sadly and apologetically, she looks back at me. I don't forgive her.

I follow Cynthia as she attempts polite pleasantries. She introduces me to Mindy, who looks like a living Barbie doll and will be tending to me. Mindy is excited. I am furious. For the next three hours, I am made over. My hair is cut. I receive a pedicure and manicure and, most humiliatingly—and painfully—of all, a Brazilian wax.

I realize, of course, that Noah is behind all of this. As he does with all things, he has arranged the situation so that there is no way for it to play out except his way.

Mindy seems not to notice that I am seething and chatters on as she transforms me. She asks me where I'm from.

"New Jersey," I say, "but I am staying at the Lucey."

"Noah Bentley's building!"

"Excuse me?"

"That's Noah Bentley's building," she repeats. "He owns the whole blessed thing. Can you imagine having half that much money?" Then she whispers, "He certainly is hotter than hot! I've only seen him in person once, but he is sure easy on the eyes." She giggles. I only sigh.

Finally, Mrs. Middleton and I are out on the sidewalk. Liam is waiting for us. Mrs. Middleton explains that I will go with Liam, and she will walk back to the apartment. I remain silent and don't bother asking where I am going.

Ten minutes later, Liam and I arrive in front of Trump Plaza. Liam escorts me into the dining room, where Noah is waiting. As I approach the table, a waiter pulls out the chair, and Noah stands courteously until I am seated. Liam disappears.

Once we are facing each other, Noah says, "You look lovely."

I glare and say nothing.

"Is something wrong?"

"I am not a dog to be taken to the groomer," I say, seething.

"Certainly not," he answers without skipping a beat. "You are a lady to be pampered."

"I didn't want any of this." I am boiling mad. "My body is *my* body."

His lack of agreement is obvious.

"You certainly did have them scrub all of the New Jersey off of me," I sneer furiously.

"Not my intention."

"Stop changing me!"

"Keep your voice down."

A salad that I didn't order is placed in front of me. I want to scream. Noah is unfazed. He picks up his utensils. Then, with a look full of warning, he whispers, "Get over it. And eat your lunch."

༄

The next week seems endless. I try to count the days, but they begin to run into one another to the point where I have to ask Mrs. Middleton which day of the week it is.

Much to my dismay, Noah and I fall into somewhat of a routine. We start the day together with breakfast at eight. He departs shortly after, leaving me with a chaste kiss on the cheek and a long day in front of me. I fill my time by watching game shows and reading, but there is only so much of that I can do. When Noah returns promptly at six, I am determined to make his life miserable enough that he will let me go.

However, my tactics don't seem to be working. Noah only seems to be getting stronger, while I am growing tired. He is unflappable. My pouting and sulking go unnoticed, and outward signs of anger are either ignored or met with a challengingly raised eyebrow that, I am embarrassed to say, puts me in my place.

We alternate our dinner schedule. We have dinner out at a restaurant of his choosing one night, and the next night, we eat at home. On the nights when we eat at home, after dinner, we go into the great room. Noah is consumed by the news—particularly the stock market. Afterward, he chooses a show for us to watch. Usually, he settles on a documentary, which bores me to tears but makes it easier to keep the practiced, miserable look on my face.

On the nights when we go out, the dinner is always fancy. Instead of going right home afterward, we ride around in his convertible with the top down, and he shows me Manhattan. Some places are familiar, but most I have never even heard of. I love this drive, but I try hard not to show it. Still, I know that I look around like a wide-eyed little girl. Sometimes I catch him looking at me and get embarrassed, but he lets it go and just places his hand on my thigh.

At midnight, Noah walks me to my room and gives me a not-so-chaste kiss goodnight, and then we part.

"I won't be satisfied with this arrangement for long," he warns me. "But I can be patient for a while."

These words only make me want to hasten my escape.

※

"I do wish you would remove your elbows from the table."

"I'm sure you do." I am relatively safe to be a smart-mouth for the moment, because we are out to dinner in public, and I know that Noah will not make a scene. Noah wouldn't scream if he were on fire.

He sighs and runs his fingers through his gorgeous black hair. "You are a lady, and ladies do not position their elbows on top of the table," he tells me so patiently that it irks me. I find it condescending.

"So the next time you are a lady, you can be sure to keep your elbows off the table," I say.

His eyes blaze, and he is just about to respond, when we are interrupted.

"Why, Noah Bentley!"

The voice belongs to the largest man I have ever seen. He is tall and round. He is a misplaced cowboy, standing in the middle of this New York City restaurant with a cowboy hat, Texas belt buckle, and boots. The only thing missing is a horse.

"You dog!" The cowboy bellows so loudly that the entire restaurant hears. "You've been keeping this pretty little lady a secret!"

"Charles." Noah's greeting is a million decibels lower. He wipes his mouth with his napkin and stands, always the gentleman.

"Charles Hunnicut," Noah says, "this is Gabriella Rossi."

"Like 'em nice and young?" He guffaws.

I am instantly a bright shade of pink.

"Well, it's a good thing I didn't get to you first," the giant man says, laughing heartily.

I am mortified, but Noah saves me. "Well, you didn't," he says flatly, though with a tinge of good nature. "I got to her first."

The man reaches out and shakes Noah's hand before tipping his hat to me. "Miss," he says, "a pleasure."

Still dumbfounded, I say nothing.

The man turns to Noah, saying, "Keep her," and he smacks Noah on the back before walking away.

"I plan to," Noah says, now looking squarely at me.

૭

I'm a little worried. I might have pushed him too far. He got tired of my elbows being on the table, and we left without having dessert.

"Young ladies who do not behave during dinner do not deserve treats," he told me.

Apparently, we are not taking a ride either. I'm disappointed because I like the rides, even though I'd never admit this. When we enter the apartment, I can tell he is still angry. "Bath and bed," he orders.

I frown.

He tosses his keys onto the entry table. "Go!" he barks, pointing toward my bedroom when he notices I've hesitated. My heart skips, and I dart off. At least he didn't order me to the study.

Once alone, I undress slowly and wonder if what I'm doing even matters. He's always in control. Even when I've somehow succeeded in making him angry, I'm still the one who loses.

I draw a bath, add a dollop of bubbles, and climb in. I linger there for a while, playing with the suds. My thoughts are scattered, and my mind races. I have been pretending to have a grand plan, when in reality, I have no idea what I'm doing. I know that I don't want to be here. I know that I want to go home. But I also know that Noah has to be the one to give in, and so far, that's not looking likely. I act self-assured around him, but in truth, he rattles me and leaves me off kilter. Just his presence disarms me—so much so that as soon as he appears, I turn into a horrendous, smart-mouthed brat. I try to remind myself that he is only a man, but maybe that is the issue. I have such little experience with men that I am at a total disadvantage.

I get out of the tub, dry off, and dress for bed. I'm startled to see Noah standing in the bedroom when I enter. His expression is softer than before. He comes closer.

"Come," he says.

Taking me by the hand, he walks me out of the room, down the hallway, across the great room, and to the balcony. He takes a quilt from the back of the couch and wraps it around me. The door is open, and he leads me out. He sits on an oversized love seat, pulls me onto his lap, and wraps me in a hug. I try to resist, but there is little fight in me, and in spite of myself, I settle in on his lap.

"This city is yours now," he whispers softly in my ear.

I want to object, but I don't have the strength. He holds me tightly. After a while, my body betrays me, and I melt into him.

༄

The next evening, Mrs. Middleton lays out a ruby-red sequined gown with matching pumps and handbag. I have never touched such clothing, let alone worn anything like it.

She comes to check on me. I am still wrapped in a towel, fresh from the bath. The look of trepidation on my face must be obvious.

"I don't think I can," I tell her, wagging my head.

Her smile is soft and maternal. "Certainly you can," she says as she helps me into the dress.

A few minutes later, we stand in front of the mirror together, studying my image. "It looks like it was made for you," she tells me.

"But it wasn't."

"Let's just wait and see."

Noah is waiting in the foyer, checking his watch. It is almost unperceivable, but I think his face softens when he sees me. He is silent except for a nod. He grasps my hand and leads me into the elevator.

Downstairs, Liam is waiting. Within moments, we are part of the city nightlife. Doe-eyed, I look out the window of the limo at the myriad of lights.

"Do you like the ballet?" Noah asks me.

I blink. My heart skips. "I've never been," I say quietly.

"New things are good."

The ballet! Seeing the ballet in New York City has always been a dream of mine. My sisters and I grew up dancing. We couldn't afford lessons, but we paid the owner of the neighborhood dance studio in pizza. Ballet was always my favorite.

Liam pulls up to the curb. We step from the car and onto the sidewalk. Noah takes my elbow and leads me through the crowd and into the lobby of the hall. We are shown to our seats in a private box.

"Enjoy the performance, Mr. Bentley," the usher says, and then he nods at me. "Miss."

For the next three hours, I am mesmerized. I am in another world. When it is over, I am speechless.

Liam collects us out front.

"Did you like it?" Noah asks.

I nod.

"I'm glad you enjoyed yourself. "In December, we'll see *The Nutcracker*," he adds.

My eyes widen. He laughs at my reaction. Realizing what I have just done, I flush with embarrassment. He caresses my cheek. "There are perks to behaving yourself, Gabriella."

I look down, and in the moonlight shining through the sunroof, I study my fingers. I nod.

"I'd like to hear your voice," he says. "Say, 'Yes, Noah. I understand.'"

I swallow and will the words to come out of my mouth. "Yes, Noah. I understand," I manage quietly.

He nods, satisfied. He takes my hand and laces our fingers together. We drive home in silence.

I feel as if I am in a dream. I just can't tell if it's a nightmare or not.

Chapter 8

The next week passes slowly. One night, I wake to the sound of arguing voices in my room. It takes me a moment to realize that the voices belong to Noah and Mrs. Middleton.

"Noah, she is just a girl," I hear Mrs. Middleton plead. "She needs a mother."

"Helen," he says, "she needs to learn to rely on me for all things, especially comfort."

They call each other by their first names when they think I can't hear them.

"Noah, please!"

"Helen, leave."

I am awake now, and I sit up in time to see Mrs. Middleton leave the room. Noah is sitting on the edge of the bed. I am wet with perspiration, and the bed covers look as if I have been fighting with them. "What happened?" I say.

"You were having a nightmare." He reaches out and pushes my hair away from my face.

"Sorry," I mutter, embarrassed.

He hands me a glass of water. I take a sip.

"Do you remember what the nightmare was about?"

"I think someone was chasing me," I say. That much I remember, if vaguely.

He nods understandingly. "Well, no one is chasing you now," he says softly. "Lie down," he adds. I comply, resting my head on the pillow. He straightens the covers a bit. "You're home, safe," he tells me.

I almost react to the word *home* but am too tired to argue.

He covers me gently with the comforter and looks me in the eye. "Gabriella," he says, "you are always safe with me. Now, sleep." Then Noah pulls a chair up to the side of the bed.

When I wake the next morning, he is still sitting there.

ꕥ

"Um, Mr. Bentley? Excuse me, sir."

We are out to dinner again at Noah's favorite restaurant, Il Mulino. We come here often. Everyone knows him here, and he seems less on edge in this setting. A young man about my age appears at our table. He looks nervous and is dressed in a suit that's too big for him. He holds a paper in his hand.

Eduardo, who apparently saw this coming, jumps in front of him and tries his best to intercept him. "Mr. Bentley is a most valued guest and will not be disturbed," Eduardo says snootily, blocking the poor kid's view of Noah.

I think this is ridiculous, but I have to give the young man credit, as he begins popping up and down, trying to keep Noah's attention. "Mr. Bentley, if I could just give you my résumé …"

Noah puts down his utensils. Eduardo is now snapping furiously at his staff, who seem to have no clue what to do. I sit back and enjoy the show.

"Mr. Bentley," the boy says again, jumping up even higher.

Finally, Noah calls off an exasperated Eduardo.

"Um, thank you, sir," the young man blurts out. "It's just that you're my dream—I mean, it's my dream to work for you, sir, and this is my résumé, and ever since I was a little kid, I've wanted to be you, and I'm a real hard worker. I just graduated and …"

Noah takes the paper from his hands and glances over it quickly. The kid is now obviously holding his breath.

"Thank you, Jason," Noah says. The kid gasps at the sound of his own name coming from Noah's mouth. Noah takes a pen from his breast pocket and scribbles on the paper. "Take this to my building tomorrow at ten," he tells him, "and see Claudia in personnel. She will take care of you."

Jason's eyes bug out. "Oh God, thank you, sir! I don't know what to say, Mr. Bentley. Thank you, sir. Thank you."

"Go enjoy your evening," Noah says, nodding for him to leave.

"Yes, sir!" the boy says, and he darts off.

Eduardo is visibly annoyed and begins to speak. "Mr. Bentley—"

Noah cuts him off with a wave of his hand. "It's fine," Noah says, shooing Eduardo away. He clears his throat, picks up his utensils, and begins eating again. On his second bite, he looks up at me and notices that I haven't begun eating yet. He raises an eyebrow and nods toward the plate.

I have been lost in my own thoughts. I pick up my fork and begin to eat. I wonder what it is like to make or break people, to control the lives and emotions of people with a moment or two of your time and attention. I look up at Noah and study his face. "What will happen to him tomorrow?" I ask.

"He'll get a job," he says.

"For sure?"

"For sure."

"What kind of job?" I ask warily.

"Don't worry. A decent one. One with a livable wage and room for growth. It will give him a chance. Then the rest is up to him."

I nod, taking this all in. This seems more than reasonable—actually, generous—and I'm glad.

"Fair enough?" he asks with a smirk.

"I guess," I concede.

"I'm not a monster," he says seriously.

I look at him but say nothing.

Noah removes the napkin from his lap, folds it, and places it on the table. "Would you like to take a ride?" he asks, and I nod. "Words," he reminds me.

"Yes. I would like to take a ride."

He nods at my obedience.

Once in the car, we ride in silence for a while. The top is down, and the warm evening air feels wonderful. Noah navigates the steering wheel with his left hand. His right hand, as always, never leaves my thigh.

After about twenty minutes, we stop in what appears to be a bad part of town. "I want to get your opinion on something," he says. He stops the car in front of a dilapidated building. There are signs marking the place as condemned. "It's coming down next week. What should go in its place?" he asks.

"You want *me* to tell *you*?"

"Yes, I do," he says seriously. "Pretend you're me."

I decide to play along. I crane my neck, looking out the window of the car. Nothing but poverty surrounds us. "Something pretty," I tell him. "If it belonged to me, I would put something pretty here, like a park. The people who live here don't own anything beautiful." He looks at me puzzled. "You know, a real park," I say dreamily. "With lush grass, magnolias, and birch trees, gazebos and benches, and even a place for the kids to play."

He considers this. His expression is not exactly a frown, but it's close. "Would have been my last choice," he says with a small smile.

"So no park?" I say sarcastically.

"I didn't say that. I'm a reasonable man," he insists, taking my hand. "It's just that putting a park here is not exactly a revenue-generating venture. But on the other hand, everyone needs to own something beautiful."

I try to pull my hand back, but he only tightens his grip. "After all," he says, "I own something beautiful. I own you."

֍

"I want to see them," I announce one night at dinner. I can tell that Noah hasn't had the best day and is working on controlling himself.

"Whom would you like to see?" he asks.

"My family." I'm annoyed, since he knows full well whom I am talking about.

"Too soon," he says.

I've been in New York three weeks. I think I've waited long enough. "I need to know that they are okay."

"They are all fine," he insists.

"How do you know?"

"I know," he says with a pause that warns me to watch my tone, "because I have someone checking on them daily."

Puzzled, I ask, "Why would you do that?"

"For your comfort. If there is ever anything you need to know, I will tell you. And though I know that you are averse to using the apartment landline, you are welcome to it at any time."

I ignore the offer. "Do they know that you have someone checking on them?"

"Certainly not."

"How are they?" I ask softly.

Noah stops eating and gives me his full attention. "They're quite fine," he assures me. "Keeping track of Mia is a little bit of a challenge but not anything my security can't handle."

I frown, worried. "What's she doing?"

"Nothing serious," he says. "Let's just say that she could choose her suitors a little more selectively."

"You can say that again. And the others?"

"Fine. Just the normal comings and goings," he says.

"And Poppy?"

"Seems fine. But he needs to get out of that shop and retire," he says. "This sale is long overdue."

I am quiet. "Just a visit?" I say, pleading now.

"The question was asked and answered," he tells me evenly.

I pout.

"Do you need something to really pout about?"

I gulp and shake my head.

"Privileges are earned with proper behavior," he reminds me. "Have you been good?"

I cringe. By now, I am well aware of the rules.

"Then you have something to work on."

I frown. He always wins.

༺ঌ༻

"Does everyone always do what you say?" I ask him at dinner one night.

I have watched all evening long as everyone from

Liam and Mrs. Middleton to the waiters, the maître d', the water boy, the valet, and even people on the other end of the phone seem to jump at his every command.

He seriously contemplates the question. "For the most part."

"Why?"

"For different reasons," he says. I wait for him to go on. "Money is probably the biggest. I have a lot of it, and people want some of it. Other people want the power that I can give them."

"Because of the power you have?"

"Because of the power I have. Opportunity is another reason," he adds. "I am able to give people opportunities that they might not normally have."

"Are people afraid of you?" I ask.

"Some," he says.

"People shouldn't be afraid of people," I insist.

He nods. "Maybe not. But it's how things work."

Our conversation is interrupted by a sultry voice. "Hello, Noah."

The voice belongs to the most voluptuous blonde creature I have ever seen. She is tall—five foot six or seven in stilettos—and has a killer body. I am instantly envious of her curves. With amazing hair and makeup, she is movie star pretty. She is not particularly young, but it hardly matters. I am mesmerized and almost shrink at her arrival.

Noah greets her impassively. "Grace." He stands courteously and offers his hand. He's being too formal. He's not glad she's here.

She turns to me. "And what do we have here?" she asks, batting her amazing eyelashes. She looks me up and down and smiles condescendingly, as if she's meeting a toddler.

"Who we have here," Noah says, obviously finding her choice of words disrespectful, "is Gabriella."

"Gabriella," she croons, adding more syllables to my name than necessary. "A pleasure." She offers a white-gloved hand.

Good God, she's wearing gloves! Who wears gloves?

We shake hands lightly.

"How are you, Noah?" she asks, her attention now fully back on him.

"Very well. Thank you," he answers. "And you?"

"Well," she says.

They exchange icy stares. One could cut the tension with a knife. Without Noah's cooperation, the conversation stalls. She makes a noise in her throat and smiles insincerely. Again, she turns to me. Not expecting this, I sit up a little straighter.

"Gabriella," she says. "I'll remember your name."

I blush, having no response. As always, Noah saves me. "It's the only name you'll ever need to remember," he tells her coldly.

Her face drops. "Very well then," she says. "Noah." She nods.

"Grace," he says.

With that, she turns and walks off. I watch as she disappears into the restaurant. We sit in silence for a few minutes, sipping the wine he ordered. Then, thinking I have nothing to lose, I ask, "An ex?"

"Yes," he says. "A former girlfriend."

I nod and dare to go further. "Was it serious?"

He pauses before he answers. I'm surprised at his patience. "It was at one point for a very brief time."

"What changed?" I ask.

"Last question," he warns with a slightly amused smirk. He seems to weigh his words. "She became insignificant."

"Insignificant? People are not insignificant or significant," I say, appalled. "Everyone matters!"

"Not in my world," he says flatly.

I shake my head. His ego astounds me. He smiles at my reaction, which further irritates me.

"If it is any consolation," he says, "you happen to be highly significant."

I don't accept the compliment. "Did Grace become unafraid of you and powerful and rich on her own? Is that why she became insignificant?" I ask snidely.

He raises a warning eyebrow. "None of the above," he says. "And you're out of questions."

Chapter 9

It's a Monday night, which is usually a night at home, but Noah called at one and told me to be ready by six. Mrs. Middleton has laid out jeans and a sweater, which is odd. I have to admit I'm curious.

Noah races into the apartment at the last minute and changes into casual clothes, and we are off. He gives me no clues as to where we are going, preferring for it to be a surprise.

I gasp and almost squeal when Liam pulls us up to the entrance of Madison Square Garden, where the marquee flashes, "Rangers vs. Devils, Play-Off Game #4." I love hockey.

"Yay," I whisper to myself.

"I heard that," Noah whispers back. "Maybe I've found something you won't pout through."

Maybe.

The irony of the game being between the Devils and the Rangers is obvious to both of us.

"New York or New Jersey?" he asks playfully.

I roll my eyes.

"How about you take New Jersey, and I'll take New York?" he teases.

From the moment we climb out of the limo, Noah holds my hand protectively in his. We join the crowd of people and make our way through the entrance. I am so excited that I actually have butterflies in my stomach.

As I would have expected, our seats are front row, center ice. We couldn't get any closer to the action.

The game is three hours of excitement, with the score teetering back and forth between the two teams. I have never enjoyed myself more. The entire time I watch the game, Noah watches me. Finally, the place erupts as the Rangers win the game in a shoot-out, six to five.

I collapse back into my seat, exhausted. Noah smiles and gently moves the hair away from my eyes. "Sorry." He grins, obviously not sorry at all. "I win."

I wonder if everything in his life always works out to his liking.

"You look like you played the game yourself," he tells me, and I blush. "Enjoyed it?"

I nod and then catch myself; the least I can do is answer him. "Yes. Very much."

"Good," he says. "I like to see you enjoy yourself."

He takes me by the hand, and we merge into the crowd filing out. Again, he holds my hand protectively. I'm not entirely ungrateful for this. The crowd thins a bit. When we reach the ramp, we slow our pace and walk casually. We are almost to the exit, when a group of three young guys in their early twenties who have obviously had too much to drink race by.

They are almost past us, when one of them reaches out and taps my behind. "Nice ass!"

The guy gets no more than ten steps away before Noah is on him. He grabs the guy by the shirt, winds up, and punches him squarely in the jaw. The guy goes flying. In an instant, the guy's friends jump on Noah. I scream.

For a moment, it is an unfair fight. Then, out of nowhere, Liam joins in but instead of throwing punches he attempts to break up the fight. I scream again. Fists fly, and bodies sail through the air but, thankfully, not for long. The police are there almost instantly. Liam holds his current captive in place until the police get to him and suddenly, everyone—including Noah—is in handcuffs.

Minutes later, everyone is separated into little rooms, except Liam and me who were just questioned briefly. We sit in an outer lobby of the arena's police office. I am crying and scared. Liam is trying to console me, assuring me that this will be all right. He explains that he is always just two steps behind Noah, in case something comes up. I am comforted by this, but I am sure he is wrong about everything turning out fine. However, I find out quickly that he is right, when Noah, uncuffed, comes out, escorted by six apologetic police officers.

"We are so sorry for the trouble, Mr. Bentley," one of them says. "Please don't ever hesitate to ask for an escort. We would be happy to see you to and from your seat." He adds, "We will bring the boys right in."

They leave for a moment. Noah, who, to my horror, is slightly beaten up, with a puffy lip and a cut around his eye, dismisses Liam and kneels to face me. "You okay?" he asks softly. I nod, and he smiles sympathetically. "No tears," he tells me as more spill from my eyes. Seeing Noah beat up like this disturbs me.

Suddenly, the police officers appear behind Noah with the three young guys, all of whom look pretty beaten up themselves. Noah stands to face them with an icy glare. They look at Noah and then down at their shoes. Noah steps back, so they are now standing in a row, facing me. It takes me a second to process what's about to happen. I'm mortified when I understand.

Noah clears his throat impatiently. One of the cops pushes the middle kid forward, directly in front of me. He is the one who made the comment.

"Um, miss," he says, stuttering, "I'd just like to apologize. You don't have a nice ass."

"Dude!" the guy to his left screeches.

"Wait!" He stops himself. "I mean you do have a nice—"

"Dude!" the guy yells again.

"I mean, I'm just sorry for being disrespectful!" he blurts out, finally getting a hold of himself. If it weren't so awkward, it would have been hilarious.

The cop grabs him by the collar and pushes the next one forward.

"I'm sorry for my behavior, ma'am," he says.

He gets yanked back, and the last one is pushed forward in his place.

"I'm sorry, miss" is all he manages to say.

I'm embarrassed—both for myself and for them—and have no idea what to say.

"Mr. Bentley?" one cop says. "If that's not enough, sir, they can go to jail."

Noah waves the kids away in disgust. They are practically thrown out of the room. Noah takes a couple of minutes to thank the police officers, exchanging pleasantries about the game and shaking hands. He then turns and faces me. "Ready?" Everyone files out of the room, and he kneels down in front of me again, looking serious. "Mine," he says emphatically. "You are mine. No one touches what is mine."

I have never seen eyes more serious in all of my life. I gulp and nod.

He takes my hand, and minutes later, we are back in the car and on the way home.

I've never felt more like a possession.

⑨

The weather is unseasonably warm. We sit on the balcony after a dinner at home. The golden setting sun amid the New York skyline is spectacular. I longingly watch the people below.

"Would you like to go for a walk?" Noah has an amazing ability to read my mind.

My heart leaps. "Yes, I would," I tell him.

He smiles. I run for my shoes. I can hear him laugh.

Two minutes later, we're almost out the door, and Mrs. Middleton is chasing me with a sweater.

"Don't need it," I call over my shoulder.

"Take it without a fuss," he tells me.

I huff and make a face.

"Without the face or the fuss," he warns.

I take the sweater and offer Mrs. Middleton an apologetic look. She smiles and forgives me.

The street below the apartment is still crowded with people, so of course Noah's grip is like a vice. But once we get to the nearby park, he holds my hand more gently, and we walk casually with his fingers laced in mine. I inhale the warm night air. I've been with Noah for a month now, and our time together has been a roller coaster, mostly because of me. I can't seem to get a grip on myself. I argue with him at every opportunity. I find myself fighting with him constantly. But at times like this, when we are doing something normal, I forget myself and settle in.

We stroll through the park. I study the people. I wonder if any of the other couples have an arrangement like ours. I'm sure not. I am intrigued by the children. I love children.

One day, I think.

"One day what?" he asks.

Startled, I cringe. I didn't realize I'd spoken out loud. "Nothing," I mumble.

"I'd love to know what you want someday."

Cornered, I shrug. "Just normal things," I tell him. "Marriage, kids—the traditional."

He nods, taking this in. "Those are good things."

"I think so," I say. "And you?"

"Let's say I'm kind of a traditional-plus sort of guy," he tells me, grinning.

"I think you might be right." I roll my eyes.

He takes my hand, the one he has been holding; raises it to his mouth; and kisses it. I sigh and look off into the distance. I wonder which direction New Jersey is.

"It's that way," he says, pointing left.

I flinch. *He can't possibly know what I'm thinking!* "What is?" I ask, sure he doesn't know.

"New Jersey."

The night air becomes cool quickly, and I am grateful for the sweater.

The street by the apartment is nearly deserted when we get back. When we reach the side of Noah's building, I hear a rustling in the alley. I turn to see a homeless man huddled under a blanket. He makes eye contact with me.

"Please, miss," he says, holding out a filthy hand. I stop and try to pull away from Noah, who instantly tightens his grip and yanks me closer to him.

"No!" he barks, holding firmly on my arm.

I tug harder. "Why can't we help him?"

"Because he is here by virtue of his own choices," he says, pulling back.

"That's an awful thing to say!" I yell as he practically drags me down the sidewalk away from the alley. I look back, and my heart breaks to see that the man's hand is still out.

We are now in front of the main entrance, and Noah's grip is even tighter. I stop short with all my strength and plant my feet. "Why can't we just help him?" I shout.

He is out of patience with me. "Have him removed," Noah orders the security guard.

"No!" I wail.

"Yes, Mr. Bentley," the guard answers, and he instantly darts off toward the alley. "Let's go, Simon!" I hear the guard say to the man in the distance. Somehow, knowing his name makes it hurt more. My heart falls.

Noah has now dragged me into the building and the elevator, but not before I make a scene for the lobby staff. Once inside the elevator, he lets go of my hand and grabs me by the shoulders. "First, that man is there because of his own poor choices. Second, it is not our place to help him. And third, no matter how you disagree, you are to do as you are told. You do not cause a scene!"

I glare at him. Tears of fury drip from my eyes. "First, we all make poor choices!" I scream. "Second, of course it's our place to help him. It's what good people do! And third, I have my own mind!" The elevator reaches the apartment. He pins me against the elevator wall.

"You don't understand how dangerous someone like that can be!" he yells.

"I understand completely!" I scream back. "I understand that you're mean!"

"You have no idea just how mean," he warns.

I wiggle free from his grip and dart past him toward my room

"Go near him again, and you will be sorry and sore for a month!" he yells after me.

The roller-coaster ride continues.

Chapter 10

"Mrs. Middleton!" I call. I jump when I see Noah appear in the doorway instead. I didn't even know he was home. Even though I've been with him for a month, his sudden presence still unsettles me.

"Gabriella, what's wrong?" he asks, seeming genuinely concerned. "What do you need?"

I shake my head quickly. "Nothing," I mutter, my voice barely audible. "I'm fine."

"You called for a reason," he says. "Now, what do you need?"

Stubbornly, I shake my head again. I don't feel as if I'm ready to trust him completely. I feel vulnerable when letting him solve my problems.

His eyes are fixed on me, studying me. Mrs. Middleton shows up behind him. I look at her pleadingly. He catches me looking, and annoyance covers his face. "Go," he tells her without turning around. Instantly, she is gone. I gulp. I want her. He kneels down. "You called for a reason," he says again, speaking emphatically. "Now, what do you need?"

I am mute and can't speak. He is angry but trying to act patient. My noncompliance is infuriating him.

"You must trust me with all of your needs," he says. "There is nothing that I can't fix. There is no need Mrs. Middleton can tend to that I cannot tend to," he insists. "Tell me what is wrong."

I draw in a bit of breath and close my eyes, weighing my options. He continues to analyze my face. Then he pulls out his trump card. "Do I need to send Mrs. Middleton away permanently?"

"No!" I say instantly, looking at him for the first time.

A look of satisfaction that he has finally gotten my attention crosses his face. "Well then," he says, aware that he has won, "tell me." Waiting, he reaches up and tucks a loose strand of hair behind my ear.

I draw in a breath and then let it out in a small sigh. My eyes fill with tears. "I have a stomachache," I whisper. He nods and takes this information in, considering it. I'm embarrassed at how seriously he considers it. I do have a stomachache, but it's probably not that bad.

"Come," he says, taking my hand and leading me to the bed. He begins to undress me. Not knowing what else to do, I let him. "If you're ill, you need to be in bed," he tells me. I open my mouth to protest, but when the words don't come, I simply give in.

He redresses me in one of his long flannel tees.

I am grateful for the warmth. He tucks me in with extra bedding and pillows. He leaves my side for a few minutes and returns with a hot water bottle and some liquid medicine in a burgundy-colored bottle. As if I'm a child, he feeds me the medicine from a spoon and demands that I lie down. He places the water bottle on my tummy.

"Too warm?" he asks, and I shake my head. "Open," he orders, and he places a thermometer in my mouth. He studies it but says nothing. He disappears for another minute and then returns and tells me, "You need to rest for a while."

"I'm not tired," I say.

He moves onto the bed beside me and gently touches my stomach. Soothingly, he caresses it. I feel myself beginning to relax and drift off. I don't know long I sleep. I wake to his touch. He is gently pushing my hair from my eyes.

Someone else is in the room. Noah sits on the edge of the bed. The stranger, a man holding a black bag, stands to the side. My heart lurches. It's a doctor. I'm not in love with doctors. I wag my head just as Noah begins the introduction.

"Gabriella, this is Dr. Sinclair."

"I don't need a doctor," I croak.

"Just for a checkup," Noah says.

The doctor stands there trying to look friendly.

"I don't need a doctor," I say again.

"She'll cooperate," he tells the doctor over his shoulder. Then, facing me, he says, "You will cooperate." His voice is both soft and stern. "Nothing will hurt," he assures me.

I feel trapped, and my eyes fill with tears. I'm angry for becoming so emotional.

"No need for that," Noah says quietly. He gets up from the edge of the bed, and the doctor takes his place and proceeds to examine me. Noah never leaves my side. The whole thing is no big deal—it is just a check—but having no say in what is happening to me has me shaken. As Noah sees Dr. Sinclair out, I pull the covers up to my chin and try not to cry.

In a moment, he's back on the edge of the bed, stroking my cheek. "You did just fine."

I'm angry about someone touching me without my permission.

He reads my mind. "I would never let anyone else touch you unless it was for your own good," he says.

I refuse to look at him.

"Now, sleep," he directs.

I pout and decide that I won't sleep, because he can't make me, but in time, my body betrays me again, and my eyelids become heavy. I lose again to sleep.

I wake just in time to see the digital clock next to the bed turn over to 3:00 a.m. Noah is sleeping, still in his clothes, on top of the covers next to me. He has never left my side. I have slept for more than four hours. I try to move the heavy, protective arm he has flung over me without waking him, but his eyes open instantly. "How do you feel?" he asks.

"Better," I insist.

He checks the time. "It's been hours since you've eaten. You need to eat something."

He reaches over and checks my forehead. I'm sure that I'm fever free.

"Come," he says, taking my hand. He leads me into the kitchen. On the island are two place settings. Mrs. Middleton has left out a snack of fruit, cheese, and crackers.

Knowing what I'm thinking, he says, "Don't worry; she's gone only till the morning."

I nod gratefully.

We sit there silently, eating. I don't know what to do with all of my emotions. I'm conflicted. When he's demanding and stern, I'm committed to keeping my distance and decide I will simply tolerate this arrangement, but when he's kind, as he is now, I find myself curious and drawn to him.

"I won't let harm come to you," he finally says, breaking the silence.

I look up at him, and I believe him. I should say something but don't.

"Back to bed," he says suddenly.

Tucked back in bed, his arm across me again, he falls asleep first, his breathing regular. I replay the day in my head. I don't know what to think. All I know is that never have the needs of a stomachache been more thoroughly tended to.

Occasionally, when the August heat makes it too warm to eat on the balcony, we have our dinners in the formal dining room. Noah insists upon this. A crystal chandelier with muted lighting hangs overhead. Mrs. Middleton floats in and out, serving courses on gold-plated china.

Noah sits at the head of the table, and I sit to his left. He's had a bad day. I'm playing with fire.

"I want my phone back," I say.

"So you are demanding your phone?"

I know that this is a trick question. Inside my head, I scream, *Yes, I am!* but I know what he wants me to say. I want my phone back badly enough to sell myself out. "May I please have my phone back?"

"Better," he says, taking a bite of his meal. "But the answer is still no. You may use the home phone anytime you wish. Furthermore, you may give out the number to anyone you'd like."

Inwardly, I boil. Outwardly, I slam my fork on the table.

He stops and frowns. "That will not be tolerated," he says.

"Sure it will!" I shout. "Because it just was!"

"Done!" he says, and in one swift motion, he has lifted me up out of the chair. I am over his shoulder, and he is carrying me down the hallway to the bedroom. He swats me on the bottom so hard I see stars. He tosses me onto the bed.

"A bath and to bed. Now," he says coolly. "Or there will be more!" He leaves the room, slamming the door behind him.

With nothing else to do, I do as I am told. That's one thing about Noah: he arranges and controls everything in his world to such a degree that it's nearly impossible not to cooperate.

I linger in the bathtub, surrounded by lavender bubbles, and wonder where this is all going. I have been here almost six weeks and have made no progress at all. I know that I am not wearing him down even the slightest bit and have no idea where to turn. Being uncooperative doesn't faze him; however, if I choose to cooperate, I'll never get out sooner than six months from now.

Without warning, the bathroom door slowly opens. It is him. I slouch lower in the tub so that I am covered up to my shoulders. He takes the decorative gold chair from the corner and sits on it, facing me. I have no idea what to make of this.

"Would you like your dinner?" he asks.

I shake my head.

"What would you like?"

I am tempted to say, "My phone," but I don't feel as if I am in a position to provoke him.

"Why don't you get dressed? We'll go out."

I don't know what to make of this gesture, so I don't react. He smiles down at me with a warm, sexy grin. Then he scoops a handful of bubbles from the tub and blows them into my face. I jump back, startled. He looks amused, and I can't help but smile back.

Once I am sure he is gone, I get out of the tub and

towel-dry my body and hair. I dress and go out to the great room. He is reading the paper, waiting.

"Ready?" he asks. I nod. He grabs his keys, and we go.

He gives no indication of where we are going, and I haven't a clue. We drive with the top down. He asks me if I am cold, and I say no. Actually, I love the way the air flows through my hair. Besides, my fairy godmother—Mrs. Middleton—laid out a sweater for me to wear over my short cotton dress. He drives with one hand on the wheel and the other on my thigh. It doesn't bother me anymore, and I wonder how I've grown accustomed to it. We drive in silence. I am relaxed, paying little attention to where we are going. Noah seems to do the thinking for both of us. I close my eyes for a few minutes to enjoy the wind, and when I open them, I can't believe where we are. I look at him in amazement. My jaw drops.

"I figured if you were going to act like a child, maybe I should treat you like a child," he says with a grin.

We are at Coney Island Amusement Park. I look from him to the park that awaits us. The sun has set, and the park is aglow with light. My tummy tingles as it did when I was a kid. My mouth is still open in shock.

"Well, let's go!" he says, laughing. Surely he is laughing at me.

He holds my hand in his as we walk through the park. I am quiet as memories flood me. I came here once every summer with my sisters, and the memories we created are among the best of my childhood. I know I must look like a kid in a candy store with my wide eyes and a huge grin.

"Been here before?" he asks.

"Once every year with my sisters," I tell him. "But not since I was little. It has a whole different feel to it now. You?"

"A few times," he says.

"When we were little, we used to dream of owning the park," I tell him with a giggle. "Between the six of us, we thought we could pool our money, buy it, and then walk through here like little queens."

Noah smiles. But the smile disappears quickly, as if he is uncomfortable.

"What?" I ask.

He tries to nod me off, but I won't let him. I stop walking, facing him.

After a pause, he looks at me and says, "Sometimes the crazy dreams come true."

Taking his words lightly, I agree and continue walking, until something dawns on me. I turn to face him. "You don't," I say incredulously.

Noah looks uncomfortable.

"You do!" I gasp.

"Not an owner, an investor," he whispers, trying to silence me.

"You own Coney Island Amusement Park!" I squeal loudly.

"Gabriella, quiet," he admonishes, and then he repeats, "An investor."

I just stare at him. "No difference!" I screech.

Noah grins at me as if he is secretly enjoying my reaction. He picks my hand up again and forces me to begin walking. "Now, hush," he orders, "and walk like a queen. What's mine is yours."

For the next three hours, we do it all: we eat, we ride, and we play games.

Noah isn't big on rides, so we only ride three. *More control issues*, I decide. *If he's not driving it, then he's not interested.* But I get him on the merry-go-round. Actually, he stands beside my horse as I ride, but he is still on the ride. I can't believe I actually get him on the teacups. He laughs and enjoys it but promises never again. Then he kisses me on top of the Ferris wheel.

We eat corn dogs, ice cream, and cotton candy.

"Little girls who get dismissed from dinner shouldn't get treats," he teases playfully as we sit on a bench. I'm eating cotton candy, and Noah is watching me.

I redden a little, embarrassed at my behavior. Dinner seems like a lifetime ago.

He laughs and wipes my face with a napkin. "You're getting it all over you," he says, shaking his head. "Here," he says, and he leans in, kissing me deeply. I melt into his kiss. When he finally pulls back, he says, "That should help."

I blush and say, "Now you're sticky."

"That I am," he admits before leaning in and kissing me again. "Ready to go home?"

I shake my head, taking another bite of cotton candy. "You haven't won me anything yet," I tease.

He points to the goldfish, who I have ceremoniously named Guppy, in a plastic bag of water that I won because the man guessed my weight wrong. I have been carrying it around with me all evening. "I won this myself," I tell him, checking on the fish.

"I'll buy you something."

"Not the same," I say. "You have to *win* me something."

He makes a face with a look that says I am pushing it. Then, after a grinning stare-down, he says, "What would you like?"

"A bear," I announce excitedly. "A pink one!"

"A pink bear," he mutters as we begin to walk through the park again. We enter the game arcade. After walking for a few moments, I spot my prize.

"There!" I point to a humongous pink bear sitting on a shelf, surrounded by bears of many colors. "We have to hurry!" I shout, taking his hand and trying to drag him. "It's the only pink one left. All the other good guys got here first."

It is a traditional baseball-pitching game. You get three chances to knock down a pyramid of milk bottles. If you knock them all down using all three balls, you get a small bear; if you knock them all down with two balls, you get a medium bear; and if you knock them all down with one ball, you get a giant bear.

We step up to the counter. No one else is playing. Noah places a dollar on the counter. The teenager managing the game gives him three worn baseballs and nods at the pyramid.

Noah gives me a warning look. I giggle.

He winds up and rifles the ball into the pile of bottles. They all fall except two. Without hesitation, he throws a second ball. The ball goes off course and thuds against the mat behind it. I wince. Noah, undeterred, stretches his arm and plants the next ball directly between the two bottles, knocking them down.

The teenager takes a small bear from the shelf and tries to hand it to Noah, who waves him off. "Reset them!" he barks while offering me a glare. I burst into laughter.

The boy resets them and hands Noah three more balls.

"I'll take three too," a voice says. It comes from a muscular guy somewhere in his early twenties. He is wearing a T-shirt that has the words *Monroe Baseball* on it. He and his girlfriend have stepped up beside Noah and me to play the game too.

"I want the big pink one," the girlfriend announces, snapping her gum.

"Me too," I whisper playfully so that only Noah can hear. He shoots me a not-so-kind look. I giggle.

Noah steps back to allow the younger guy to take a turn. With awesome force, the ball he throws explodes through the stack of milk bottles, but surprisingly, it only knocks down three.

Noah grins. Then his face grows serious. He winds up and throws the ball. This time, all but one bottle topple. I grimace.

"Reset them," Noah orders.

"But you still have two more—"

"Reset them," Noah repeats. The boy shrugs and resets the bottles.

It is almost a race against the clock as the men alternate firing baseballs at the bottles. It has become obvious that they are both going for the largest bear. The pressure builds. Noah has stopped looking at me, and the younger guy has stopped looking at his girlfriend; they concentrate on the challenge at hand. I am beyond nervous, and I have stopped enjoying the game. The other girl glares at me. When I am just about to tell Noah that it's okay and that we can go, he winds up and, with a single ball, sends the milk bottles toppling to the floor.

I jump and squeal.

Noah closes his eyes and rotates his shoulder. "The pink one," he tells the boy with a sigh. The boy laughs, pulls the huge stuffed bear from the shelf, and hands it to Noah, who hands it to me.

"Jerk," we hear the young guy's girlfriend sneer as we walk away hand in hand.

We both burst into laughter.

When we are a safe distance away, I stop and do something I never dreamed I'd do. I turn to Noah and give him a kiss on the cheek. It is the first time I have ever initiated intimacy. At first, he looks shocked, but then his face dissolves into a gentle smile. He accepts my kiss and then takes my hand, linking his fingers with mine.

Like a queen, I walk out of the park, holding my prize.

We drive home in a comfortable silence. When we get there, he walks me to the door of my room. I think he might say something, but he doesn't. Instead, he holds my head gently and kisses me deeply and firmly. I am used to this now. I like how it feels.

He pulls away. His eyes grow darker, and he studies me. Without taking his eyes off of me, he lifts the hem of my too-short sundress just a touch so that he has access between my legs. Pushing my panties aside, he reaches inside of me with one finger and feels how wet I have become. I gasp, flushed and embarrassed. I try to pull away, but he holds me in place with a firm grasp of my arm. With his other hand, he raises my dropped chin, and his piercing blue eyes are on me.

"Good girl," he says, and he walks away down the hallway to his room.

※

The next morning, still exhausted from the park, I sleep late. Noah is already gone by the time I wake. I check my night table for a note. There is none. Usually, he leaves one even if it is only to remind me to behave. I force myself not to feel disappointed. He'll probably call at noon to check on me, as he always does. So why am I anxious to hear his voice?

I spend the morning on the balcony, the place where I do my best thinking. I have a lot to think about. For the first time since I've been here, I have to admit that I'm a little confused. My heart and my head are at war. My hard heart has softened a bit—Noah can be awfully nice when he chooses to be—but my head reminds me that I am here for one purpose only: to help my family. My heart thinks of the pink bear sitting in the corner of my bedroom. My head tells me to stay the course. Finally, I decide to try not to think at all.

Noon comes and goes without a call. When he doesn't show up by six, I'm pacing. Finally, at seven, Mrs. Middleton appears with the phone. It's him.

"Gabriella," he says almost formally, "I'll be away for the night. Business."

"Oh," I say, taken aback by his curtness. He seems not to notice.

"I'll see you tomorrow," he says, and he hangs up.

Chapter 11

I spend the evening alone. Dutifully, I stay locked on the Discovery Channel and watch a documentary on bears. Then, at eleven, as Noah would, I switch over to the news. I watch halfheartedly. The last story is the "About Town" segment. I am just about to click it off, when my heart sinks.

The announcer's voice comes blaring through. "Seen at tonight's black-tie event were Mayor De Blasio, Senator Gillibrand, entrepreneur Noah Bentley, and fashion designer Grace Blattman." A photo of Noah and Grace together flashes on the screen. I'm glad I am alone, as my eyes fill with tears of hurt and rage. Finally, I throw the remote across the room. It hits an antique vase and shatters it. I'm glad.

"Get a grip," I tell myself. "You are here for a purpose. He means nothing. Don't fall. Whatever you do, don't fall."

I sleep fitfully, tortured by nightmares. In them, I

am lost, I am being chased, and I am trapped. When I wake up, I realize that they were all fitting.

By the next morning, I have made a decision: I'm going home. But I'm going home on my terms. I will make him release me.

Screw him, his penthouse, and his money. Screw his rules and punishments. Screw his fake kindness. Screw my heart.

୭

He calls at noon, just as he always does. He acts completely normal. "Gabriella, I'm back in town," he says hurriedly. "I'm in a rush, but I wanted to tell you that tonight we are going out to dinner."

I can tell that whatever this is, it is important to him.

"We will be joined by friends of mine. Actually, they are dear friends of mine. The gentleman was my mentor, and his wife was almost like a second mother to me. I owe them a lot," he says. "And I would like them to meet you. It is very important that you are on your best behavior."

I say nothing, which immediately puts him on edge.

"What's wrong?" he asks, annoyed.

I remain silent. I can practically see his eyes closed in exasperation. I can hear people in the background. He's busy.

"I don't have time for this now," he mutters. "We will deal with whatever it is later. Mrs. Middleton will help you choose the appropriate clothing, and I will pick you up from the downstairs lobby at seven. Be waiting."

The phone goes dead.

Well, he could have hardly explained his vulnerability more clearly. I know exactly what to do.

I spend all day rehearsing my plan in my head. I shudder to think of pulling it off, but then I remind myself that if I am going to get him to release me, I might have to go to the extreme.

Dutifully, at seven o'clock, I am waiting in the lobby with Mrs. Middleton.

"You look very nice, Gabriella," she says. I smile a thank-you. She has chosen an all-white, form-fitting dress, a cotton shawl, and black Gucci pumps. She has even outfitted me with a sequined handbag filled with tissues and mints.

When the car pulls up, Noah gets out to open my door, as he always does. Not once since I've been here have I opened a door for myself. He prefers to be the one to open my door, even when Liam is around.

He dismisses Mrs. Middleton with a nod and smiles warmly at me. "You look lovely, Gabriella," he says. Instant guilt washes over me, but in my head, I preach to myself to stay the course.

With Noah's hand on my thigh, we ride in silence the few short blocks to the restaurant.

Doors are opened for us, and we step out. Noah, as always, guides my movement with his hand on my back. We enter the restaurant. It is one we have never been to, but it looks much like others we have eaten in, except with more than its share of crystal chandeliers, golden fixtures, and expensive paintings.

Mr. and Mrs. Fielding are already seated, the maître d' explains, and he leads us to a table occupied by an elderly couple. Impeccably dressed and groomed, they drip money. The man's white hair is full and in waves atop his head, while hers is cut into an expensive bob. Diamonds are everywhere.

The gentleman stands upon my arrival. My guilt is suffocating me. *Stay focused,* I scold myself.

Noah handles the introduction. They invite me to call them Doris and Harvey. I sit, and Noah reaches over and gently squeezes my knee. This is important to him.

I close my eyes and say a silent prayer that my plan works. If it does, I will be back in New Jersey by midnight.

My plan is to do absolutely nothing. And that's what I do.

For three hours, I am mute, refusing to speak and offering only half nods when spoken to. I take part in none of the conversation. Noah and the Fieldings all but stand on their heads for me, trying everything in the book to include me. I will have none of it. I eat nothing. Noah is mortified. The Fieldings are confused and almost apologetic, as if they have done something wrong, but I am unshakable in my resolve.

One could cut the tension with a knife. The discomfort is beyond words. I have succeeded in making it an unbearable evening for everyone. Finally, Noah ends the evening by saying, "It is obvious that I must get Gabriella home." The Fieldings agree sympathetically, which makes me feel like a heel. They are truly nice people.

As the valet retrieves their car, Noah takes Mr. and Mrs. Fielding aside and apologizes profusely for my behavior.

Liam arrives, and Noah all but pushes me into the car. We drive home in silence. I have never seen him this way, and I know I have gone too far. I am scared of his reaction, but I'm sure I will be going home tonight. Noah is dead silent as we exit the car, navigate the lobby, and ride the elevator.

Once we are in the apartment, he has me by the arm. He forcefully pushes me down the hall to his bedroom. We pass Mrs. Middleton, who is there to greet us, but he waves her off. She reads his signal and retreats.

In his room, he tosses me onto the bed. "It's time for you to learn a lesson," he says. "Those two wonderful people have done nothing to you. It is me you hate!"

I am scared to death. I scoot back up against the headboard only to realize that there is no place to escape to. I tuck my legs up to my chest and hug them with my arms.

Never taking his angry glare from me, Noah undoes his belt in one swift motion, pulling it out from his trousers and doubling it over. He stands above me furiously. "What in the world where you thinking?" he thunders. "What would possess you to behave in such a fashion? Do you hate me that badly that you would purposely choose to humiliate me?"

Feebly, I manage to shake my head.

"Then what?"

When I don't answer, he becomes even more enraged. Suddenly, he strikes the belt to the bed with all his strength, and with a terrifying swoosh, it cuts through the taffeta comforter.

"Speak!" he demands so loudly that the sound shakes the room.

I have never been more scared in all my life. My eyes are filled with tears of fear, and my mouth refuses to open. I can't even swallow.

"I just ... I just thought ... I just thought you would send me home." It is all I can think to say, because it is the truth—the only truth.

"Well, you thought wrong!" he shouts. "You don't know me well, Gabriella, but you know me well enough to understand that I don't lose!"

I nod.

Still enraged, he strikes the bed again, making another cut in the fabric. This time, I scream, shaking uncontrollably. Then we make eye contact, and thankfully, something connects us. Through his rage, he seems to actually see me, and he stops. He mutters something that I can't make out and throws the belt across the room. I don't know what to make of the unheard words but am glad that the belt is gone, if only for now.

My eyes are glued to his, waiting for his next move.

He sighs deeply and runs his hand through his hair, shaking his head. Then he comes closer to the bed and grabs my ankle, forcing me to unravel. He crawls on the bed to meet me. I am still visibly shaking, and he sees this. He grimaces and lies down next to me.

With a sudden, misplaced gentleness, he stares down at me and tucks my hair behind my ear. He looks at me with an expression I have not seen before, cups my head in his hands, and kisses me. Softly yet firmly, he parts my lips.

"Open," he tells me. Again, I am learning. I begin to relax and melt slowly into the bed. As always, his tongue explores. He has done this before, but tonight he is more urgent.

He reaches down and undoes his zipper with one hand. The sound terrifies me yet makes me tingle at the same time. He senses that I tense up and says, "Easy, baby."

Then he gently pulls my panties from my body and pushes my dress above my hips. He moves on top of me. I wriggle a bit, but he holds me firmly. He reaches down and places a finger inside of me. As usual, I am wet for him. He nods and shakes his head back and forth. Then, like the exasperated man that he is, he sighs.

He looks down at me as he continues touching me, learning every curve and crevice. I squirm even more and can't help but let out a moan. A small grin spreads across his face, but I only see it momentarily before his wandering fingers make me arch my back in delight. My body pulses, begging for him not to stop. I feel him hard against my thigh.

He spreads my legs with his and is about to take me, but he pulls back and looks deep into my eyes. "Ready?"

I nod because I am. He carefully places himself inside of me.

The sensation feels foreign. He fills me completely, deeply. Slowly, he begins a rhythm. I am tight and can't help but whimper each time he plunges forward. He makes it last a long time, kissing me softly all the while. He kisses me first on my lips, but as my breathing becomes heavy, he moves to my neck. He teases, plunging deeply before pulling almost completely out. He quickens almost to the point of climax and then slows and begins again. Finally, he is groaning, and with one final, deep thrust, he comes inside of me.

When he is finished, he is panting with his head on my chest. My body goes limp. I let go of the breath I have been holding. My hands rest on top of his thick black hair. His breathing is regular now. He leans up and looks me squarely in the eyes. He shakes his head. "Very few people give me a run for my money," he says, but he is no longer angry. I blush, assuming that maybe I have. He rises from the bed, and he is about to say something else, but his voice fades as his eyes fall to the blood on the sheets.

His eyes widen as if he is seeing something unimaginable. He looks back at me in shock. His mouth gapes open. I can see him swallow. Then, with a voice hoarse with disbelief, he says, "You were innocent." The words come out as a whisper.

I am once again wrapped up in myself on the farthest point of the bed. I blush. I can't look at him and instead stare down at my painted toenails. The blood on the bed mortifies me. I can still feel his stare upon me. He drops to his knees at the foot of the bed. I let myself look up. I have no idea what he might do. His expression is still one of shock. He closes his eyes and grimaces. Then he speaks.

"I would have never. Not like this." His voice trails off.

I have never seen him like this.

"That's why you wanted to leave so badly." Again, his voice fades.

He rises carefully, as if he is trying not to scare me, and stands at the end of the bed, staring at me for what seems to be forever. Finally, he is broken from his trance.

"Let's get you into a bath," he says so gently that I am mesmerized by him.

He holds out his hand. I leave it hanging there in the air before finally reaching up to touch his fingers and allow him to take my hand and guide me off of the bed.

Once in the bathroom, I stand barefoot with only my silky, now-stained, short white dress on. I shiver.

"God, you're cold." He curses. He turns the knobs on the tub, and it begins to fill. He searches the shelf in the corner, finds some bubble bath, and dumps a dollop into the tub. Instantly, it foams up. He turns to me and looks into my face, but I can't look at him. He reaches down and pulls my dress up.

"Lift your arms," he says soothingly. I obey. He lifts the dress off of me and tosses it onto the floor. I am naked. Gently, he takes my hand and helps me into the tub. The warm water feels good but burns a bit when it touches the area between my legs.

"Kneel," he says. I don't know what else to do, so I do as he says.

He begins washing me gently. He starts at the top and works his way down, washing my neck and then each arm. Gently, he circles each breast. He orders me onto all fours to wash my bottom, and then he is in between my legs. I close my eyes. My head is spinning. *What have I gotten myself into?*

He rinses me clean and then helps me from the tub. Just as thoroughly, he dries me.

Noah guides me to the dressing room and chooses a pale pink silk baby-doll nightie. It has spaghetti straps and falls just below my belly. The matching panties have ruffles on the bottom. He puts them on me. He lifts my chin and looks directly into my eyes.

"Now you are really mine," he says with molten blue eyes. "My beautiful girl."

Chapter 12

The next morning, I awake in Noah's bed. Never has an escape plan backfired more perfectly. He is already gone. I don't know how I feel about this. There is a note on the night table.

> I'll be early.
> N

I eat my breakfast alone as Mrs. Middleton goes about her business. I am lonely and confused. For the first time, I begin to understand the magnitude of what I have agreed to. I shiver at the thought.

I never expected my first time with a man to be like it was. But admittedly, I liked it.

I long to talk to my sisters, and I contemplate using the house phone to do so, but I refuse to succumb to the urge. For all I know, he can probably listen in.

I am puzzled by our arrangement. I am confused, unsettled, and scared—probably because he confuses me, unsettles me, and scares me. I still don't know what he wants. Does he really think that after 180 days, I will choose to leave my entire life behind and be with him? It's illogical and unrealistic.

Mrs. Middleton interrupts my thoughts by bringing me a sweater. She is always keeping an eye out for me. I wonder what she knows.

"Mrs. Middleton?" I ask as I pull the sweater on. "Has he ever been married?"

She looks at me and frowns. "I'm not at liberty to discuss Mr. Bentley's personal life," she says apologetically.

"Had kids?"

Again, she says nothing, and she begins to walk back into the apartment.

"Murdered someone?" I call after her.

She appears back in the doorway, and we both dissolve into laughter.

"No, no, and no," she says, still smiling, and then she scurries off to continue her work.

၆

When Mrs. Middleton goes on her daily shopping trip to the market for the night's dinner, I ask her if I can please go. She tells me that Mr. Bentley has already said an emphatic no to this request, and although I can tell she feels badly for me, she leaves me behind as instructed.

While she is gone, I rummage through the kitchen drawers and find what I am looking for. I take six pieces of paper, a marker, a ruler, and some tape and head to the walk-in closet. I sit on the floor in the spacious room and make a homemade calendar. I use one piece of paper for each of the six months: July, August, September, October, November, and December. I pray that I will be long gone before using them all, but seeing the days disappear might help me stay inspired or at least focused. I mark off the days that I have already been here. *Time served.*

I push a bottom row of clothes aside and tape the papers to the wall. I then push the clothes back to hide them. I hear the front door; Mrs. Middleton must be back. I scurry to gather the scraps of paper and the supplies to return them to the kitchen. When I stand up, I am not looking where I am going, and I bump right into Noah so hard that I bounce off of him and fall to the floor. He tries to catch me before I fall, but I land on my bottom anyway.

"What are you doing in here?" he asks. I look up, embarrassed, and don't speak. "I thought you might be unsettled, so I came home to check on you." He glances to the spot where the clothes are slightly out of place. "What are you hiding?"

"Nothing," I say, finding my voice.

But he reaches down and parts the clothes, revealing my makeshift calendars. He frowns and sits down so that we are both facing each other with our legs stretched out. "That bad?" he asks.

I stare at my knees. He reaches over and realigns the clothes, hiding my embarrassment. For a moment, we just sit there together, which is odd. He has invaded my safe haven.

"I know what you need," he finally says, getting up off of the floor. "Come," he orders.

He doesn't seem mad, but the last time he gave me what I needed, I was sore for days.

I follow him out of the closet.

"Shoes," he calls over his shoulder. I scramble back to slide my sandals on, wondering where we are going.

On our way out of the apartment, we pass Mrs. Middleton. She addresses Noah formally and then looks at me, puzzled. I shrug.

We enter the elevator, and he takes my hand in his. When we get outside, his car is waiting at the curb. He opens my door, and I climb in. He walks around and gets in, and off we go. He calmly navigates the city traffic. His hand rests gently on my knee. After a short ride, he announces, "Here we are." I have no idea where here is, but I am intrigued.

He opens my door, and I step out into the bright sunlight. I look up through the glare and discover that we are someplace I've only seen in movies. I keep myself from gasping but know that my eyes are wide. We are at Tiffany's.

I look at him, confused, but before he can say anything, an entourage of people are out on the sidewalk, greeting us. They welcome Noah as if he is some kind of royalty. We enter the store through a welcoming committee of employees who part down the middle.

The life of Noah Bentley certainly is a remarkable one.

Noah is gracious with all of them, shaking each and every hand.

"Mr. Bentley," says a man I presume is the manager, "you are generally accustomed to shopping after hours. Are you sure you are at ease with the other people?"

"Perfectly," Noah answers. "This is a bit of an emergency, Thomas."

"I understand, sir." Thomas nods seriously.

I am glad that he understands, because how someone could have a Tiffany's emergency is beyond me. But since I have been told I possess a smart mouth, I keep quiet and go with it.

"And what are we in the market for?" Thomas is almost jumping out of his skin with excitement.

"The lady needs a timepiece," Noah says, looking at me now.

I cringe.

"Wonderful!" Thomas exclaims, and he claps his hands. He is really into this.

Thomas leads us to the correct area while dismissing the extra employees who have gathered. He almost shoos them away, and I kind of feel bad for them. He leads us to a counter with a huge array of watches. There are too many to count, constructed of gold, silver, and diamonds. Each is prettier than the next. My eyes almost water at the beauty.

"What kind of watch are we looking for?" Thomas asks. I flinch and come out of my trance, realizing that his question is directed to me. Helplessly, I look at Noah.

He steps closer to me so that his hand is on the small of my back. Usually, I don't like this, but this time, I am grateful.

"Well, it has to be something special," Noah says. "Very special." He gives me a wink and a grin. "The lady," he says to Thomas, "is really into time. I mean really, really into time."

I try to stifle my grin. He is playing with me.

"She needs to know exactly what time it is at all times. It is very important to her."

Thomas nods so seriously that I think I might burst out laughing. I look at Noah, who looks at me, and we grin.

Thomas is suddenly frantic. He lays a soft cloth out on the counter and begins to lay watches on top. He begins to babble. "We have gold, silver, and platinum." The words fall out of his mouth in a rush.

In my opinion, they are all amazingly beautiful.

Noah looks discouraged. Thomas is reading this reaction.

"Thomas, I don't believe you realize just how into time this beautiful girl is," Noah says.

"Oh, I do, sir. I really do," he assures Noah, and he quickly makes more watches appear. Thomas, who is beginning to sweat, looks expectantly at Noah.

Mercifully, Noah lets Thomas off the hook and offers him the proper clue. "Diamonds," he whispers softly.

"Oh! Yes, sir!" Thomas snaps at his assistants to remove the present array of watches, as if they are all a bad idea. They do as they are told, and the cloth is empty again.

"Diamonds," Thomas repeats to Noah.

Noah nods. "Lots of them."

Thomas looks as if he might pee himself. He fishes keys from his pocket and turns to a cabinet behind him. He opens the cabinet and then a safe within. He removes an aqua-colored box and carefully carries it to the counter. Some of the employees have stopped what they are doing and are watching him. He sees this and shoots them a look, and they all pretend to continue what they are doing, but each of them still has an eye on us.

Noah steps closer to me, still with his hand on my back.

Gently, Thomas opens the box and takes out the most amazing thing I have ever seen.

My eyes widen. It is a floral-cut diamond cocktail watch. The entire platinum face is encrusted with brilliant round diamonds. The lid unlocks the face of the watch to reveal the time. I never knew that such a thing existed.

"Total carat weight is fourteen point fifty-one," Thomas tells Noah discreetly.

Noah nods. "It is the lady's choice," he tells Thomas.

Thomas nods and looks at me. Taken aback, I look at Noah and shake my head. My mouth opens as I begin to say that I never could accept such a gift, but Noah warns me off with a look.

"Do you like it?" he asks softly.

"I've never seen anything more beautiful." It's all I can manage. Beyond that, I am speechless.

"Then you should have it."

"Noah, I can't—"

He stops me again with a look. I gulp.

"So is it the lady's choice?" Thomas asks tentatively.

Noah looks at me and grins with raised eyebrows. "Is it?"

I let out the breath I have been holding. I don't know what to do or say. I look at Noah to help me, but he won't. He is enjoying this. Finally, I just nod.

Thomas lets out a relieved smile and bounces backward on his heels.

Noah moves his hand down from my back to my bottom. I don't mind.

We refuse gift wrapping, and twenty minutes later, I am walking out of Tiffany's with a $200,000 watch on my wrist.

I hear the employees whisper among themselves as we leave. One says, "I know who he is, but who is she?"

୭

That night, we are back at Il Mulino. The maître d' is scurrying, as usual. Water has been poured, and menus have been placed gently in our laps. We are both worn out and mellow.

Noah surprises me by asking, "What would you like to eat tonight?" He has never asked this. He has always just ordered for the two of us. But most of our meals so far have been a little volatile, with me belligerent and him unflappable.

Tonight we are at peace.

I open the menu and scan through it. I realize that before, whenever I was not given the choice, I cared, but now that I have it, I don't care much at all. I close the menu. "Whatever you choose," I say.

Noah takes a moment to try to read my face. He is trying to decide if I am being uncooperative or defiant. I am being neither. I am growing accustomed to him making choices for me and don't entirely dislike it. *How did this happen?*

He reads my mood correctly and nods. His face softens. I am glad because I don't feel like fighting.

The waiter appears.

"We will both have the veal piccata," Noah tells him.

The menus are whisked away. Noah looks at me across the table and gives me his full attention. "You look lovely tonight, Gabriella," he says.

On a different night, I would have made some snide comment about the clothes being chosen for me, but not tonight. "Thank you," I answer.

"You're a very beautiful girl," he remarks.

I look into his eyes, and for a moment, we connect. For just one moment, it is as if we are out on a date or even married—just like all of the other people in the restaurant. Tonight I don't feel the arrangement between us. The elephant in the room has taken the night off.

He places his elbows on the table, folds his hands under his chin, and rests on them. He stares at me as if he is intrigued. He is gorgeous. His intense gaze makes me blush, and I have to look away. My eyes drop to my own hands, which lie upon the folded napkin on my lap.

"Truce?" he asks softly.

This one word and the manner in which he says it startle me. I lose my breath for a moment. In spite of myself, I raise my eyes to meet his. His blue eyes are soft, and he waits for my answer. I weigh the offer. I know now that fighting is no use. He is stronger than I am. He has proven that in a hundred ways. I am no match for him. I gulp and search for my voice. At first, I manage only a nod. Then I whisper, "Until December."

He unfolds his hands and lays an arm out on the table with his palm up, waiting for me to take it.

For a moment, I allow his outstretched hand to lie there, and then, slowly, I do something I never dreamed I'd do: I reach out and gently place my palm in his.

He nods at the gesture. Then he draws my hand up to his mouth and gently kisses it. "Good girl."

Chapter 13

The next morning, when I wake, I check the clock. It is after eight. I am hoping he is gone already. I need some space. I think it will do me some good to be alone. But when I reach the kitchen, he is still at the island with the newspaper.

"Good morning," he says. I can't read his tone. "You must have been tired; you slept in."

I nod. For many reasons, I can't look at him. I've agreed to stay, but I'm still apprehensive. This entire scenario is surreal. I'm confused by my feelings. I'm fighting it, but I am finding myself drawn to him. Even though I've agreed to a truce, I don't know where we stand. I go to sit in my place, but he stops me.

"Walk me out, Gabriella," he says. "I need to go."

I follow him. He leads me to his study. I take in a breath. The memories of this room are difficult for me. I think he knows that.

"Today," he says, leading me to the desk, "you will sit here and write an apology note to Mr. and Mrs.

Fielding." He motions toward a pen and stationery he has laid out for me.

I redden with embarrassment.

"Have it done by the time I get home," he says. "We'll put it in the mail in the morning."

I don't answer and only look down at my feet.

"And," he says, raising my chin so that our eyes meet, "you are grounded with no privileges. We will begin again today. Understood?"

So last night meant nothing. We are back to exactly where we started from. He is as stern and demanding as ever. He waits for my response. By now, I know he wants eye contact and compliance—obedience.

I swallow back tears of frustration and fury but give him what he wants. "Yes," I answer. However, he is not willing to let this be enough. He keeps his eyes on me and waits for more. He wants me completely in my place.

"Yes," I say. "I understand."

"Good," he says, and he turns and walks out of the apartment.

At noon, when Mrs. Middleton takes her daily trip to the market, I give in and do something I promised myself I wouldn't: I use the apartment phone and call home. It has been six weeks, and the homesickness has gotten to me.

My heart squeezes, and my resolve to see this arrangement through heightens when I hear Poppy's and my sisters' voices. I'll do anything for them. I keep up my lie about the secretarial job and insist that all is going well. It is only my oldest sister, Angela, who doesn't seem to buy my story.

"I don't know what exactly is going on, Gabby," she tells me, "but please know that whatever it is, I'm here for you."

My voice breaks as I thank her.

If only I knew what was going on. My original plan is lost now. He's not going to send me home. That's not going to happen. At the same time, I'm finding it difficult to come to terms with what I've agreed to instead. I'm scared.

When Noah comes home promptly at six, he finds me in the library, sitting on the floor with a book laid out in front of me. He stares down at me. I say nothing. He is holding the apology note I wrote to Mr. and Mrs. Fielding. I gulp and look at him expectantly.

"Adequate," he says. My heart sinks, and I frown. I shouldn't have expected more from him, but somehow, I did.

He looks down at the oversized book lying open before me. It is the most glorious book I have ever seen. It is called *The History of Art* and contains amazing photographs and biographies of famous painters. It tells about their lives and their works. I am fascinated and have been exploring it for hours. Suddenly self-conscious, I rush to close it.

He sees my reaction and says, "I told you the library was open to you. I'm actually pleased to see you making use of it. Do you like art?"

"Love it," I murmur honestly.

Ever since I was a little girl, I have dreamed of being a famous painter. The funny part is, I haven't held a paintbrush in my hand more than a few times. I've always been too intimidated even to try.

"So much to discover," he says, looking at me, intrigued. At first, I think he means about art, but then I realize he's referring to me. I flush.

"Put the book away," he tells me. "Dinner is ready."

I nod and feel heartbroken to have to part with it, but I do as he says and follow him into the dining room.

Everything feels different to me because of last night, yet nothing seems to have changed for him. He is still stern. A million jumbled thoughts run through my head, but I say nothing. Last night has me confused. I feel as if I might cry. I hate myself for this.

"You're unhappy," he says.

His words make my throat swell. I shrug.

"Words," he says, reprimanding me.

"Yes," I say, and he nods. I pick at my food.

"Elbows."

I take them from the table.

He stares at me. "What can I do to help?"

Let me go home, I think, but I don't say it.

"You already are home," he says, somehow knowing my thoughts. "You'll adjust." His expression is neither cold nor sympathetic. It is matter-of-fact.

"In time," he adds. His words and the definitive way in which he says them send a chill up my spine.

Finished with his meal, Noah lays his utensils neatly on his plate. After dabbing his mouth with his napkin and laying it to the side, he raises his hand, links his fingers together, and settles his arms on the table. He focuses his full attention on me. "Game over, darling," he says.

I am unable to speak. My eyes are riveted to his. I only nod obediently.

※

Now that I share his bed, rare is the night that Noah doesn't make love to me. We finish watching the eleven o'clock news that night, and as is our routine, he goes to his office to check his e-mail and close down his computer while I go to the bedroom and wait for him. Before we part in the living room, he kisses me gently on the lips.

"Go," he orders, motioning toward the bedroom. There is something different about him tonight. I swallow and wonder what I am in for.

When he comes in, I am sitting in the middle of the master bed, as he likes me to be. He circles the bed like a panther eyeing its prey. He never takes his eyes off of me but comes closer, undressing as he does.

"Do exactly as you are told, Gabriella," he says, finally reaching the bed.

I nod, casting my eyes downward. My body tingles with a mix of anticipation and excitement.

"Let's take this off," he says, lifting off the top of my teddy. Obediently, I raise my arms. "And these too," he says, removing my panties and tossing them aside.

He leans into me and begins to suck my breast,

drawing soft circles with his tongue. When the nipple becomes hard, he growls with satisfaction and then moves to the other breast. Once both breasts are pointed, he begins moving slowly and methodically down me with his mouth. He kisses the center of my stomach, and I begin to wriggle.

"Still, or I will cuff you," he warns. I think of the cuffs that I know are just inches away in the night table. We have never used them before.

He reaches my pubic hair and rubs it with his five o'clock shadow. The friction sends electricity through me.

"Lie back, and spread your legs," he orders. I don't move. My legs are nearly locked together. I am still kneeling. He leans up and looks at me sternly. "First, lie back," he tells me, breaking his order down into pieces.

Slowly, I take my legs out from under me and lie back.

"Now spread your legs," he says. When I hesitate, he begins to lose patience. He reaches over and retrieves the leather cuffs from inside the night table. After pausing for a moment, he grabs a second pair. "These will help you," he says. My mouth goes dry.

Swiftly, he cuffs one hand to the other and then cuffs both hands to the bedpost. I open my mouth to object, but he leans in and kisses me fully.

"Let it happen," he whispers, leaving me silent. Instinctively, I pull on the restraints, but it only makes them tighter.

"Now spread your legs," he tells me again. I am

helpless, and he could easily pull my legs apart himself, but I know that he wants me to obey his commands. I close my eyes and spread my legs, submitting to and trusting him completely.

"Wider," he orders.

I oblige.

"Wider," he growls. When I am slow to react, he reaches to the opposite night table and retrieves another set of cuffs. "Do you need more help?" he asks.

Unable to speak, I shake my head. I'm not ready for another set of cuffs. I spread my legs so that I am completely exposed.

He kneels between my spread legs. He spreads me apart with his fingers, exposing my clit. "What do we have here?" he says playfully.

Slowly and mercilessly, he begins to rub in circles. He brings me almost to the point of climax and then slows. Each time, I arch my back as he pulls his hand away, involuntarily rising to meet his escaping touch. He holds his hand just out of reach and laughs teasingly.

"Tell me, honey," he croons. "This?" He begins to rub again.

I moan and nod. I arch my back and pull at the cuffs, but they are at their tightest and hold me firmly in place.

"Please?" he asks.

I groan.

"Words," he insists, slowing.

"Please," I moan softly.

"More, please," he corrects, quickening his pace. I am almost there.

"More. Please," I gasp.

"Again," he orders.

"More, please. More, please. More, please!" I cry.

I beg until I come violently, quivering as I do. Done, my body goes limp, my eyes still closed. I can feel him undo the cuffs. He gently rubs my wrists. When I open my eyes, he is above me, smiling faintly.

"That's my beautiful girl," he says. "That's my beautiful girl."

Chapter 14

When Noah said I was grounded without privileges, he meant it. I am confined to the apartment for days. We eat breakfast together at eight. He leaves me until six. I entertain myself as best as I can with television and the library. Most days, I am bored to tears.

One day he shows up unexpectedly in the middle of the day. I'm out on the balcony. I've happened upon a butterfly perched on the ledge. I am leaning in and studying it in wonder. The colors are astounding. I watch as it randomly opens and closes its wings.

"Beautiful, isn't it?" His voice startles me. I jump but quickly collect myself and nod in agreement. "Looks like a monarch," he notes.

I don't know what kind it is, so I don't comment.

"Do you like butterflies?" he asks.

Again, I nod.

"Words," he says.

"Yes," I say.

We watch together silently for a few moments.

"Go get a sweater," he tells me. I do as he says. When I return, he's on the phone.

"We'll be there in thirty," he tells whomever he's talking to.

He hangs up and takes my hand, and we are gone. He leads me to the Mercedes, which is parked at the curb. He opens the door and allows me in.

Being out of the apartment feels amazing. I have no idea where we are going, and frankly, I don't care. *I'm out!*

The ease with which Noah maneuvers the traffic always surprises me. Twenty minutes later, we pull up to the curb in front of a huge gray building. I read the sign. We are at the American Museum of Natural History. Noah puts on the car's flashers, and as is always the case with Noah, magic happens. A man appears.

"Mr. Bentley. A pleasure to have you, sir," the man says. He takes the keys.

Noah gets out and comes around to open my door. I step out of the car and onto the sidewalk. The car disappears. Noah takes my hand and leads me toward the entrance. "I think you'll like this," he tells me.

I have no idea what we are doing until we reach the main doors and I see the sign: Butterfly Conservatory. I gasp. My mouth drops.

"Good idea?" he asks.

I nod and then answer, "Yes."

We spend the next two hours exploring the exhibit. He never lets go of my hand. It is glorious. I never knew there were so many varieties of butterflies. Seeing them all in one place is amazing. The colors are spectacular. They fly all around us and sometimes land on us.

He points out his favorite and asks me which is mine. He always seems genuinely interested in my thoughts. In this respect, I have never met anyone like him.

"Not too many butterflies in New Jersey?" Noah asks me teasingly.

"No." I grin.

"Not too many in Manhattan either," he says. "Had enough?" he asks when we reach the end of the exhibit.

I nod.

"You'll like dinner," he promises.

We dine at the Rainbow Room. I try not to appear amazed but give up and look around wide-eyed. Each place he takes me is prettier than the place before.

Everywhere we go, he is known—not only known but also respected and liked. He is always greeted by name and led to a favorite table, where whatever he wants seems to appear magically.

We have oysters. He insists I try one, but I decide that I don't like them.

"No worries," he tells me softly.

I try to catch glimpses of him when I think he is not looking. He's becoming familiar, but for the most part, he is still a stranger. I wonder what he sees when he steals glances at me.

Once we are at home, he leads me into the bedroom. He turns me around and, from behind, nuzzles my neck. I arch as tingles run through me. He growls, knowing the power he has over me. He unzips the zipper that runs the length of my dress and peels the dress from me as he nibbles my earlobes. He kisses my neck as I step out of it. Deftly, he unclips my bra. My ample breasts spring free. The bra drops to the floor. He turns me and leans down, sucking each breast, taking his time with each until my nipples are hard. I am dripping wet for him. I begin to wriggle as my sex aches. He looks at me and smiles.

"I hear you, baby," he says. Taking my hand, he guides me to the bed. He pulls my panties off. "Like this." He turns me so my back is to him. "Climb on the bed on all fours," he says. "I want to take you from behind."

I hesitate. All of this is new to me.

"Don't think. Obey," he whispers.

I climb onto the bed.

Noah kneels behind me and reaches inside of me with one finger, discovering how wet I am. He makes an approving noise in his throat. "Bend down, and put your cheek on the bed."

This is too much for me. I am too vulnerable.

"Gabriella." His voice is stern.

I close my eyes and lean over, resting my cheek on the bed. My bottom is up in the air, exposed. He rubs it with both hands and growls. Then he holds me by the hips and firmly enters me. I whimper. It feels good.

In this position, he is deeper than before. He plunges slowly at first. I grip the comforter tightly as his pace becomes more urgent. Moments later, I close my eyes and feel the room spinning as we come together.

Chapter 15

It's Noah's mother's birthday. He says it's time I meet his family. I think otherwise. I protest a bit but know I am not going to win.

"We will go and spend just a short time," he assures me.

On the elevator ride down to the car, he pulls a small box from his breast pocket. He opens it and shows me the contents. I cringe and blush when I see that it is the pendant I was caught wearing on my first day.

Noah raises an eyebrow. "Our gift."

Embarrassed, I nod.

It's warm, and we have the top down on the ride out of the city.

"What's your family like?" I ask him. He has never spoken about his family before.

He thinks for a moment and then chooses his words carefully. "Well," he says, "let's see. My parents are wonderful. My father is a retired college history professor."

"That's why you like history so much," I say.

Noah nods. "And my mother never worked out of the home."

"Brothers and sisters?" I ask.

"Five brothers," he tells me.

"Wow!" I exclaim. "Just like my five sisters."

"My brothers are not quite as wonderful as my parents, I'm afraid."

"You don't like them?" I ask, slightly astonished, thinking about the love I have for my sisters.

He mulls this question over. "No. I guess I don't," he admits. "Let's put it this way: I don't respect my brothers. I don't approve of the way that they live their lives. They are unable to control their vulgar wives or their unruly children. They are takers, and they are mediocre employees."

"They all work for you?" I ask, surprised.

"Every single one of them." He sighs.

"Are you the oldest?"

"Youngest."

"But you're the one who achieved the most," I say.

He nods. "I have the drive, determination, and focus that they lack."

"So the entire family kind of lives off of you?" I ask.

"Not kind of," he says. "They do live off of me."

"Does that bug you?"

"I do it as a favor to my parents," he says as we pull into an exclusive neighborhood of expensive homes with brick and stone exteriors, immaculately manicured gardens, and long, winding driveways leading to fancy front doors. Each home seems more impressive than the last.

Finally, Noah pulls into a stone driveway that leads to a stately looking home constructed of red brick. It is huge. It has eight windows that face the street—four on the top story of the house and four on the bottom. The shutters and front door are bright white.

Suddenly, I am nervous. Reading my mind as always, Noah says, "There's nothing to be worried about." He gently touches my knee. "We hold all the cards. Trust me." Then he pulls me in for a kiss.

He exits the car, and I stay frozen in the passenger seat. He arrives on my side and opens the door. I shake my head firmly. He laughs and then takes my hand and helps me from the car.

His parents greet us at the door. I like them instantly. They look like average, everyday people, which comforts me.

"Mom, Dad," he says, "this is my girlfriend, Gabriella Rossi."

My mouth drops open at the word *girlfriend*. Noah has never introduced me like this before. My mouth must still be open as they each shake my hand, because Noah leans in to me and tells me to close it. I look at him, red faced and astonished. He grins and squeezes my hand before leading me into the dining room.

What greets us is nothing short of mayhem. I can't begin to count the number of people present, but there seem to be a zillion: there are his five brothers, their wives, and troops of children. It is chaos. They are already at the table, beginning to pass plates of food. The bedlam ceases for a moment when Noah walks into the room. At first, I think they are staring at him, but then I suddenly realize that they are staring at me. I want to sink into the floor.

"Everyone," Noah says, "Gabriella Rossi. Gabriella, everyone."

I say nothing and force an embarrassed smile as they respond practically in unison: "Hi, Gabriella."

Sensing my discomfort, Noah ushers me to the table, where there are two empty seats for us. "Don't worry," he whispers. "We won't stay long."

I nod and let out the breath that I am holding.

The children run rampant throughout the entire dinner, doing everything but hanging from the chandelier. The brothers guffaw obnoxiously to one another and laugh hysterically at stupid jokes. They seem like frat boys. It's difficult to imagine them as Noah's brothers. He couldn't be more different. The sisters-in-law are as loud as their husbands, except for when they huddle together and whisper with their eyes focused on me. Being stared at is making me uncomfortable, and I am fidgeting. Noah reassuringly holds my knee.

When the meal is over, we all go into the family room, where the adults have after-dinner drinks. I look at Noah pleadingly. I want to leave. He reads my face. "Just a little longer," he tells me quietly.

I frown. "Restroom?"

"Right down that hallway." He points.

Nervously, I leave his side. The restroom is right

off the kitchen, which is empty. I scoot through it and enter the bathroom.

I freshen up a bit, putting on fresh lip gloss and fluffing up my hair. I sigh at my reflection. I look as stressed as I feel. I am just about to reach for the doorknob, when I hear the wives enter the kitchen noisily. They do nothing quietly.

"I wonder if good old Gabby knows she's the flavor of the month," one of them screeches.

"She'll find out soon enough!" another says.

"She won't last long. None of them do."

"I mean, gosh, what does he actually see in her? She's practically an infant."

"He'll send her back to her mother soon enough!" one predicts. This brings a collective barrage of laughter.

I gulp. That comment hurts. But I will not cry.

I grab the handle of the bathroom door and fling the door open so that it hits the opposite wall. Shocked, they turn and see me. Obviously, they did not expect me to appear. They part as I walk through them. There is dead silence.

I find Noah where I left him, talking to his father in the family room. They both smile warmly as I approach. Noah's face drops as he sees the look on mine.

"I want to leave," I tell him bluntly. He knows I am serious. "I want to leave now."

He nods, looking a little puzzled but reading the urgency in my statements. "Let me say good-bye to my mother."

I tolerate a collective and uncomfortable good-bye

with the rest of them. Minutes later, we are back in the car. Only when we are back out on the highway do I let myself breathe. I am too angry to speak.

He lets the silence linger between us for a while, as if sensing that I need some time. Then, finally, he speaks. "Would you like to tell me what's wrong?"

I don't answer. I stare out the window.

"If you don't tell me, I can't make it right."

I continue to stare.

"I can make anything right," he says.

This statement drives me crazy and makes me burst. "Well, you can't make this right," I snap.

He stays level and calm, as always. "Try me. Did someone do or say something to you?"

I can't contain my rage any longer. "They called me the flavor of the month!"

Hearing this, Noah suddenly swerves across two lanes of highway traffic and stops us with a screech on the side of the road. He throws the car into park and confronts me. "They called you what?" he thunders.

"The flavor of the month," I repeat, feeling glad that he is furious.

"Which one?"

"All of them."

I don't know that I've ever seen him so mad. He shakes his head. "Don't worry. I will take care of it." Furiously, he pulls the car back onto the highway.

"You don't have to," I murmur. "I can take it." Just knowing he is upset makes me less upset.

"Well, I can't take it!" He drives like a maniac back

to the apartment. I don't dare to approach him when he is like this, so I say nothing.

Once we're inside the apartment, he orders me to take a bath and disappears into his study, closing the door. Fifteen minutes later, Mrs. Middleton appears. I am already bathed and dressed for bed.

"Mr. Bentley would like to see you in the study," she tells me. Without a clue as to what he might want, I nod and go.

When I reach the study, Noah is sitting at his desk, on the phone. When he sees me, he rises from the sleek leather desk chair and motions for me to take his place. He hands me the receiver of the phone. I furrow my brow, puzzled, and hesitate, but he nods for me to say hello. When I do, there is a slight pause, and then, suddenly, I can hear a crowd on the other end. I blink, shocked. It takes me a moment to realize that the crowd is all of the sisters-in-law. It is a conference call between the five of them and me.

I look at Noah, wide-eyed, as they all begin to apologize at once. The five of them frantically beg for my forgiveness. I have no idea what to say, so I say nothing at first. I just stare at Noah, whose face is only slightly less furious than it was earlier. I guess that when he says he is going to take care of something, he means it.

Finally, I find some words and tell them that it is okay. I am slightly mortified. With nothing else to say or listen to, I hand the phone back to Noah. As they continue to gush, he simply hangs the phone up.

"It won't happen again," he says with finality.

I nod. Once again, I am taken aback by his power.

Later that night, after making love to me, he cradles me in his arms. We lay in silence for several minutes. I promise myself that I won't ask the question that continues to pop into my mind. I toss and turn. As always, he reads my mind and knows just what my restlessness is all about.

"Settle, baby," he says, tightening his grip. "You are not the flavor of the month, darling. Anything but. Anything but."

Chapter 16

We spend most of our evenings at home, just the two of us, but a couple of times a week, Noah seems to want to introduce me to his world. First, I met his family, and now I will meet a few friends.

It's a Saturday night. We are having dinner with three of his fraternity brothers from college and their wives in Chinatown. We drink green tea and eat family style from huge platters in the center of the table. It's a new experience for me.

It's a fun evening. They are nice people. The guys are highly successful, as Noah is. They are charismatic and interesting. It's difficult for me to know exactly what they do for a living, but I'm pretty sure it has to do with money—and lots of it.

The women are all beautiful and genuinely nice. None of them seems to work outside of the home, and they talk a lot about their houses and children. They're self-assured without being arrogant.

It's obvious that Noah thinks a great deal of

everyone there, and they of him. I enjoy listening to their stories about college escapades, rowdy adventures, and funny mishaps. It's difficult for me to imagine Noah ever standing in the dean's office being scolded or performing community service as a punishment for his misdeeds, but apparently, he has done both. Every once in a while, when I hear a story that truly shocks me, I shoot Noah a silly look. He simply shrugs and rolls his eyes.

I find it interesting to see Noah in this element. In some ways, he's the same Noah, cool and composed, but in another way, he's different—a bit more relaxed and boyish.

Still, he knows that these situations are always a little bit intimidating for me, so he stays close with one arm around me protectively. I'm grateful for this.

It's nearing the end of the evening, and I have pretty much managed to stay under the radar until now.

"So, Gabriella, how'd you manage to meet this guy?" Noah's friend Clark asks.

I immediately bristle. In all of the time we've been together, no one has ever been so direct. I'm frozen.

"Serendipity," Noah says, gently squeezing my shoulder reassuringly. I relax.

"A noun!" announces Grant, another friend, jokingly. "The faculty of making fortunate discoveries by accident. S-e-r-e-n-d-i-p-i-t-y—serendipity."

Grant introduced himself to me at the beginning of the evening as the smartest member of the group, bragging that he had once claimed the state title in middle school spelling. He has been shouting out spellings and definitions of random words all night long. Everyone groans.

"Just thought you people should know," Grant says. We all laugh.

"Actually, Gabriella's father and I have done business together," Noah says. "And she certainly was a fortunate discovery," he adds, brushing my cheek. I blush. He's never shown such a public display of affection before.

"Well, you certainly must be very special to Noah," one of the wives says, "because in all the years that we've been meeting, he seldom brings anyone."

"I was thinking the same thing," another chimes in.

I nod appreciatively.

"Well, we hope to see you again, Gabriella," says the third wife.

Satisfied, they go back to their conversation. The spotlight is off of me. I relax and lean back against Noah, nestling under his arm.

"Much longer?" I whisper.

He shakes his head. "No. Something wrong?" he asks quietly.

"No," I tell him. "I'm just ready for home."

"That's my girl." He kisses the top of my head. I know that me calling the apartment home pleases him.

"Serendipity." I giggle.

"S-e-r-e-n-d-i-p-i-t-y," he whispers back playfully.

The waitress comes with the check and some fortune cookies. Noah slips away to pay the bill for the table, and everyone else pounces on the cookies. Instantly, they begin munching and noisily announcing their fortunes. They roar with laughter over each one. I laugh, enjoying their fun. Noah returns. There are two cookies left.

"Ladies first," he tells me, motioning for me to choose one. I do. I open the wrapper and slide out the thin piece of paper from the cookie. I read my fortune and begin to nibble. He watches as I roll my eyes. It is as if he wrote it himself. He snaps his fingers and holds his hand out for me to hand him the slip. When I hesitate, he raises his eyebrows. I hold it out. He takes it. It reads, "Obedience is the root of all learning."

He throws his head back and laughs. I close my eyes and cringe.

"Your turn," I tell him.

"Okay." He sighs and takes the remaining cookie from the table.

I bet he doesn't believe in fortune cookies. He removes the cookie from the wrapper, slides out the paper, breaks the cookie in half, and pops part of it into his mouth. I study his face as he reads. He reveals nothing. He crumples the paper and tries to toss it away, but I'm too fast; I catch the paper midflight. He tries to snatch it back, but I hold on to it and unfurl it. I hold it away from him and read: "Don't be afraid to lose control. It is in that loss that we often gain."

I gasp. He rolls his eyes and takes the paper from my hand. He then deliberately deposits the paper into the flame of the candle in the center of the table. Together we watch it burn. I frown. *Message received.*

༶

Noah has just gotten home from work, and he is in his study. It's kind of an unspoken rule that I am not supposed to interrupt him there. After a long day, it takes him some time to unwind.

However, the way I see it, it's now or never. I stand in the doorway, nervously waiting for him to look up. It takes a few moments before he does. *God, he intimidates me so much.* I watch him as he takes a sip from the drink that Mrs. Middleton set out for him. He takes off his reading glasses to give me his attention.

"Yes, Gabriella?" His formality scares me, and I have the urge to run away.

"I have something to ask you," I manage.

He nods.

Gosh, he is not making this easy.

"What do you need?" he asks.

I walk into the room and approach the desk. My bare feet pad against the hardwood floor. I stand next to him and suddenly feel like a child. I can't find words, so I just hand him the flier.

He puts his reading glasses back on and scans the paper. I stare at his face. He shows no reaction as he is reading. When he is done, he looks up at me, removes the glasses again, and waits for me to speak. He raises his eyebrows and lets the silence linger between us.

"I want to go to it," I say nervously.

He cocks his head to one side. "Is that how you ask?"

I shake my head. "May I please go to this?" I say, looking at him. "I've been good," I add now that I've gathered a slight bit of courage.

"I can recall a few smart-mouthed comments just recently," he says. "And some pouting and sulking as well."

My heart drops. My eyes begin to fill. I don't know what to say to this.

He puts his glasses back on and scans the paper again.

I wait nervously. Does this mean he's considering it?

"This is tonight." He frowns. "In an hour."

I nod that I know this.

"Gabriella," he scolds.

"Please, Noah," I plead, finally finding my voice. "I'll be good forever."

He stops short of a smile. "Forever?"

I grimace at my own choice of words.

"What about dinner?" he asks.

"We could eat after!" I say.

He tosses his glasses aside and stares at me, propping his chin on his hand. I bounce nervously from foot to foot.

"You're squirming," he notes. I blush, embarrassed.

He moves the papers he was working on from the center of the desk and pats the empty spot, motioning for me to sit. Dutifully, I climb onto the desk. Without taking his eyes off of mine, he pushes my dress above my hips and removes my panties.

"Let's see if we can't make you squirm some more," he says, rising from his chair and unzipping his trousers.

He leans down and kisses me thoroughly, his tongue exploring my mouth. Moving to my neck, he chooses a spot and sucks hard. My back arches. Growling, obviously enjoying his power over me, he reaches up my dress and cups each breast, working them until they are sore and the nipples are pointed. He leans down and sucks one of them and then the other. I moan. Pushing me back so that I am lying flat on the desk, he reaches down and spreads the folds of my sex open wide. He lowers himself and kisses my bud. I gasp, and he laughs. Inserting two fingers, he finds me wet and ready. He makes an approving sound and then enters me hard. He rams me again and again. Moments later, we come together.

When we are done, he kisses me gently again and, with his lips still on mine, whispers, "Go get ready."

I jump up from the desk and grab my panties. For good measure, he smacks my bottom, and I squeal with delight as I run from the room.

"Don't make me regret this, Gabriella," he warns. But I am halfway down the hall, so I don't bother answering.

At 6:55, we pull up in front of Creative Creations Gallery in the heart of the city. Earlier, I made the mistake of suggesting that Liam take me. Emphatically, Noah told me that he would be the one escorting me.

My heart is pounding. I can't believe I am about to take my first art class. I am over the moon with excitement but also nervous out of my mind. I figured that since being in New York has been all about new things, why not take the leap into painting?

We park on the curb—illegally, of course—and Noah takes me into the building. Right inside the front door is a registration desk manned by a young girl about my age. Her homemade nametag reads, "Free Bird."

"May I help you?" she says.

Noah nods at me to speak.

"I'm here for the painting class," I tell her.

"Your name?"

"Gabby Rossi," I blurt in my excitement. Noah gives me a warning look. Instantly catching my misstep, I grimace and say, "Gabriella Rossi."

The girl writes my name on a pink slip of paper. "Will you be paying for just one class or the entire course?" she asks.

I look at Noah expectantly, praying that he will say, "The entire course," but I am not surprised when he tells her, "Just one." Then, to me, he says, "We'll take it a week at a time." I nod, a little crestfallen, but I'll take what I can get.

Noah pays her. She stamps the piece of paper, hands it to me, and nods to the classroom just to our right. It is directly in front of the building, and its windows open to a view of the sidewalk. "Go right in," she says. "Your instructor is Philip. You'll love him. He's cute." She giggles.

I want to die. I'm too afraid to look at Noah, who

has just made an unhappy growl, so I don't. I take the paper and turn to go in.

"I'll be waiting out front," I hear him say behind me. I know he will be.

For two and a half hours, I am free. This class is the most amazing thing I have ever done. I've dreamed my entire life about being in a painting class, and now I am. I am instantly engaged and soon forget that Noah is right outside the window, watching my every move. I don't care.

Philip, who is wonderful, has us spend the class "playing with color," as he calls it. He plays classical music and meanders around the room, offering each of us individual attention as we create our first paintings. When he gets to me and observes my work, he laughs and jokes about spying potential in my painting. He thinks I might have talent. I laugh too. But then he says seriously that I might have a gift to explore.

When the class is over, Noah is out on the sidewalk, leaning against the car. I call good-bye to a few of my classmates. We promise to see each other next week.

I present myself in front of Noah with my painting behind my back. I am bouncing with excitement.

"Well, let me see." He smiles.

I squeak and pull my painting from behind my back. He takes it from me and inspects it thoughtfully.

"It started out as fruit," I explain excitedly. "A pear, actually. Then it turned into an apple, but when that wasn't working out, I just made it a flower."

"Good move." Noah laughs. "Fruit-a-floria," he jokes. "It's lovely."

"Thanks," I say with pride.

That night, all through dinner and the ride home, I can't stop talking. I chatter endlessly about the class, the other students, the classical music, playing with color, and my budding potential. Noah listens attentively, amused, and nods throughout my entire spiel.

Finally, I have exhausted myself, and I fall into bed. He still has a meeting to prepare for in the morning, so he tucks me in before retreating to his study.

He kisses me gently on the forehead. "I'm glad you had a good time," he says.

I nod. Then realize that I forgot something. "Noah?" I say as he turns out the light. "Thank you."

"You're welcome, baby," he says over his shoulder through the darkness. Then he closes the door gently, leaving me to my sweet dreams.

꽃

The next morning, I am the last one in the kitchen.

Noah is already done with his breakfast and is sipping his coffee and reading the paper when I enter.

"Good morning," he says with a smile. "Sleep well?"

"I did," I tell him, smiling back.

I am just about to sit down, when I catch sight of the refrigerator door. I smile, embarrassed. Mrs. Middleton has hung my flower painting from art class on the door with a magnet. I smile at her, and I am just about to say thank you, when she nods me off and tilts her head toward Noah.

I realize she didn't hang it. He did.

The sweet gesture takes me aback. I stare at him, but he is engrossed in his newspaper. I want to say thank you but don't know how. I'm tongue-tied.

Noah checks the time on his watch and refolds the paper before rising from the island. He walks over and kisses my forehead. "Brilliant art needs to be on display," he says, and he turns and walks out of the apartment.

I stand there in the kitchen as giddy as a three-year-old.

Chapter 17

I'm blubbering like a baby when he walks in.

"Gabriella, what's wrong?" he asks, alarmed, dropping his suit coat on the floor.

I'm in the great room, curled up in a blanket on the couch, surrounded by a hundred discarded tissues. It's after midnight, and I'm sure he expected me to be asleep.

"What's happened?" he says, kneeling and taking my hands. I wag my head, too distraught to speak. I crane my neck to see the television around his head. Puzzled, he turns and looks over his shoulder, studying the screen. Putting it all together, he frowns and faces me. I continue to sob and point at the TV in my own defense. I'm watching *An Officer and a Gentleman* on the Movie Channel.

"I've seen it," he tells me, letting go of my hands and retrieving his jacket. He stands and watches a few seconds more of the movie before becoming disinterested. "It works out just fine," he calls over his shoulder as he heads out of the room to change out of his work clothes.

I know it does, but I am still inconsolable. The part where they break up always devastates me.

A few minutes later, Noah comes back with a bowl of ice cream and two spoons. He settles in on the couch next to me. I rearrange the blanket so that it covers him too. I'm a little better now that things are starting to work out. We watch together, passing the bowl back and forth.

"That's exactly what you need, young lady," he tells me. "Some time working in a factory to make you appreciate how good you have it around here," he jokes.

I giggle. We watch in silence for a bit, and then comes my favorite part.

"Wait. Look!" I gasp. "He's coming for her. Oh my God! And look. Look! All her friends are watching him come in all dressed up and handsome. And watch how he carries her out!"

Noah throws his head back and laughs.

"Oh my," I squeal. "It just doesn't get any better than that!" I collapse back onto the couch.

"No, it does not," Noah says sarcastically and emphatically.

I punch him. "You just don't know about love." I look back at the screen. People cry tears of joy. Music plays. The credits roll.

Noah clicks off the TV. I'm exhausted. He takes the empty bowl and spoon from me, sets them on the coffee table, and pulls me close under the blanket.

"So that's the ultimate in romance, huh?" he asks.

"Pretty much," I say.

"I'll keep that in mind," he says with a grin. "So, Miss Gabriella, tell me about love," he teases.

"Okay, Mr. Noah," I say, playing along. "What would you like to know?"

"Let me see," he says thoughtfully. "Here's a question. Does love find you, or do you find love?"

It's a good question. Now it's my turn to think. "Mostly, love just happens," I tell him.

He nods and accepts this. "Is there love out there for everyone or just some people?" he asks.

"Absolutely for everyone," I say. "There's someone out there for everyone. You just have to be patient."

"Just one someone?"

"I think so. That's why it takes a little while sometimes."

"Have you ever been in love?" he asks cautiously.

I wasn't expecting this question. "Um, well, I don't know," I say, trying to avoid the question.

He is not so easily put off. "You said you were going to teach me about love," he insists playfully. "If you have firsthand experience, you should let me know."

"No is the short answer," I say.

"I'd like to hear the long answer."

"Okay." I laugh. "Well, I thought I was in love in kindergarten with a boy named Gill Wheat. He had the blondest hair and the most beautiful blue eyes."

"Ah, a blond." Noah nods as if he understands. "What happened to old Gill?"

"I don't really remember," I tell him. "All I know is that he kept stealing all my crayons." I laugh.

"Thief!" Noah exclaims. "And after him?"

I think back. "Well, in third grade, I thought I loved Nathan Weiss," I say.

"All right," Noah says. "What was Nathan's redeeming quality?"

"He was a great kickball player. Over the fence every time!"

"An athlete!" Noah croons.

"But he was kind of dumb," I admit. "He was always asking me how much I weighed and would try to lift me up over his head to prove how strong he was."

Noah makes a face. "And then?"

"Nothing till seventh grade."

"A love drought! What happened in seventh grade?" he asks.

"Mario Valente and my first kiss," I tell him.

"I hate Mario Valente," Noah says instantly, only half kidding.

"Me too," I say. "He kissed everybody. His goal was to kiss every girl in the seventh grade."

"Bastard," Noah says. "Go on."

I say nothing.

"And then?"

"And then nothing. Just boys here and there," I say.

"Really?" he asks. "Boys in love with you?"

"Some," I admit. "But mostly just boys."

He nods. I can tell he is pleased but trying not to act

too pleased. "Did you ever dream of that kind of thing happening to you?" he asks, referring to the movie.

"Of course!" I tell him with a laugh. "When we were little, all we ever dreamed of was the love of our lives showing up at the pizza shop one day out of nowhere and carrying us away from it all to live happily ever after! I mean, it was all we ever dreamed." My voice trails off as I realize what I've just said. I stop and am silent. I'm embarrassed.

He pulls me a little closer and kisses the top of my head. He lets some time pass before he speaks. "So what do you think happens next?"

"For who?" I ask.

"The movie," he says. "I mean after he carries her out like this." Noah tosses the blanket off and scoops me up from the couch. I laugh and kick my legs playfully like the actress did in the movie.

"I don't know," I say, pretending to be puzzled.

"Well, I do," he tells me, nuzzling my neck and making me squirm. "I know exactly what happened next." Then Noah carries me down the hallway toward the bedroom. "And I can tell you another thing," he says, leaning in to kiss me. "He made it even better than she dreamed of!"

෯

The next morning, Noah is gone by the time I wake. When I reach the island for breakfast, there is a stack of papers at my place. They are one-page Google search printouts of each of my previous so-called loves. I gasp as I discover what has become of each of them.

Gill Wheat is still as gorgeous, blue eyed, and blond haired as ever. Unfortunately, he is also incarcerated. Apparently, he stopped stealing crayons and started stealing cars.

Nathan Weiss appears still to be athletically inclined and somewhat dumb. He works in a gym. He smiles proudly in a photo of him holding his wife above his head like a barbell. He lists his greatest accomplishment as benching three hundred pounds.

Last is the kisser. Mario Valente's profile picture shows him dressed in a pink tank top and spandex. He is kissing someone—not a girl this time but, instead, his boyfriend, Rex.

The next thirty-seven pages are a Google search on Noah. There are pages and pages of his accomplishments. He has taken it upon himself to highlight his various college degrees and his net worth, which is in the billions.

There is a sticky note on top that reads simply, "I win."

I laugh out loud.

૭

We've been getting along well lately. I haven't been too much of a brat, and he hasn't been too much of an ogre.

It's the first week in September, and we're sitting at breakfast. He takes a shiny brand-new silver iPhone 6 from his breast pocket and slides it across the counter. My eyes widen.

"Really?" I exclaim.

"Don't abuse it," he warns.

I grab it and begin to play.

"Approved numbers are programmed in," he remarks, standing and putting on his suit jacket for work.

This stops me. "Wait," I say. "What does that mean?" I scan the contacts.

"The numbers that you are permitted to call are already in the phone," he says.

I try to call a random number. "Call Failed" appears on the screen. "It's a preschool phone!" I tell him angrily.

He raises his eyebrows and, without comment, calmly takes the phone out of my hands and puts it back in his pocket.

My heart sinks. I regret my smart mouth. "Wait," I say. "I'm sorry! May I please have it back?"

He studies me.

"I'm sorry I said that; that was rude." I squirm. "I've been good."

"You've been adequate," he says.

I cringe. "I'm working on good."

He gives me a look that indicates he doubts this. "Probation," he says, and he slides the phone from his pocket again.

My smile couldn't be bigger. "Deal," I tell him.

He grabs my chin and raises it so that my eyes meet his. "Behave," he tells me.

I nod.

He's been gone for just a few minutes by the time

I'm scanning through the contacts. All of my sisters are there, plus Mrs. Middleton, Liam, the apartment number, and all of Noah's contact numbers. Noah's cell number pops up. I hesitate for a moment and then press the send icon. He answers on the first ring.

"Yes?"

"I forgot to tell you thank you," I say.

He waits.

"Thank you."

"You're welcome," he says.

There's silence.

"Bye," I say.

"Good-bye, Gabriella."

We hang up. I sit there feeling happy and content. Suddenly, the phone goes off. *My first text!* I read it and roll my eyes. It simply says, "Good girl."

۞

The following week, Noah allows me to go back to painting class even though I forgot myself and misbehaved a couple of times.

When I go inside, Philip isn't there. Instead, Free Bird is at the head of the class. She explains that everything will carry on as usual but without Philip. It seems that Philip happened upon a better opportunity, though no one seems to know what. Everyone appears a little confused. I am confused too, until I look out the window and spot Noah. Then it becomes perfectly clear.

I whip out my phone and shoot off a text: "Where is

Philip?" I watch as Noah checks his phone and glances up to see me through the window. Because of the glare, I'm not positive, but I think he is grinning.

"Don't know," he texts back.

"You do know! Where is Philip?"

"I heard he happened upon a better opportunity."

I am boiling. "You didn't have to do that!" I text.

"Yes, I did. It's Free Bird. Take it or leave it. And watch your tone," he replies.

How in the world can he tell that I am having a tone? I'm afraid to reply. He texts me again.

"Do you need to be taken home?"

"No," I text, sulking, if it is possible to sulk via text.

"Then paint."

I catch another glimpse of him through the window and then go to my seat and dip my brush in the paint. My phone goes off again. It's another text from Noah: "Stop sulking."

I sigh and resign myself to the fact that he always wins.

Chapter 18

Mrs. Middleton is gone for the day, and Noah is not due home until six. I'm restless. I've contemplated this before but always chickened out. Today, convincing myself that I won't get caught, I take the dare. I sneak out of the apartment and press the button for the forty-fourth floor. My tummy somersaults, and I tingle with excitement as I smell the chlorine. The doors open to a beautiful indoor swimming pool. I discovered it two weeks ago but never bothered asking Noah, sure his answer would be no. I know sneaking out is wrong, but if he never knows, what's the harm? Besides, I deserve a little something every once in a while. I'll be saving both of us a fight.

Since it's the middle of the day, the place is empty. *No witnesses.* I decide I'll swim just a few laps and then be done. *Just a small taste of freedom is all I really need*, I tell myself.

Having no swimsuit, I strip to my bra and panties. I

waste no time and dive right in. The water is somehow both warm and refreshing. I'm in heaven. I swim a few laps, stretching my muscles. However, instead of getting out like I promised myself, I get lost playing in the water. It's been years since I've been swimming, but like riding a bike, you never forget how.

As kids, my sisters and I were like fish to water. In the summers, we'd spend all day at the community pool. My mind drifts back to those carefree days. I close my eyes and lie back in the water and float. I think about the little girl I once was, tall and gangly, a little bit different from the rest of my sisters.

There's a picture hanging on the wall of the pizza shop that illustrates this perfectly. When the photo was taken, my sisters and I were all young. We were dressed in our swimsuits and flip-flops, with towels around our necks, ready to go to the pool on the first day of summer. Our mother, thinking we looked cute, lined us up according to age before taking our photo. Because I was a bit taller than expected, I stood taller than the sisters on either side of me. I always thought that because of this, I stood out like a sore thumb. We often took photos like this, and it always bothered me. I always felt as if I were messing up the pictures.

I'm lost in a myriad of childhood dreams, when suddenly, I am jolted back to the present as I am yanked from the water by one arm. I fly out of the water. The swat on my bottom tells me clearly that I have been caught and exactly who has caught me. When I look up, I am mortified to find not only Noah but also Mrs. Middleton and Liam.

As near as I can figure, when Noah got back to the apartment and didn't find me there, he was so panicked that he called them to help look for me. Instantly, I feel horrible. It seems I've worried all of them. Mrs. Middleton and Liam both look a little mad. They say nothing.

"I've got her," Noah mutters, and they disappear.

I don't even bother to look up in the elevator. I shiver, freezing and frightened. In moments, we are back in the apartment, in his bedroom. He tosses me onto the bed.

"What in the world were you thinking?" he says, seething. He's livid, and I'm scared. "My God!" he fumes. "Anything could have happened to you!"

"I was fine," I squeak. "I know how to swim."

"I don't care!" he yells. "You are never, ever, ever to go near that pool again!"

"Noah, why?" I ask, almost pleading.

"Because I have rules!"

I don't understand this, but he's too mad to reason with, and frankly, I'm terrified of a punishment, so I nod.

He begins pacing and running his hands through his hair. It's as if he's contemplating his next move. I watch him. Part of me understands that he's mad, but part of me is confused. He's way madder than he should be, even for him. His behavior seems like a crazy overreaction.

"I understand," I finally say, trying to diffuse the situation.

He stops and makes eye contact with me. "Do you?" he says.

I nod frantically. "I do. I promise."

He looks at me, studying my face as if trying to decide whether to believe me or not. He raises both hands to his head, as if he's composing himself. I don't think I've ever seen him like this. I'm shivering again now. "I swear. I understand," I tell him. "No pool."

Noah draws in his breath and kneels down in front of me, taking my hands. He looks straight into my eyes. "Never again?" he asks.

"Never again," I say. I don't like seeing him like this. "Never again."

Finally, he lets go of his breath. He closes his eyes, and for a few moments, he simply kneels there.

It scares me how quiet Noah is throughout dinner. We watch some TV afterward, but I notice he's not even looking at the screen.

Finally, at ten, earlier than normal, he puts me to bed. He gives me a kiss, strokes my cheek, and looks at me with sad eyes. He says he has some work to do in his study.

I wake up at two o'clock in the morning. He's not beside me. I get out of bed. The apartment is dark except for a sliver of light coming from his study. He must still be working.

I don't want to disturb him. I turn to go back to

bed, but strangely, I think I hear voices. He's not alone in there. I move closer. I hear the murmur of quiet conversation. I peek through the crack between the door and the frame and find that Noah, Mrs. Middleton, and Liam are sitting in the study and sharing a drink, talking easily.

Liam says something that makes the other two chuckle. They fall back into quiet talk that I cannot hear. I've never seen them be anything but formal with one another. Right now, they look like three friends. I watch for only a minute more, and then, feeling as if I'm intruding, I slip back down the hallway to bed. I tuck myself in and lie there, trying to make sense of it all. I can't. All I know is that there is definitely more to know.

֍

We pass an enjoyable albeit boring evening out with acquaintances of Noah's. They are an older couple, Edward and Cecilia Louis. The man, white-haired and pleasant, speaks mostly about business to Noah. The woman, pretty enough but fiercely fighting aging, speaks mostly to me, apparently feeling it's her place to school me on subjects ranging from child-rearing to how to keep men in line.

"Never be submissive." The instruction is so ironic that I almost spit out my wine. "It's a complete turnoff," she insists with a smirk.

Obviously, this woman knows little about Noah Bentley. I smile uncomfortably down into my plate as she speaks louder and louder. Her martinis are kicking in.

In situations like these, I always feel as if I am balancing on a tightrope. Other women routinely seem to speak freely and somewhat disrespectfully about their husbands and boyfriends right in front of them. I know better. As much as Noah appears to be giving whomever he is speaking with his full attention, I know that he always has one eye on me and an ear on my conversation as well.

He knows I am in an uncomfortable spot and touches my bare leg under the table as the woman goes on about "husbands in tow." I know better than to even remotely agree with her; Noah would certainly dole out the consequences of such agreement after we got home. This I don't want. I walk the tightrope with the woman while Noah massages my thigh, inching my dress up so that he has access between my legs.

I wiggle a bit as Noah pulls my panties to one side and slides a finger inside of me. I am dripping wet. Noah can make me wet with a simple word, smile, or glance, but when he is actually trying, as he is tonight, I am hopeless. He has such power over me. He knows this and enjoys it.

Finding me aroused, he turns to me with a faint smile and kisses me chastely on the cheek. "Later, baby," he says so that only I can hear. "Special treat."

I shiver with a combination of excitement and fear, not knowing what to make of this statement.

Later, I'm relieved to have made it through dinner.

We are waiting for the valet to retrieve the car. Cecilia continues to drone on and on about independence and women's rights. I'm sure there are no leather cuffs in her husband's night table.

She takes me aside and pulls a DVD from her purse. "This is from me to you," she whispers.

I look at it blankly. I'm confused.

"I've made copies for all of my friends," she tells me. "It's a gift. We're friends now."

When I don't take it right away, she takes my handbag, looks around to make sure that Noah and her husband are not watching, and slides the DVD inside.

"You watch it first. Then share what you learn with your man. These boys don't need to know where we get all our tricks," she says with a wink.

I color, realizing what she has just given me. I'm mortified. If Noah knew, he'd kill me.

The cars come. Cecilia gives me a peck on the cheek. "Enjoy," she whispers. I die.

Later, at home, as we are undressing, Noah shakes his head. "Cecilia Louis," he mutters. "What a piece of work!"

I laugh loudly. "I found her kind of interesting."

"Oh, did you?" he says.

"So you heard her?" I grin.

"Every word."

"She seems to have her husband trained," I say.

Noah shakes his head, disgusted. "That woman wouldn't last a second under this roof!"

I nod and agree. Then I ask, "Has anybody ever lasted under this roof?"

"Do you see anybody else around here?" he asks as he leaves the room to take a shower.

"No," I answer meekly.

"So there's your answer," he calls over his shoulder.

※

When we got home from dinner with the Louis's, I hid the DVD behind some books in the library. I'd like to say I forgot about it, but I never did. The moment Cecilia said, "Enjoy," I became curious.

One night Mrs. Middleton is gone, and Noah isn't due home for hours, so I dare to take a peek. After a few minutes, I am no longer peeking but instead gawking with eyes wide open.

Suddenly, Noah surprises me. I am fully engrossed and don't even hear him enter the bedroom.

"Gabriella!" he says, astounded. "What in the world?"

I jump and fumble with the remote, failing to locate the stop button. He's faster than I am and snatches the controller from my hands. He sits down and views my shame. We watch together as Bronco and Misty—the leads in this particular DVD—do some unspeakable things to one another.

Noah shakes his head in disgust. I find myself a little more fascinated than disgusted.

"Where did you get this?"

"Cecilia Louis." I giggle. "At dinner."

He mutters something about corruption under his breath, but his eyes are glued to the screen. He cocks his head to one side as if to get a better view of what's happening.

"She said it would spice us up," I explain, leaning my head to one side too.

"I wasn't aware that we needed spicing up," he says. "I don't want you watching this kind of thing."

I laugh. "Why? Are you afraid I might learn something? Cecilia said we both will."

"Oh, did she?" Noah is not amused.

We continue to watch. Bronco and Misty are getting a little ridiculous now. "Jeez, I think we are learning something," I murmur.

Noah rolls his eyes. He moves to click the video off.

"Wait!" I stop him, catching sight of something I've definitely never seen before. I'm intrigued.

He halts and furrows his brow.

"What's he going to do to her?" I ask, curious. I'm unable to take my eyes off of the screen. Noah shakes his head and stands up. He loosens his tie and begins to undress. He's blocking my view. I crane my neck, struggling to see the television. He clicks the DVD off. Bronco and Misty disappear.

"I wanted to see what he was going to do to her," I complain.

Noah crawls onto the bed and then onto me. "He was about to do this," he growls before beginning to do the unspeakable to me.

"Really?" I gasp.
"Really."

※

I can tell what kind of mood Noah is in by the way he holds my hand. When he is in a good mood, mellow and playful, he laces his fingers between mine as a boyfriend and girlfriend would do. When he holds my hand like this, I can relax.

But when he is angry and displeased, he grips my hand firmly in his, as one would hold a disobedient child's while leading him or her off to the woodshed.

Tonight I am in trouble. Noah has a firm grip on me. My hand is cupped firmly within his, and I have no idea what I have done wrong. We had what seemed to me to be a pleasant-enough time with his family. As usual, they were all there—his parents, his troop of brothers, and their unruly wives. Things are a little bit better between me and the other women. We even had a little girl talk on the deck of his parents' home.

"What have I done?" I ask as Noah all but yanks me to the car when leave his mother's house. He practically tosses me into the passenger seat of the car and slams the door. He drives in silence the entire way home. Even the radio is off. I am really in trouble.

Once we're back at the apartment, the valet takes the car, and we walk through the lobby with the usual amount of fuss from the staff. Noah ignores them all. As we head to the elevator, I want to be anyone but me.

In the apartment, he grabs my hand again and pulls

me through the rooms and into the bathroom. I am confused. He drops my hand, swiftly picks me up, and plops me down harshly on the countertop between the two sinks. My shoes fall from my feet.

"Open," he orders. I don't know what he means. "Open your mouth!"

I have no idea what we are doing and stare at him, wide-eyed.

"So help me, Gabriella!" he says when I don't comply immediately. He grabs my chin in such a way that he forces my mouth open, and in one quick motion, he squirts some liquid hand soap into my mouth.

Immediately, I begin to spit and gag uncontrollably. The soap is bitter, and it only gets worse as it foams up. I raise my hands to wipe it out, but he stops me and holds my wrists at my sides to make me taste it awhile longer. The soap is beginning to burn, and I wag my head back and forth, attempting to spit it out. I am gagging.

"My brothers' wives are trash," he says, seething. "You are not! I do not wish to kiss an ashtray!"

Finally, I understand. He caught me smoking with his sister-in-law Nancy. When we were out on the deck, she offered me a drag off of her cigarette, and I took it. This is all over one puff.

I am desperate for my hands, so I nod that I understand.

"Are we clear?" he thunders.

Again, I nod furiously. Finally, he lets my hands free. My eyes are watering uncontrollably, and tears spill down my cheeks.

He tosses me a hand towel. I take it and wipe my tongue off. I feel as if I might throw up. He fills a glass from the tap and hands it to me. I take it and glare at him. I take a sip but don't know if the water is making it better or worse. Now I am furious.

"It was one puff!" I yell at him.

"Obviously one puff too many!" he hollers, louder than before.

"I am not a child!" I scream.

"But you are mine!" he shouts. "And you will behave appropriately!"

"It was one puff," I squeal again.

The minute I say this, I regret it, because I know that I am only making him madder. I rarely argue with him. His eyes are menacing.

Please, not a spanking too, I silently plead.

"Do you need more to see this my way?" he shouts, grabbing me by one wrist and pulling me off of the counter.

"No!" I shriek. He halts. "No," I repeat. "I understand. I was wrong."

He turns and eyes me warily. For a moment, our eyes are locked. As always, he is in control. The next move is his. I silently pray that we are done. He closes his eyes and makes a face of exasperation. He grabs me by the elbow, spins me around, and swats me once so hard on the bottom that I yelp and nearly see stars.

"To bed!"

I nod with my head down, my eyes dripping with tears from the sting of the spank. He releases me, and I am relieved that there is no more punishment. I hurry to the bedroom before he changes his mind. He heads toward the living room to make himself a drink and, I guess, to count to a million.

I swear I taste soap for a week.

۶

"What's sixty-nine?" I ask on the ride home from a function one night.

"Good God, Gabriella," Noah scolds, slamming closed the partition that separates us from Liam.

I look at him expectantly.

"Who told you about that?" he asks, wide-eyed.

"No one told me about it," I say. "Caroline Matthews is going home to do it with her husband."

Noah grimaces. "Caroline Matthews," he mutters. "Always the epitome of discretion."

"Tell me?"

"Okay," he says. Then he patiently explains what it means to sixty-nine. I nod, taking in the information. It doesn't sound like much compared to what Noah and I have done.

Noah waits for my reaction. When I am quiet, he says, "You don't seem impressed."

"I'm not." I shrug.

He smiles and then laughs. "Well then, let me get you upstairs to see if I can impress you," he says as the car comes to a halt in front of the apartment.

I giggle, betting that he can.

Later that night, after Noah has thoroughly

impressed me, I lean across him in bed and reach for the phone on his night table.

"Who are you calling?" he asks.

"Caroline Matthews," I deadpan, "to tell her that you're better than her husband."

Noah throws his head back and laughs loudly before he tackles me and begins tickling me. I roll around on the bed, squealing in delight.

Chapter 19

"Five minutes," he tells me.

It's a Saturday morning after breakfast. Noah folds his newspaper and takes the last swallow of his coffee. He rises from the island.

"For what?" I ask.

"For you to be ready and waiting by the door," he says.

I pause, trying to find a clue in his face, but there is none. Still, I know that when he says five minutes, he means exactly five minutes, and I know he won't tell me twice. I jump down from the stool and scurry to the bedroom for my shoes and sweater. Four minutes later, I am waiting by the elevator door.

He meets me and smiles. Nothing puts a smile on his face like obedience.

Downstairs, the car is waiting for us. We drive for a while. It is a beautiful day. I am intrigued and have no idea where we are going.

Once we leave the city, he demands that I keep my

eyes closed, telling me that if I open them even once, we will head straight back to the apartment. He assures me that I will like where we are going and wouldn't want to blow it.

I nod and dutifully keep my eyes closed. Finally, I feel the car coming to a slow stop.

"Keep them closed," he warns. I have no idea where we might be. "You've been good lately. I thought a privilege might be in order," he says.

I am nearly dying of anticipation. The car comes to a complete stop.

"Okay. Open," he tells me.

When I do, I can't believe my eyes. Before me is the most beautiful sight: the Rossi's Pizza sign. He has brought me back to New Jersey for a visit. I gasp and then look at him. My smile couldn't be brighter.

"You have exactly three hours," he tells me sternly. "Not a second more."

I am still in shock and tongue-tied and am afraid to move.

"Well, get going," he says. "You're wasting your time!"

I squeal and jump out of the car. Noah drives away.

As I burst through the shop door, the chimes crash above my head. Mia is the first to see me, and she screeches hysterically, "Gabby's back!"

The others come running and surround me in seconds. Everyone is hugging, kissing, and crying. I've missed them all so much. It's been three months since I left, but it feels as if it's been forever.

Poppy hugs me tightly. "My Gabby," he says with tears falling from his eyes.

I explain that I can't stay long and tell them we'd better make the most of the time we have, and for the next three hours, we do. Everyone chatters at once. Each sister catches me up on what is going on in her life. I love hearing it all.

"But the biggest news," Mia tells me, "is that we have a buyer for the shop!"

I try to act surprised.

"There's been a man here almost every other day since you left!" she exclaims.

We all know that this is bittersweet news. The business is dying, so we have no choice but to sell. Still, how do you let go of a place you've called home for your entire life?

I wonder whom Noah has working on the deal, but I guess it doesn't matter. I am just grateful that he has given my family hope for a brighter future.

We sit together, gabbing nonstop while we eat pizza, just as we always did. They catch me up on the local gossip, and I lie my way through when the conversation turns to me. They ask about me and my new life. I insist that my heart is always right there in New Jersey with them. They playfully make fun of my fancy new clothes.

"Hey, whatever happened to Knightly?" Gina asks.

I fib and tell them that I see him around.

"I'm telling you," Teresa says. "You should have made a move. It was obvious that he liked you."

"Yeah, you should've seen how he looked at you," Maria says.

I feel my face reddening as I try to redirect the conversation.

Too soon, three hours is up, and Noah's car parks illegally along the curb. I check the time. I have just two minutes. I know if I ever want to come back, I'd better hurry. Abruptly, I tell them that I have to go. They protest, but I insist, grabbing my sweater and giving out quick hugs, the longest to Poppy.

"Don't worry, Poppy," I tell him. "I have a really good feeling about this deal coming through."

He nods at me and my encouraging words. "God willing," he says as he dabs his eyes with his handkerchief.

"Please hang in there, Poppy," I plead, and I give him a kiss on the cheek.

Then I turn and race out of the shop and into the Mercedes. When I look back, I see all five of my sisters' faces plastered against the storefront window. They stare out in disbelief as they realize that Knightly is driving me away.

As we leave New Jersey, I begin to weep softly. Noah puts a comforting hand on my knee. We drive in silence the entire way back to the apartment.

Later that night, I tentatively peer around the corner of the kitchen into the great room. I am already dressed for bed, and Noah is out on the balcony, working. The door is open. He is reading with only a small light above his head and the moonlight. He is deep in thought, so I have the chance to study him.

Still dressed, he has on his worn Saturday jeans and a V-neck black T-shirt. His feet are bare. He looks amazingly hot. I feel myself tingle. I can't believe I live with this man—this man who can be so infuriatingly arrogant and as hard as steel in one moment and then a tender lover the next.

Suddenly, he glances up. I try to step back, but I am not quick enough. "Gabriella," he says.

Embarrassed, I come out from my hiding place.

"Come," he says.

I walk across the living room to the balcony door. When I stop short, he grins in a way that draws me closer. I can't help but smile back. He holds his hand out. I take it. He pulls me in front of him so that I am standing between his legs. He holds my hands and plays with my fingers. He raises an eyebrow. "Do you need something?"

I shake my head, fidgeting from one bare foot to the other. Finally, I gather my courage. "I wanted to thank you for today," I manage shyly. I am embarrassed. The moonlight shines on his face in such a way that I can see that his eyes are soft.

"You're welcome," he says, continuing to caress my fingers. His molten eyes stare right through me. He licks his lips. I have to look away.

I kneel in front of him. Once kneeling, I tuck my hair behind my ears. I look into his eyes. He takes my head in his hands. He leans forward and gently yet completely kisses me. As he does, I reach down and unzip his jeans. He is already hard.

"You don't have to," he whispers. I can tell he is taken aback by my boldness.

"I want to," I say.

He leans back slowly and closes his eyes. I lean down and gently place his cock in my mouth. He holds my head gently and pushes himself in more deeply.

I slowly begin to suck him. He groans and glides his hips back and forth. His pace quickens, and I can feel him growing even larger. He is huge inside my mouth. The rhythm increases, and he holds me more forcefully with his fingers tangled up in my hair. With one final groan, he comes inside my mouth. I swallow. Still holding me, he groans again and arches his back. His eyes are closed. As he pulls out slowly, a small, satisfied smile crosses his lips. He leans forward and tilts my face up to his. He kisses me gently.

"Good girl," he whispers quietly. "Good girl."

※

"Please, Noah," I beg. "I'll be super good!"

"No," he says flatly.

We're arguing over the phone. Noah is in Chicago and has been for two days. He's not due back until tomorrow night. I've been bored and lonely without him. His sisters-in-law are going out for a girls' night, and they've asked me to go along.

"Why?" I ask. "It will be harmless. Just some girl time!"

"Gabriella, you know how I feel about those women."

"I do. But they're family," I remind him. "They're only going out for a drink or two and maybe a movie. You have to start learning to trust me."

"I trust you. Not them," he says.

"Please, Noah," I say again. "Just for a couple of hours."

He's silent on the other end of the phone. My heart flops. *He's actually thinking about it!*

"A couple of hours," he finally says. "But I want to know where you are at all times. You must be in constant contact with me. Keep that phone on!" he barks.

"I promise I will. Thank you. Thank you so much!" I say, knowing I'm overdoing it a bit.

"Don't make me regret this!"

"You won't! I promise," I say confidently.

The girls decide on dinner and a movie. We agree to meet at the TGI Fridays near the theater.

Tame enough, I think.

Of course Noah insists that Liam take me.

We meet there at eight, and the six of us take Fridays by storm. I thought Noah's sisters-in-law were wild at family events, but I haven't seen anything yet. They drink like fish and swear like sailors. I alternate between sitting in shock with my mouth gaping open and laughing hysterically at their antics. They sing to the overhead music, dance in the aisles, flirt unmercifully with the young waiter, and throw cheese sticks at one another. A manager finally suggests that we leave. Apparently, this is not the first time, because they seem unfazed and simply pay and sashay out of the restaurant as if they own the place.

Noah has been texting me relentlessly. I admit nothing and instead describe a boring evening out, dotting my texts with plenty of I-miss-yous, thank-yous, and heart emoji.

Out on the sidewalk, I wait for them to finish the last chorus of "Wild Thing" before I ask, "What movie are we going to see?"

At first, there is a collective silence, and then all at once, they burst into laughter.

"Oh, Gabriella!" one of them shrieks. "A movie? Really, girl?" They wail and then grab me by the arms and drag me down the sidewalk.

"We've got better plans than that," another promises.

I open my mouth to protest, but nothing comes out.

Before I know it, I am front and center at the Hunk of Male strip club. I'm mortified. I have never been to a place like this before. The only naked man I have ever seen is Noah. I'm dying. I've got to be fifty shades of red.

Thankfully, Noah's sisters-in-law don't even notice I'm here. I don't know how often they do this kind of thing, but they certainly seem at home. They have each come with an endless supply of one-dollar bills, which keeps the action down at our end of the table. So far, we have been entertained by a sailor, a cop, a doctor, a construction worker, and an astronaut.

Noah continues to text. In honor of the astronaut, my favorite, I tell him that we're seeing *Gravity*, starring

George Clooney. I ramp up the cute emoji and increase the number of I-miss-yous. The guilt is killing me.

Every time I think we might be nearing the end of the evening, another naked guy takes the stage, more shots are passed around, and the lunacy begins again. What shocked me before, I am now becoming immune to. These girls, on the other hand, never seem to tire of it.

I honestly think that the night would never have ended if it had not been for Becky's misstep. Who knew these places even have rules? Apparently, no matter how drunk you are, you may not toss your shirt and bra and storm the stage to grab the penis of a dancing cowboy. It's frowned upon. Again, we are asked to leave, and with heads held high, we find ourselves out on the sidewalk again.

"Next?" says Bridgett, the organizer, looking out over the street.

"I've got to go!" I announce, frantically searching for my phone in the bottom of my purse.

"Oh, Gabby!" They groan collectively.

"No. Really, I've got to go," I insist, finally locating my phone. I feverishly press buttons to text Liam to pick me up, only to realize my phone is only a few mere percentages from dying. "I've got to borrow someone's phone," I say in a panic. "I have to get home!"

They exchange glances. One at a time, they raise their hands as if to say, "Not me." I swear they are the mean girls from middle school.

"One more stop!" says Bridgett.

"I need a phone!" I say again.

"Oh, Gabby. We all know he's got you in a cage. Escape for one night!"

This comment touches a nerve. "I am not in a cage!" I fire back.

"Prove it," one of them mutters.

"I don't have to prove anything," I sneer.

They are silent. The tension on the sidewalk is palpable. I cave.

"Fine, one more stop," I say, seething.

They cheer and surround me.

Noah's going to kill me.

I am next wagging my head no in the middle of Paco's Piercing and Tattoo Emporium with a newly dead phone.

"Pick something, Gabby," says Bridgett. "We're all getting something to remember the night by."

Noah's going to give me something to remember the night by.

Nancy is already up in the chair with her rear end exposed, getting a daisy tattooed on her derriere. "Brent's going to love it," she remarks.

The rest of the girls are leafing through large sample books of tattoos. I'm the only holdout.

"I can't," I say. All the while, I'm thinking, *I'd love to.*

When my sisters and I were little, we would cover ourselves with temporary tattoos. When we were older, we experimented with some henna. It has been so long since I've done anything like that, and I've always wanted a tiny real tattoo.

"Oh, caged one," sings one of the girls.

"Stop it!" I snap as another girl jumps into the chair. She's up for a skull and crossbones on her breast.

"My kind of girls," says Paco as his heavily pierced and tattooed assistant offers us shots.

What kind of tattoo parlor serves drinks? I take one, thinking I should be allowed at least some fun.

Each tattoo takes about thirty minutes. Meanwhile, the drinks keep coming. Becky gets a rose. I'm jealous. I take a shot. I've always wanted a rose.

Cali gets angel wings on her shoulder. I take a shot.

Tina gets a snake on her wrist. I take a shot.

Five tattoos later, I'm woozy.

The girls surround me, chanting, "Gabby! Gabby!"

"There's got to be something you like," Paco insists with his pen poised. I'm compromised.

"Nope!" I slur.

"No special someone we need to remember?" he asks.

I make a face.

The chanting continues.

I don't remember much about the next few hours, but what I do remember clearly is Noah and Liam bursting through the doors of Paco's Piercing and Tattoo Emporium, dragging me out, and throwing me into the car. I also remember throwing up all over the limo.

When I wake up, Noah is standing over me. I'm home and in bed. His arms are crossed in front of him. He glares at me. "Paco's Piercing and Tattoo Emporium?" he yells.

I'm horribly hungover, and his yelling his killing me. This might be the point of his shouting, I realize. "Sorry," I squeak.

"Sorry?" he hollers. "Sorry! Thank God for the locate-my-phone app. You deserve a preschool phone! You were this close to getting something pierced. This is not over!"

I nod that I understand.

"Thank God I showed up," he says. "I'm surprised you didn't get yourself a tattoo!"

I blanch, remembering.

He almost misses the grimace on my face but catches it just before he stalks off. "Tell me you did not!"

I cringe.

"Where and what?"

I'm frozen.

"Where and what?"

I slowly remove my hand from my ankle, exposing a fresh tattoo.

He grabs my leg and examines it. I've not often seen him confused, but as he studies it, a mix of emotions I can't decipher fills his face. He's still angry, but there's more there. He's slightly disarmed. He lets out his breath as he runs his thumb over a tiny red heart with the initials NB in the center.

He looks up at me and simply says, "Go take a shower."

Chapter 20

"Such beautiful eyes," Noah says. The words make me flinch. I try not to, but I recoil. I try to pull farther back, but he holds me firmly. "What is it, Gabriella?" he asks urgently.

I won't make eye contact with him. I wriggle, trying to get away.

"What have I said? Why is that wrong?"

"It's nothing," I insist.

Noah releases me but still has me cornered on the bed. I scoot back up against the headboard and wrap my arms around my knees, assuming my safe position. I will myself to be smaller.

"Tell me, please," he whispers, looking genuinely concerned. "Tell me, Gabriella. Why was that the wrong thing to say?"

I am frozen. My eyes are filling with tears. I gulp and wag my head. I want him to let me go. I want to be alone, but I know he won't let me. He edges his way closer.

"All I was saying is that you have beautiful blue eyes," he repeats. "You're the only one of your sisters to inherit them." He is trying but is saying exactly the wrong thing.

It is more than I can take. I collapse and break into sobs. He gathers me in his arms, and I let him. He holds me and rocks me back and forth as I cry uncontrollably. I cry enough tears for twenty-one years.

Finally, I am all cried out. He is relieved that I have stopped but is still confused and concerned. I look at him and decide to trust him. I decide to tell him. I take in a shuddering breath and say, "I am not a sister."

He is trying his best, but I know he doesn't understand.

"I'm not really a sister." I shrug.

"The girls aren't your sisters?"

I shake my head. "I'm no one."

He wants more explanation but is hesitant to push. I look into his eyes and find them not cold or callous but caring, so I tell him. I tell him the story that has rolled around in my head all my life but that I've never told another living soul.

"She left me."

"Your mother?"

I nod and sigh. "I know nothing about her except that she left me on the front steps of the church. She knew someone would find me. The priest brought me to the Rossis. I guess the priest figured, *What's one more?* And amazingly, the Rossis felt that way too. And they took me in." My eyes fill with tears.

"You know," I continue, "in some ways, they were right, and in others, they were so wrong. I mean, they took me in and loved me and treated me like their own. They gave me everything. But they were wrong, because they should have at least tried to find my mother," I tell him, wanting him to understand.

"You just can't do that. I mean, not try," I whisper. "I mean, I always knew that as much as I seemed to fit, I didn't. And my mother! What was she thinking? You just don't leave a baby on a doorstep."

Tears well in my eyes again, and for the first time in my life, I let myself be angry. I let myself be angry instead of grateful.

"You just don't leave a baby on a doorstep!" I scream at him. Then I say what I have felt my entire life to be true. "Because it makes them no one."

Noah shakes his head. "No, Gabriella," he says. "You are not no one."

Now I shake my head at him. "Don't tell me that!" My words are biting. "You don't know."

"I do know," he insists, matching my passion. "Because I know you, and you are a beautiful, amazing someone."

"A beautiful, amazing someone who has no idea who she is. I mean who she really is," I say. I look at him through watery eyes. His kind, sympathetic gaze looks back at me. "Will you help me find her?" I ask.

His face drops, and he stops short of grimacing. "I don't know if that is the best idea."

I frown and turn my back on him.

"I'm not sure it's what's best," he says gently.

"It's all I've ever wanted," I tell him.

He turns me around to face him. "It may not even be possible."

"That's a cop-out," I tell him. "You can make anything possible. I've watched you!"

This stops him in his tracks.

"And you know it's true." I stare into his eyes and challenge him to tell me that I am wrong.

He sighs and runs his hand through his hair. "Gabriella—"

"Please," I say before he can go further. I wait for his response, never letting my eyes waver from his.

"Okay." He nods. "We'll try to find her," he says softly.

"When?"

He sighs again. "I'll put somebody on it in the morning."

I fall into him. He takes my exhausted body and pulls me onto his lap. He cradles me in his arms and rocks me back and forth.

"You are someone," he says softly, and he kisses my head.

༄

The next morning, I walk Noah to the door as he leaves for work.

"You won't forget?" I ask him pleadingly.

"Of course not," he tells me. "But these kinds of things take time."

I nod, but my impatience makes me bounce nervously from one foot to the other. He sees this and frowns.

"We should also be prepared for answers that we may not expect," he cautions, though I've already thought of this.

"Hope for the best. Prepare for the worst," I say, pretending that it's that simple.

"Exactly." He leans in to kiss me good-bye.

ඹ

It's the third night in a row that Noah hasn't come home for dinner. I know it's just business, but I'm still bored and lonely.

Mrs. Middleton has rushed off to be with her grandchildren, and I'm alone. I'm already bathed and dressed for bed. I decide to watch TV. I scan the channels. Finding nothing, I click it off. I spy my phone on the night table.

"Hi," I text Noah.

"What's wrong?" he instantly replies.

"Nothing," I type back.

"Then go to bed."

"Not tired."

"I'm busy," he says.

"Doing?"

"In a meeting."

"When will you be home?"

"Hours. Got to go. Bye."

I set the phone down. I miss him. I watch the clock.

I let two minutes pass, and then I pick up the phone again.

"Hi," I text again.

"Gabriella!"

"I miss you."

"I miss you too. I will be home as soon as I can," he writes.

"Do you really miss me?" I ask.

"Of course."

"Then come be with me."

"I am in a meeting. Go to bed!"

"If you really missed me, you would come home," I type.

"No more texting."

"Just one more?"

He doesn't respond. I try again. "Just one more?"

He types back, "?"

I gather my courage, find the camera function on my phone, slip off my panties, put the camera between my legs, and snap a picture. I view the photo and laugh to myself. I press the send button.

Twenty-two minutes later, he walks into the bedroom.

ෆ

It's Halloween. We are at Noah's parents' house. Apparently, every year, they have a huge Halloween party for the grandchildren. They go all out with decorations and treats. I think this is great. Noah does not. According to Noah, it is just another opportunity for the already-unruly children to run amok. This year, the weather is wonderful. It is unseasonably warm, and they are hosting the party in their expansive backyard.

Everyone is in costume except us. I snag a tiara from one of his nieces, and at least he lets me wear that. His father is dressed as Professor Plum, and his mother is dressed as Raggedy Ann. His brothers are ugly things, such as werewolves and gorillas, and his sisters-in-law, according to Noah, look more like prostitutes than anything else. I giggle at this observation. He's kind of right.

We are standing in the yard, enjoying the sunshine, and sipping apple cider. The children are making a game out of asking Noah if he is able to tell what they are dressed as. They run rampant around us. Every once in a while, one will stop running long enough to present him- or herself boisterously to Noah, demanding, "Guess me!"

After he corrects their language and posture, Noah guesses. Most are easy. The boys are a variety of superheroes. The girls are ballerinas and fairies. Once he guesses correctly, he rewards them for their costumes with a dollar bill from the wad of money he has brought specifically for the occasion. So far, he has guessed all of them correctly except one. His five-year-old nephew Adam is dressed just as he always is, in shorts and a T-shirt, but with one addition: a red necktie flung loosely around his neck. He has presented himself twice to Noah so far, demanding, "Guess me, Uncle Noah!" Each time, Noah has told him to return later. By the third time, Noah's response is the same. Adam stomps away.

We continue to sip our drinks. "Not a big fan of Halloween?" I ask.

"Not at all."

"Why?"

"They should be encouraged to become the best realistic versions of themselves that they can be," he tells me.

"So they should be running around as little doctors, lawyers, and businessmen?" I laugh.

"Not bad goals," he says.

"Oh, Noah," I say. "They should be allowed to be anything they want one day out of the year!"

"These children have no goals any day of the year," he mutters. When I ask him why he's so hard on them, he says, "I just hate to see wasted potential. They each started off as a clean slate with endless possibilities. Then, year after year, thanks to poor training and bad habits, they've turned into what you see here." He waves his hand in disgust.

"Noah, they're kids!" I say.

"Kids are goats. These are children, and children need training."

"Like girlfriends," I say, rolling my eyes.

"Exactly," he says, unaffected.

I groan.

"Not acceptable," he warns.

I'm about to push further, but instead, I just take another sip of my cider and watch the joyful chaos in front of me. "Did you ever dress up for Halloween?" I finally ask him.

"Only when I was very young and my mother made me."

"Really? What were you?"

"A pumpkin, a ghost, and a cowboy," he tells me. "In that order."

I laugh that he remembers it so clearly. "Did you enjoy it?"

"Not at all," he insists, shaking his head.

"Why? You were a little boy!"

"Because I didn't wish to be a pumpkin, a ghost, or a cowboy," he grumbles.

"Oh, Noah," I say, feeling kind of sorry for tiny cowboy Noah.

"Did you dress up for Halloween?" he asks.

"Every year!"

"And what were you?" he asks.

"The same thing every year," I say. "A princess."

He smiles and nods. "Of course."

"Always had a pretty pink dress with frills and a tiara," I say, straightening the tiara on my head.

"And it was fun?"

"It was great fun!"

He takes my hand and kisses it. "Well, it must have been good training," he says, "because you're the perfect princess now."

Suddenly, Adam appears again. He's panting and out of breath from running. He seems to have somehow lost his shoes, and his face is covered in some sort of red candy. "Guess me yet, Uncle Noah?" he asks.

"Almost, Adam," Noah says. "Come back just one more time."

The child wails and runs away. I'm enjoying this, because he actually has Noah stumped. "He's adorable," I say.

"Why is he adorable?" Noah asks. "He's filthy. His mother needs to tend to him."

"You're so stern! Why won't you guess what he is?"

"Because I don't know what he is!" Noah confesses with a laugh.

I don't either.

We watch Adam a little longer. He runs around, periodically stopping to straighten his tie. Then, suddenly, I figure it out. I gasp. I know exactly what—or, rather, who—Adam is.

"I think I've got it," I say.

"You know what he is?"

"I do!" I laugh.

Noah studies Adam intently. He shakes his head. "Is it something I would know?"

"Very well."

"Is it good or bad?"

"It can be both," I say.

"Is it a superhero?"

I laugh. "Sometimes, yes."

"Okay," Noah mutters, trying to put the pieces together. "It's something I know very well that can be both good and bad and is a superhero." Finally, he shakes his head. "I give up." He sighs. "Tell me."

"He's you!"

Noah's face drops. A small smile creeps across it as it becomes clear that this is exactly who Adam is dressed as. "Hey, Adam!" he calls, waving the boy over. "I'm ready to guess now." He pulls a five-dollar bill from his wallet.

To me, Noah whispers, "This one still might have some potential."

Chapter 21

It's after one o'clock in the morning. I can't sleep, so I've snuck out of bed. Noah's sleeping soundly. I'm out on the balcony, trying to find stars in the horribly foggy sky.

The days are running into one another, and time is passing. I know this is a good thing, because six months will be over soon, and I will hold all of the cards.

However, at the same time, as much as I try to deny it, I'm adjusting to all of this. I promised myself that I wouldn't and tried to fight it, but somehow, this odd world that I'm living in is becoming natural to me. He promised me I would adjust. I promised him I wouldn't. He's proving to be right. I'm proving to be wrong. Bit by bit, he has lured me into his world.

What keeps me up on nights like this are the thoughts of my old life drifting away from me. My poppy and my sisters are becoming more and more distant. How have I become confused, when I was so sure at the start? When did I lose control? How have things changed without my knowing it?

Suddenly, I feel Noah's hands on my shoulders. "You shouldn't be out here," he scolds softly, wrapping a blanket around me.

I shrug.

"Can't sleep?"

I nod.

"You were quiet all evening," he says.

I was. I didn't think he noticed.

"Why don't you tell me what's on your mind?"

Strangely, part of me wants to. Part of me wants to let it all out. Part of me wants to scream, yell, cry, and tell him how scared and confused I am. Part of me wants to tell him that one minute, he looks like my problem, and then the next, he looks like my solution. I'm pretty sure he's both.

"For us to be the best we can be," he tells me, "you need to trust me with what you're thinking and feeling."

"Sometimes I don't know what I'm thinking or feeling," I admit.

He nods sympathetically. "Fair enough, but I can fix almost anything if you just give me the chance."

I face him. "What's that like?" I ask, genuinely interested. I want to know what it's like to have that much power.

He's thoughtful. "I try to make it a good thing," he says. Noah looks out into the dreariness of the night. "Not much to see."

"I know," I say sadly.

We sit silently for a while, looking at nothing but blackness.

"Ever since I was a little girl," I say finally, "I've snuck out of bed at night to look at the stars when I am sad."

He nods, taking this in. "So you're sad," he says, stroking my hair. "That's going to happen sometimes. What can I do to help?"

"Nothing."

"Tell me how the stars help."

I've wondered this myself. "I don't know exactly," I say.

"Well, what do you like about them?"

I think. "I like the light. I like how it goes on forever. I like how no matter who we are, we're all looking at the same sky."

"New Jersey or New York," he says with a grin.

"Exactly," I say, grinning a bit too. "The stars comfort me," I finally say.

"So let's go find some stars," he says, taking my hand and guiding me up. "Go get dressed."

"It's almost two o'clock in the morning," I remind him.

"I didn't ask you what time it was. I told you to go get dressed."

Fifteen minutes later, we are driving in the city. The streets are almost deserted.

"We won't see any, no matter where you drive to," I say cynically, looking out into the black night.

"We'll see plenty," he assures me.

Thirty minutes later, we are sitting inside Hayden Planetarium. It's been opened just for us. The man who lets us in asks, "What would you like to see, Mr. Bentley?"

"Lots and lots of stars," Noah replies.

Soon Noah's fingers are laced with mine, and we are looking into a glorious star-filled sky. We watch as the constellations take turns dancing across the dome above our heads. We listen as a soft, soothing voice explains the history of each.

"Do you know about astronomy?" I ask Noah.

"A fair amount," he says. "I took a few courses in college, and I've spent some time here. How about you?"

I shake my head that I don't. "As much as I love the stars," I say, "I'm afraid not."

"I'll teach you," he promises.

We watch as a few more constellations go by.

"Do you have a favorite constellation?" I ask.

"Of course," he says with a grin. "He's actually coming up right about now."

I giggle as the constellation Hercules appears above us.

"Hercules is a constellation named after the mythological hero of the Greeks and, later, the Romans, made famous for his strength," the announcer says.

"My guy." Noah sighs.

I laugh. We continue to watch. "Which constellation would you pick for me?" I ask.

"Easy," he says. "She's actually coming up now."

"Virgo is one of the constellations of the zodiac," the voice tells us. "Its name is Latin for *virgin*."

I giggle and punch Noah's arm playfully. He intercepts my hand and kisses it. Silently, we watch the rest of the presentation with me nestled under his arm, my head on his shoulder.

"How do you make things like this happen?" I ask him on the ride home.

"I want you to be happy, Gabriella," he says. "I'll make anything happen for you. Even if it means making the stars come out at night."

I catch a glimpse of his gorgeous profile against the beautiful rising sun. I trust him just enough that I believe him.

৬

Fresh out of the shower, I enter my bedroom in only a towel. Noah appears in the doorway after a long day at work. I grin at his timing.

"Hold that thought." He smiles, already beginning to undress. Naked, he disappears into the bathroom. I hear the shower turn on. Less than ten minutes later, he's back, his body clean and glistening.

He joins me on the bed, taking the towel from me and tossing it onto the floor. I'm on my back. He turns me sideways. "How was your day?" he asks as his hand travels teasingly down my body until he finds what he is looking for. A finger explores me before I realize I have yet to answer.

"Good." I sigh, settling in as he adds a second

finger. Slowly, he plays, pulling his fingers in and out. I wiggle a bit, feeling myself becoming wet. "How about yours?" I manage.

"Getting better all the time," he says coolly.

He adds a third finger, going deeper with each stroke. Continuing the rhythm, Noah reaches over to the night table and pulls out something that I've never seen before: a simple pink blindfold. I'm guessing by its color that it is for me.

"Let's try this," he says.

I eye him and the mask warily. I'm not sure how I feel about this. I always get a little apprehensive about new things. But I've liked everything we've done so far.

He smiles at me, enjoying my contemplation. "Trust," he whispers softly as he straddles me. He puts the blindfold over my eyes.

The mask is in place. I can see nothing. I quiver with excitement.

"Trust," he whispers again in my ear. His hot breath makes me tingle, and I shiver. I can feel him moving on the bed. He is beside me again. At first, he does nothing, and I squirm with anticipation. I know he's making me wait on purpose. He chuckles.

"Just feel," he says, tracing my breast with one finger. The circles are large at first, and then he narrows them until he reaches my nipple. It becomes hard and erect. He gives it a firm tug with his teeth. I jump. Then he begins the same process with the other breast: he makes large circles around and under until the nipple is pointed. I try to brace myself for the tug but am surprised when it comes anyway.

Again, with just one finger, he traces a path down my tummy and around my curves. This makes me wiggle, and I am not surprised when he hisses, "Still."

I try to stay still, but with the mask on, my other senses are heightened, especially my sense of touch. I'm beginning to understand the point of the blindfold. Suddenly, he stops, and I wonder what is next. I feel nothing at first, and then I tense and shiver instantly when I feel him separate my folds. I feel a coolness as he opens them. He rubs his five o'clock shadow on my mound, and I am instantly soaked. I ache with anticipation. I gasp when I feel his warm, wet tongue begin to lick me.

He starts with long, gentle licks. I will myself to stay still because I don't want him to scold me or stop. He narrows his field until he is licking my bud, darting his tongue on and off, teasing me. I groan, waiting for more. He obliges by taking my whole clit into his mouth and sucking firmly. I moan louder. He lightens up a bit, keeping my orgasm at bay.

Never losing touch, I feel him change positions. Then, firmly, he pulls my lips apart and goes to work again.

Suddenly, I feel something grazing my face. I don't know what it is at first, but then I realize it is his shaft. He is straddling me backward. Still down on me, he lowers his hips. I open wide and take him into my mouth. He continues to lick. I begin to suck him.

He becomes hard and long in my mouth. He plunges deeper into me while pumping his hips and using my mouth. Not able to hold off any longer, I convulse and come. Just as I do, he deposits his cream into my mouth. I swallow.

I was wrong about sixty-nine. It is a big deal.

෨

"You like the fairy tales," he says, coming up behind me and kissing my neck.

"I do." I sigh.

He has found me in the library. I spend many afternoons here. I am sitting on the floor with a half dozen books spread out in front of me. He takes the vintage copy of *Goldilocks and the Three Bears* from my hands and begins to leaf through it. "One of your favorites?" he asks.

I shrug. "Not really. It bothers me," I admit.

He drops down beside me and pulls me into his arms. I settle onto his lap. Like most things lately, the book leads my thoughts back to my search for my mother. "It always bothers me that her mother never came after her," I tell him.

He nods sympathetically.

"I mean, she's out in the world all by herself, surrounded by bears," I say, only half joking.

"Maybe her mother comes along after. Maybe we don't know the rest of the story," he says, cuddling me.

I take this in. "Do you think I'll ever know the rest of my story?" I ask him.

He hesitates. I know he's choosing his words carefully. "I don't know," he finally says.

My heart sinks a bit, and my spirits fall. Then he lifts me with one word: "Maybe."

༶

"When the cat's away, the mice do play."

I jump at the sound of Noah's voice coming out of nowhere. Instantly, he is beside me. I close my eyes and cringe. When I open them, I look to Mrs. Middleton for help. She offers nothing; she simply takes her plate and disappears. Noah takes her seat across the island from me and frowns.

We have been caught.

He was supposed to be gone, in Chicago for the day, but obviously, he changed his plans and ended up back at home. When he is away, we do play. Today we have been eating junk food and watching reruns of zombie TV—things Noah disapproves of.

He eyes my plate of hot dogs, macaroni and cheese, mashed potatoes, and tater tots and raises his eyebrows. I shrink. I never know which way these kinds of things will go. Sometimes he lets them go, and other times, he does not. He opens his mouth to say something but stops short when he is distracted by the blaring television. He squints. "Are those heads rolling on the ground?"

They are. I grimace.

"Good God," he fumes, grabbing the remote and clicking it off. He shakes his head and faces me.

I'm pale by now. He admonishes me with a look. Then, thankfully, his mood seems suddenly to change. He reaches over, grabs a tater tot from my plate, and pops it into his mouth. He stands up and tosses everything—plate and all—into the garbage can.

"Come," he says, taking my hand. I'm grateful that he links his fingers in mine. "I want to show you something."

It's a nice afternoon for a drive. I don't know where we are going and don't much care. Noah says it's a surprise. His surprises are always interesting. He promises that I'll like it, and I trust him because he's never been wrong. It's amazing how well he has gotten to know me in such little time.

Then again, he knows me because he studies me. He watches every move I make. He's completely in tune with me. I know he's discovering exactly what makes me tick. He knows what makes me happy or sad, what I like, and what I don't like. He reads my moods, saying, "I'm sorry you're unhappy," "I'm glad you liked that," or "You'll be fine," without me having to say anything.

Of course, he anticipates my every move too. He'll say, "Stop sulking," "I wouldn't go there if I were you," and "Don't even start."

He even analyzes my words, listening carefully to everything I say. He will often say, "Tell me that just one more time," so he can completely understand exactly what I am trying to say. He knows when I need to see my family, butterflies, or stars. He knows me in the bedroom just as well. He can make me wet and responsive with one touch, one word, or even the sound of his voice.

At first, I found his intimate knowledge invasive and unsettling, but slowly, it's become comforting.

"Close your eyes," he says.

"Really?" I ask.

"Just for the last mile," he says. "I want you to be surprised."

"Okay." I close my eyes, playing along.

I relax and lean back in the seat. We ride for a while. Finally, I hear the turn signal. I feel the car slow and then stop.

"Open," he says, squeezing my thigh. I open my eyes and look around. I can't place where we are. "Take a minute," Noah says. "You've been here before."

I'm confused. I look around again. He watches me, amused.

"There," he says, pointing across the street.

Then I see it: a beautiful new park. It all comes together. We are in the same poverty-stricken neighborhood that he took me to months ago, where he showed me that dilapidated building. At the time, he asked me what I would build in its place once it was torn down. I gasp, realizing. He has torn the building down, just as he said he would, and replaced it with a park, just as I suggested.

When I look closer, I see that it is not just any park. It is the park I described that day in the car. He listened to every single detail. It has green grass, magnolia and birch trees, beds upon beds of daffodils, a gazebo, lots of benches for sitting, and a small play area for young children. It has everything I imagined. It's wonderful to see the park filled with people.

"It's amazing!" I turn to face him. "You listened?"

"I always listen, Gabriella."

I nod that I know this. "It's just perfect," I whisper. "Why?"

"Why not?" He shrugs.

"Not exactly a money-generating venture." I grin.

"Not exactly," he agrees. "But that's not a problem."

"Thank you," I say, and I kiss him on the cheek. "It's really, really special."

"Just like its visionary," he says. He takes my hand and kisses it.

I lean back in the seat, ready to relax, but when I catch a glimpse of the sign at the entrance, I jump. It reads,

Gabriella's Park
Land Donated by Bentley Industries
Park Designed by Gabriella Rossi

I gasp, speechless. He kisses my hand again.

"Noah," I whisper, managing only that one word.

He offers only a wink and a grin before starting the car and pulling away from the curb. I lean back and relax and feel myself falling further for this man.

Chapter 22

"Stop. Now," Noah warns me from across the table.

We are out to dinner. I'm angry, and I'm showing it. The people from my painting class are going out for drinks to celebrate the end of the term, and I want to go. Of course, when I ask Noah if I can, he answers with a resounding no.

"I said please," I point out.

"You can say please all you want," he tells me. "You do not barhop."

"It's hardly barhopping," I say, exasperated. "It's one bar and one drink!"

"It's one bar that you won't be going to and one drink that you won't be having," he says.

I stare at him, and he ignores me. "Why not?"

"The question was asked. The question was answered," he says.

"I hate that answer," I sneer.

"Gabriella." His voice is stern. "The conversation is over."

I make a face. I know I should stop, but I don't. Instead, I do what he hates. I slouch back in the seat and go into a full-on pout. He glares at me, his eyes hard. He says nothing, but his eyes say, *Back down.* In my head, I weigh my options. I make my decision. I glare back.

"Done," he says, tossing his napkin onto the table. He calls for the check. We haven't even gotten our entrées yet.

"Not tolerated," he mutters, yanking me out of the booth and cupping my hand in his as he leads me out of the restaurant. He deposits me in the passenger seat of the car, and with a slam of the door, he is in the driver's seat beside me. He takes my chin in his hand and turns me so that I am facing him. I can't help but look directly into his eyes.

"You are done," he tells me emphatically. He lets go of my chin and puts the car in gear.

"Maybe I am. Maybe I'm not," I respond.

"And now," he says, speaking slowly and deliberately, "you are done painting until further notice."

He's just about to pull out into traffic, when I do something I shouldn't. I kick the dashboard of the car. I don't kick it hard, but I do it intentionally. I have shocked myself, and I sort of wish I could take it back. I'm afraid to look up—and probably for good reason.

He freezes, takes a breath, and runs his hand through his hair. He takes a moment and then lets the breath out, and suddenly, he slams the accelerator. We're off like a shot. He drives erratically, and I'm scared to death. Red lights and stop signs mean nothing. In what seems like minutes, we are at the curb in front of the apartment. He pulls me out of the car, pushes me into the elevator, and tosses me into the apartment so fast I'm reeling.

Once inside, thankfully, we separate. I go to the bedroom, and he goes to his study—I'm sure for a much-needed drink.

I bathe, dress for bed, and fall asleep alone.

The next thing I know, it's midnight. My empty stomach wakes me up. I'm starving. Noah's in bed, sound asleep beside me. I study his face. He doesn't look like such a monster now. I lie there for a few minutes, quietly contemplating if I should risk it or not. I decide to go for it. I slide out of bed and down the hall to the kitchen. I rummage through the refrigerator. In a moment, Mrs. Middleton joins me. It is one of her nights to sleep over.

As my accomplice fixes me a snack, I tell her about the evening. The kitchen is dark, and I whisper the details. As always, she doesn't take sides. She simply nods and, every once in a while, says, "Tsk" or "Oh, you two." She has just gotten done saying this, when suddenly, the kitchen light flashes on, startling us both.

"Absolutely not!" Noah thunders, entering the kitchen. "Not under my roof! She gets nothing!"

"Noah," Mrs. Middleton pleads.

"She pouted and misbehaved through dinner. She

gets nothing. Throwing tantrums and behaving like a spoiled child will not be tolerated!"

"Noah, she's hungry," Mrs. Middleton says.

"Helen, she's spoiled!" he yells.

"Noah!"

"Helen!"

"She's going to bed!" he says, looking directly at me.

I wilt and disappear.

۞

The next morning, Mrs. Middleton and I are in the kitchen first. She is cooking scrambled eggs on the stove, and I am sitting on the countertop next to her. She is feeding me the eggs directly from the spatula. Noah appears in the kitchen and sees this. His jaw drops in disbelief.

"Tell me she's not spoiled!" he yells.

Mrs. Middleton and I both jump. I hop down from the counter and scurry to my place at the island. Mrs. Middleton puts the eggs on a plate in front of me.

Once served, we sit there alone. He's reading the newspaper. I study him. He's dressed for work in a suit and tie, looking incredibly hot. He's gorgeous. He's ignoring me.

"Good morning," I squeak.

He looks over his newspaper and scowls at me. For some reason, this makes me giggle. He closes his eyes in exasperation and then looks at me. I grin. His face softens.

"Good morning," he says. "You're bad."

I smile at him. He shakes his head, folds the newspaper, and starts to leave.

"Stay with me," I say.

He looks confused.

"Be with me," I repeat. "Don't go to work."

He frowns and reaches out to smooth my messy hair. "I can't do that. I have about ten meetings."

"You can do anything you want," I say. "You're the boss." He opens his mouth to speak, but I silence him. "Be with me," I say again, my eyes pleading.

He sighs. I've worn him down. "What do you want to do?" he asks.

"Yay!" I squeal. I jump up, throw my arms around him, and kiss his neck.

He laughs. "You're so bad!"

I run out of the room. "I'll be ready in five minutes!" I yell over my shoulder.

"Any longer and I'm changing my mind!" he yells back.

Ten minutes later, we are in the car. I actually get him to promise to let me design the day. When he agrees, I simply hand him the address of our first stop. I'm proud of him. This goes against everything he is about. He never gives up control. However, he follows the commands on the GPS.

I can't sit still. I'm excited. Since I've been in New York, I've rarely been out in the world on my terms. Today it looks as if I am.

I blanch when I catch sight of the mark that my

heel left on the dashboard the night before. He sees it too. I dare to look up. He frowns and shakes his head. I shrink. "Sorry," I whisper.

He nods and takes my hand, linking our fingers. I'm forgiven.

Thirty minutes later, we are seated across a booth from one another.

"Good God, Gabriella! Where are we?" Noah groans, looking around uncomfortably.

"IHOP," I squeal excitedly. The commercials have been getting to me all week.

"Yes. But why are we at IHOP?"

"Because IHOP is wonderful!"

"This was a bad idea," he growls.

"Why?" I ask him. "We didn't wait long, and we got a good seat."

"We stood up in a line for twenty minutes, and we have a view of a fire hydrant surrounded by mulch."

"You're a snob," I tell him.

"Yes. I like that about me. This was a bad idea," he says.

I laugh too hard, and he shushes me. He shakes his head in disgust. I can't stop smiling. "Just go with it," I say. "Remember your fortune." *Don't be afraid to lose control. It is in that loss that we often gain.*

He closes his eyes as if he's getting a headache.

"And let me order for both of us," I insist. "I know the menu!"

"Which disturbs me," he grumbles.

I lean across the table and kiss him on the cheek.

My lipstick leaves a smudge. I am just about to wipe it off, when the waitress appears.

"I'm Doris. Welcome to IHOP," she says in a singsong voice.

Doris is somewhere in her sixties, heavyset, and a little rough around the edges. I can tell by the way she greets us that she has been doing this for forty years.

"What can I get you?" she asks, looking off into space and snapping her gum.

Noah is obviously taken aback by her demeanor and looks at her with a combination of annoyance and puzzlement. I intervene before the two of them make eye contact.

"We'll have the Red, White, and Blue Pancakes," I tell her, "and two hot teas. Thank you."

Doris does not bother to write the order down. "Got it, honey," she says, and she cracks her gum again. She starts to turn away but is distracted by something on Noah. She furrows her brow and then reaches out with her thumb and forefinger and rubs the smudge of lipstick off of Noah's face. He is frozen, grimacing, no doubt appalled at being touched. "There you go, gorgeous," she says when she is done. She turns and goes to put our order in.

I laugh so hard that I almost pee.

As we eat, I chatter on about everything and nothing. Noah listens in amusement. We would sit longer, but a family with four kids sits behind Noah, and the children begin kicking his seat.

"Ready?" he asks, rolling his eyes.

"Yes." I giggle.

We get up. He drops a hundred-dollar bill on the table for Doris and takes my hand. I love him for this.

"Did you like it?" I ask.

"I liked it just fine," he says. "What's next, boss?"

I reach in my purse and hand him an advertisement that I tore out of the newspaper that morning. He studies it. It's an ad for an outdoor fall arts festival in the park.

"This I can do," he tells me.

It's a beautiful day. The festival has more than three hundred vendors. Leisurely, we walk through hand in hand, exploring each booth. We watch glass being blown, clay pots being made, and candles being molded. We laugh at caricatures of celebrities and study the more serious art.

"One day," I promise him, "this will be me. One day my paintings will be for sale."

"This is nice," he says, "but your art belongs in a gallery."

I mull that dream over as we walk, but suddenly, the sight of the last booth shakes me out of the dream, and I squeal, "Oh my gosh! Look!" I point at the sign above the booth: Adopt-a-Pet.

In my excitement, I attempt to let go of Noah's hand and dart off, but he tightens his grip and yanks me back. "Absolutely not," he says.

"We'll just look." I try to pull away again.

"Gabriella," he warns, holding on tightly to my hand.

"We'll just look. I swear."

He frowns at me warily but lets go of my hand and allows me to run over.

Forty minutes later, I'm in love. He is black and white and only six weeks old. He is the cutest kitten I have ever seen. I'm not letting go.

"I said no," Noah says firmly.

I attempt my best pouty face.

"Not working."

"Please," I beg.

"I said no," he says.

"And I said please. You won't even know he's there."

"Because he's not going to be there."

Forty-five minutes later, we are in the car, driving back to the apartment. I'm afraid to look at Noah. He's furious. After a few miles, I carefully sneak a peek at his face. He catches me looking and scowls. "You are so spoiled," he growls.

"Thank you," I whisper, picking up my new kitten. I kiss the top of his furry head.

Noah glares at me and shakes his head. We drive in silence for a while.

"What's his name?" Noah finally asks, breaking the tension.

I grin. "Paul," I tell him excitedly.

"Paul?" he exclaims. "That's no name for a cat. What about Mittens or Boots or Fluffy?"

"Nope," I insist. "His name is Paul."

He sighs. "Well, tell Paul not to get too comfortable, because the first time he acts up, he's gone."

"Why?" I ask, grinning. "I act up all the time, and I'm not gone."

৯

It's a chilly evening. Noah is out of town for the night, and Mrs. Middleton is staying over. She and I are wrapped in blankets and drinking tea in the great room.

"Thank you for dinner," I tell her.

"You're very welcome," she says.

"And thank you for staying with me," I add. She smiles. "Mrs. Middleton?" I say. "Tell me about your mother."

"What would you like to know?"

"Oh, anything," I say. "Are you like her?" I ask.

"Oh, very much so," she says without hesitation.

"Tell me how."

She ponders this. "Well, I think I'm very much like my mother. We share many of the same interests. Although she was a full-time homemaker and I became educated and worked as a teacher, I think what we both loved best is caring for our homes and families."

"Which is how you ended up here," I say.

"It is," she confirms. "It's where I'm happiest."

"I'm glad you're here," I tell her. "Tell me more," I say.

"Well, let me think. She was kind. I hope I am. And sensitive. I hope I am." Mrs. Middleton pauses and smiles. I let her linger with her private thought for a moment.

"You know, you glow when you speak of her," I say.

"They tell me I have her smile," she says.

"That's so cool," I gush. "I'd love to have my mother's smile," I tell her.

"Maybe you do," she says. Then she looks at me seriously. "Gabriella, the mother you knew was your mother."

"I know," I say with a sigh. "But it would be nice to know."

"And all of those wonderful girls you've told me about are your sisters," she tells me.

"It's funny," I say, pondering this. "It can't all be nature. Nurture has to play a big part in who we are." I laugh. "Even though not being one of them always preyed on my mind, I am still very much like my sisters. We're like peas in a pod."

"Tell me how," she says.

"Well, I can be a bit spontaneous like Mia. And Gina and Maria and I all did pretty well in school, and Teresa and I are both good at dance. The sister I am most like is Angela, but that's probably because she always acted more like a mother hen than a sister," I explain, laughing. My heart aches, and I can't help but smile while thinking about all of them.

"Now who's glowing?" Mrs. Middleton asks. I know she is right.

"Me," I tell her.

§

We are snuggling on the couch in front of the TV one November evening. I'm dozing off, when Noah suddenly straightens up. He leans forward, peering at the end table on the far wall. "What happened to that vase?"

I'm instantly panicked. He's referring to the vase I shattered with the remote the night I saw him on the news with Grace Blattman.

He's now up and scanning the room, convinced that the vase has somehow just been moved. When it becomes obvious that this is not the case, he turns to me. Seeing my face, he looks at me warily. "Do you know what happened to it?"

I shrink.

"Gabriella," he says.

I nod, and he waits. "I broke it," I whisper.

He's not happy, but his face softens a touch. "Accidents happen," he says. However, apparently, I'm transparent. He studies me. "It wasn't an accident?" His voice rises.

I'm frozen.

"Answer me!"

I shake my head.

"You broke it on purpose?" He is floored. "Start talking. Now!"

I take a deep breath. "I threw the remote at the vase the night you went to that fancy charity event with Grace. I saw the two of you on TV. You were on the news."

He frowns and shakes his head. "We were not there together," he says. "She ambushed me. Cameras were there, but that's it. I stopped by early in the evening on my way out of town as an obligation."

I lower my eyes.

"And whom do I answer to?" he asks, livid.

"No one," I mumble.

"Again," he demands.

"You answer to no one," I repeat.

He's so angry that he's pacing. I sit still, scared, awaiting my fate.

"That was a fifty-thousand-dollar vase!"

I forget myself for a second. "Really?" I ask, shocked. "Who would pay fifty thousand dollars for a vase?"

"A lover of art!" he snaps.

"Seems like a waste," I mutter. I didn't mean to say that out loud. It does not help my cause.

He runs his fingers through his hair. "Go to bed!"

I jump. *Gladly.* I think I can get away without the swat, but I am wrong, and I yelp when it comes. I scurry out of the room.

I'm in the bathroom, washing my face, when he appears. I'm kind of over the entire thing. He is not. I try to slip by him. He blocks my way.

"Fifty thousand dollars," he says, seething.

I crinkle my nose, more for his benefit than anything. I've been around long enough to know that this amount of money is but a drop in the bucket for Noah.

"Fifty thousand dollars," he says again, letting me by this time.

"Says the billionaire," I say sarcastically, rolling my

eyes. I think he is farther away than he is when I say this.

"Says the billionaire? Says the billionaire!" he hollers. "Says the toddler who throws remotes when she's angry!"

I find this funny and giggle.

He shakes his head, exasperated. "That mouth," he warns.

I giggle again and put my arms around his neck to rise up on my tiptoes and kiss him. "This mouth?" I ask.

He sighs and kisses me back. "You're getting expensive," he says, scooping me up and carrying me to the bedroom.

৯

We're in his study. I'm between his legs. He likes this best in here. I don't mind. I like being needed, and besides, I love the feel of him in my mouth.

His head is back, and his eyes are closed. I love teasing him until he begs for me.

"Suck me, baby," he croons.

When he says this, I feel my own juices flow, and my panties become wet.

"That's my girl," he groans.

He's already rock hard and ready to come, but I want more and pull back.

His erection stands tall. I want all of him. I want to know what he feels like in my mouth. I push his shaft to the side and go down again, licking his balls. He shifts and moans.

I've never done this before.

After a firm licking, I take one of his balls in my mouth. I suck gently at first and then harder. Then I move on to the other sac, licking and sucking just as I did the first.

"Oh, baby!" he groans.

I'm driving him crazy. He's holding my head tightly. Knowing that he likes me to swallow, I leave his balls and take his erection firmly in my mouth. He's huge.

"Yes, baby!" he growls.

Then, with a shudder and a loud moan, he convulses and comes, shooting his liquid into my mouth. There is so much that it seems endless. I swallow again and again. I pull back and look up at him. He looks down at me and grins.

"My girl," he simply says. His words make me tingle.

ᔕ

"I thought I might find you here." It's Noah. He comes up behind me and gives me a gentle kiss on the top of the head. It's late in the afternoon, and I slipped away from the apartment. I am at the park. This is against Noah's rules, but he doesn't seem mad. He joins me on the bench.

I've chosen the noisiest, busiest part of the park. I am positioned directly in front of the merry-go-round, where a half dozen children are playing. I have come here specifically to watch them. Noah, of course, reads my behavior clearly.

"The mothers and their children?" he asks.

I nod. "Sometimes seeing them helps," I tell him.

We sit in silence for a while, watching. My heart melts as one mother dries tears over a bumped knee, and we giggle when another mother scolds her toddler for eating sand.

"Maybe my mother sits in parks and thinks about me," I say.

"Maybe," Noah says.

I look into the perfect blue sky. "I think she's close by," I tell him.

After a pause, he asks, "What makes you say that?"

"I don't know," I answer. "I've just always had that feeling," I say. But after a moment, I doubt myself a bit. "Or maybe I'm just being silly," I say.

I wait for Noah to respond. For a second, he looks as if he might and even opens his mouth to speak, but strangely, he remains silent. Instead of answering, he simply takes my hand and kisses it.

Chapter 23

The days are passing easily now. We are in a comfortable rhythm that has somehow become my life. In spite of myself, I don't want to see him go in the morning, and I wait all day for his return.

We know each other better. He makes it a point to understand everything about me, and I know what it takes to please him. I look for his approving smile. I crave his touch. I don't know how this has happened, but it has.

"This could be painful," Noah warns as we are getting dressed for an evening out.

"Where are we going again?" I ask.

"Tom Marlin, my oldest employee, is retiring," he explains. "A great guy. Ten or twelve of us to dinner to see him off. Not my idea of a good time but necessary."

"No worries," I say.

Noah generally does not socialize with his employees, but when someone has been so loyal for so many years, he does the right thing.

"How do I look?" I ask, presenting myself to him.

I am wearing a form-fitting pink dress and matching pumps. He loves me in pink. He believes pink is for girls and blue is for boys.

"You look beautiful." He smiles, pulling me in for a kiss. He caresses my bottom and growls. "Just beautiful."

"You don't look so bad yourself, Mr. Bentley."

He's dressed in a black sport coat and trousers with a pure-white open-collared shirt that sets off his jet-black hair. *Hot!*

༄

It's a twenty-minute drive to the restaurant. As always, he drives swiftly with one hand on the steering wheel and one hand on my thigh. We valet the car and enter.

"Mr. Bentley, your party has arrived."

Is there any place where he is not known?

Already waiting are Noah's employees and their wives. Counting Noah and me, there are twelve of us. They are already seated at one large table with benches on either side. They all call and wave when they see us. Choruses of "Hey, Mr. Bentley!" ring out. They greet me as if they know me.

A sequined and stilettoed women who seems to be particularly in charge rushes over to me. "Hi, Gabriella. I'm Victoria, Lance's wife—Lance from accounting. Wives down here. Hubbies down there," she says, taking me by the arm. She yanks me away from Noah.

I don't like this. Reluctantly, I let go of Noah's hand. I didn't know we wouldn't be sitting together.

Before I know it, I'm jammed between some of these boisterous women: Joan, wife of Guy from IT, and Olivia, wife of Stewart from sales.

I frown at Noah.

"I'm sorry," he mouths at me. I cross my eyes. He laughs.

One of the guys demands his attention as the wives begin to gobble me up.

"Who are you wearing, Gabriella?" Victoria asks. I have no idea what she means.

When I don't immediately answer, Joan examines the tag on the back collar of my dress. "It's Gucci!" she announces loudly enough for the entire restaurant to hear.

"I knew it!" shouts Olivia. "Lovely."

They move on to my shoes. "Great kicks," says one woman I don't know.

"Gucci too?" guesses Joan.

"I think," I stammer.

"Jesus! That's the biggest Chanel bag I've ever seen!" remarks another.

I'm dying. They are picking me apart. It's like a feeding frenzy.

"Try to not sprain your arm lifting that watch you're wearing, Gabriella," one of them remarks. They all cackle. "How long have you been together?"

"A few months," I say timidly.

"Oh, still on a honeymoon!" one says, as if this explains everything. They collectively nod.

Thankfully, a waitress arrives with drinks. *Thank God for alcohol.* They lighten up a bit and begin to concentrate on themselves. Still, I don't like what they've said about my relationship with Noah being a honeymoon. It's insulting and makes what we have sound fake.

I spy Noah across the table. One of the men is showing him something on his phone. He shakes his head thoughtfully. I love his hair. It's all mussed up and sexy. I want to run my hands through it. He needs a haircut.

I think about the fact that we have only been together for a few months. It seems much longer. My old life in New Jersey seems long ago and far away.

The waitress comes back with menus. She passes them around. I open mine and scan it. I haven't ordered for myself since I've been here. Noah knows this, because when I look across the table, he's looking back at me. We grin. I take out my phone.

I text, "?"

"What do you want?" he texts back.

"You," I reply.

He smiles. "Let's get the salmon," he suggests.

"Deal," I type, and I put my phone away.

He winks at me before his attention is once again drawn away by one of the men.

I watch him and think about the first time I ever laid eyes on him through the pizza shop window. I remember how my sisters and I laughed as he stood on the sidewalk, fuming over his limo's flat tire. I remember clearly making eye contact for the first time after my sisters scattered, while I got caught looking.

I try to settle in and get involved in the girl talk, but instead, I just listen and remain a spectator. My eyes are drawn to Noah again.

I think about the first day we met, when he took me for ice cream, and how nervous and giddy I was. I remember the butterflies I felt. I still feel them now. I think about my nervous acceptance of his offer and those first few horrendous days before the truce.

As we are waiting for the entrées to come, a family-style shrimp appetizer arrives for the table. The others begin passing the plate. Noah thinks that I might have an allergy, because I broke out in a rash the last time I ate shrimp. I disagree, mostly because I love shrimp. The platter reaches me. Our eyes meet. His eyes say no. I pass it along. He nods and goes back to his conversation.

I try to stop staring at Noah and attempt to concentrate on the women around me. They are older and have moved on to conversations about kids and school. I'm left out.

Dinner arrives. I pick at my salmon. Noah catches me. We make eye contact. He nods toward the plate, signaling for me to eat. Then he winks, and I melt. The butterflies flutter in my tummy.

My mind drifts back to the first time he made love to me. I think of how scared I was but how ready I was. It was the first time I ever saw a man, and I think about how sexy he looked. I think about how he makes lovemaking new every time. I think about all of this, and it makes me want him. I'm wet. I wish he knew. I pick up my phone.

"Want you," I text.

While keeping up with the conversation around him, Noah looks down and grins at his phone. "Want you," he texts back.

I think about the rockier times, when I was a tremendous brat and when he punished me. I think about seeing butterflies and stars. I think about crying and laughing in his arms.

As the cake is being served, I catch his eye. I mouth, "Almost?"

He nods with another wink. I feel another butterfly.

Thankfully, the evening ends. Backs are patted, good lucks are wished, and good-byes are said.

We are alone in the car. We both lean back against the headrests and sigh.

"Duty done," he says, taking my hand. He kisses it. "You are a trooper."

We drive home in a peaceful, comfortable silence. He rubs my thigh gently, which makes me tingle. I breathe in his cologne. I want him all to myself.

Back in the apartment, I'm undressed first and on the bed, watching him. He sees me and smiles. "You were awfully quiet tonight," he tells me as he undresses.

I shrug.

In his boxers, he comes to join me. "A penny for your thoughts?"

"Okay," I say.

He smiles and raises his eyebrows. "A businessman

like me can't turn down a bargain like that," he says, and he rolls over and retrieves a penny from the loose change on the dresser. He places it in my palm, closes my hand, and kisses it. "Now then," he says, "what's going on in there?"

I look directly into his eyes. "I love you, Noah."

His face becomes serious but soft. He never takes his eyes off of me. Without hesitation, he says, "And I love you, Gabriella."

We stay in the moment.

"Noah?"

He looks at me questioningly.

"Make love to me."

He nods and rises. I lie back and close my eyes. In the darkness, ever so gently, he crawls on top of me. His kisses are soft, and his caress is electrifying. I surrender completely to his touch. He manipulates me expertly, and I obey every unspoken command until I come, cradled tightly in his arms.

Chapter 24

The call comes on a Tuesday afternoon. Mrs. Middleton has gone to the market, and I am home alone. I never answer the phone, because it is rarely for me, but the caller is persistent.

It's Mia. She is hysterical, crying and screaming. I can't make out all that she is saying, but I do understand through her sobs that something is terribly wrong with Poppy. She manages to tell me which hospital and ICU he's in and says I'd better come quickly.

That's all I need to hear. I grab my sweater and cab money from Mrs. Middleton's house money jar and am out the door. Liam is nowhere to be found, so I quickly hail a cab, jump inside, and beg the driver to get me to the hospital as fast as he can.

I am grateful that he understands my panic and gets me there in record time. I throw him all the money I have and race into the hospital, following the signs to the intensive care unit. My sisters are huddled together outside in the waiting area.

When I see their faces, I know I am too late. They reach out and gather me into the fold. Together we cry.

Poppy suffered a massive heart attack that morning at the pizza shop. The hospital did all they could, but he lasted mere minutes.

The other girls have already said their good-byes. Now it is my turn. I am escorted by a nurse into the room where Poppy lies.

"Take all the time you need," the nurse softly whispers as she leaves the room.

Seeing him is almost too much to bear, but I will myself to be strong and pull a chair up to the side of the bed. With tears pouring from my eyes, I talk to him, because deep down, I know that where he is, he is hearing me.

I thank him with all my heart for taking in the baby in the basket that was left on the doorstep. I thank him for the wonderful life he gave me. Shamefully, I tell him of my secret plan to be the hero of the family and of my arrangement with Noah. I ask him to look down upon me and be my angel when he can, and I promise to care for my sisters. Then, in the silence, I sit and hold his hand.

I don't know how long I sit there. I think I am alone, until I feel a gentle hand on my shoulder. When I turn, Noah is standing there. His eyes are soft and sympathetic, but I don't see this. I am blinded by the flood of angry emotions I suddenly feel. I turn on him.

"You promised me!" I seethe. "You said you were watching over them!"

His mouth drops open. "Gabriella, I *was* watching over them. This happened too fast."

"I didn't get to say good-bye," I say icily, "because of you. I should have been home like everyone else, but instead, I was being held captive by you!" I am hurting him with my words, but I don't care.

"Gabriella—"

"Get out! The deal is off. We both lose," I hiss.

He tries to reach out and touch me, but I jump away. "Get out," I demand again.

He closes his eyes, wounded.

I take a deep breath and then repeat myself. "Get out."

I leave him no choice. He turns and walks away from me. As the door clicks shut, I bury my head in my hands and sob.

۞

The days that follow are a blur. My sisters and I band together, doing all that needs to be done. Together we have amazing strength even as we carry around our broken hearts.

Three days later, at the gravesite, we stand side by side dressed in black and say good-bye. From the corner of my eye, I see a black limo pull to the edge of the grass. I watch as Noah, Liam, and Mrs. Middleton climb out of the car. Dressed in black as well, they stay a respectful distance away.

When the service is over, I am grateful that they make no effort to come closer but instead get back into the car and slowly drive away. I watch until the car is out of sight. Strangely, my time with them feels like a million years ago. The whole experience feels as if it never actually happened.

※

Over the next week, I work at the pizza shop with my sisters. Noah calls the shop every day, but I refuse all of his calls.

"Just tell him I'm busy," I instruct my confused sisters.

Finally, the following Friday, I am working with my back to the counter, when I hear his voice.

"I'd like a Coke, please."

I gulp before turning to face him. Our eyes lock. My anger has dissolved. I realize that there was nothing either Noah or I could have done.

"Hi," I say softly.

"Hi," he says back. There is a pause. Then he says, "I'd like a Coke, please."

He waits patiently for me to react. Finally, I turn and pour him a Coke. When I set it on the counter, he slides a folded piece of paper toward me.

"Keep the change." He nods.

I pick the paper up and find that it is a check for $1 million. "Noah, I can't," I say, wagging my head.

"What did I tell you about saying no to me?" he asks softly.

Our eyes meet. The sight of him still takes my breath away. He is dressed in the same worn jeans and white button-down shirt that he wore the first time he asked me for a Coke.

"I didn't stay," I point out.

"You did what you had to."

I nod and accept this. I know that I did.

"But it would be polite of you to finish what you started," he tells me with a smile.

"Oh, would it?" I ask, smiling back at him.

"A deal is a deal. I've missed you, Gabriella," he says seriously. Then, with a grin, he adds, "Me and Guppy and Paul."

This makes me laugh.

His face softens. "I was afraid I would never hear your laugh again," he murmurs quietly.

Blushing, I take a moment, and then I look up and tell him the truth. "I've missed you too, Noah."

"You told me you loved me," he says.

"Because I do."

"You belong with me. You belong to me," he says. "You know that."

I look into his eyes, and I know he is right.

"Let's go home, baby," he says softly.

ぅ

Noah drives back to New York leisurely. I relax in the seat. He caresses my thigh gently. *God, how I've missed his touch!*

"Can I have a car and a job?" I ask bravely.

He faces me, obviously taken aback. "The answers are no. Are you out of your mind?" he fumes.

"What about—"

"Are you actually trying to negotiate with me?" he asks, exasperated.

"Um, yes. No. Maybe." I giggle.

"And that answer needs to be no," he growls.

"No," I squeak.

"The day you get a car and a job is the day you get a new boyfriend!"

I should have known better. Noah Bentley is a man you take on his terms or not at all.

"Understood?" he demands.

"Understood," I answer, grinning.

It's nice to be us again.

When we get back to the apartment, I smile when I see that he has hung my first painting from art class in the foyer. My ten-cent painting is now displayed in a thousand-dollar frame. On the bottom of the frame is a tiny plaque that reads, *"Fruit-a-Floria*, by Gabriella." I smile.

"Thank you," I say softly.

"I'm an art lover," he whispers.

I look at him and grin. He pulls me close and kisses me, cupping my bottom and squeezing. He lets out a growl. "Bath and bed," he whispers.

I nod and disappear.

When Noah enters the bedroom, I am waiting. He undresses with one eye on me. "Where do you belong?" he asks me, crawling onto the bed.

"Here," I answer quietly, lying back and letting him undress me.

"And whom do you belong to?" he asks, his voice low and raspy.

"You. I belong to you," I tell him.

I'm naked now. He stares at me adoringly, running his hands up and down my body. Then he kisses me gently before pulling back and spreading my legs. He parts my folds with his fingers and begins to explore me with his mouth.

I lie there completely exposed. He licks and sucks everywhere. I squirm. He holds me firmly until I can barely take anymore. Again and again, he brings me close to orgasm and then retreats. Just when I don't think I can take it anymore, he takes my most sensitive spot into his mouth and sucks hard. I cry out as he finally lets me come. I lie back, panting, eyes closed.

"Words," he says softly. I know what he wants me to say.

"I belong with you. I belong to you," I manage, barely able to speak.

"Never forget that," he says with a grin.

I know that I won't.

The next morning, right before he leaves for work, he leads me to one of the guest bedrooms. Oddly, the door is closed, and there is a small pink bow in the center of it. I look at him, puzzled.

"Open it." He nods toward the knob.

Cautiously, I open the door and peer in.

I gasp. The room is no longer a guest bedroom; it is an art studio. I cannot believe my eyes. Everything I could ever imagine is there. Easels, paints, brushes, and frames surround the room.

"All yours," he tells me with a kiss on the head. I open my mouth but am speechless. He caresses my cheek and smiles, and then he turns and disappears down the hallway.

※

It's three o'clock in the morning. I've sneaked out of bed, and I am Skyping my sisters from the computer in Noah's study. I started off just talking to Mia, but one at a time, each sister joined the chat.

"So what's Knightly really like?" Gina asks. All five girls now have their faces pressed against the computer screen. I shrug, not sure how to answer.

"He's …" I search for words. "He's really …"

"Tired," a voice behind me growls. It's Noah. "He's tired!"

All five girls squeal and scramble to get out of range of the camera. It's comical. I can hear them falling over each other in the background, and I find myself looking at an empty screen until an anonymous hand reaches in view and slams their laptop shut. My screen goes black.

Noah spins the chair around so that I face him. "You have all day to play with your sisters, Gabriella," he says. I nod. He points to the door. I get up and brace myself for the smack on the bottom that is undoubtedly coming. It comes halfway down the hallway.

※

He's in the shower. I watch his figure. He's got his head back, and he's letting the water run over his face. He's beyond sexy. I'm horribly turned on. I want him. I strip.

I gently open the shower door. He shakes the water from his face and opens his eyes. He looks at me questioningly.

"I'm dirty too," I tell him.

He grins. "I can take care of that." Noah takes my hand and guides me into the stall. "Let's see how dirty you are," he teases, placing me under the stream of water.

As the water rushes over us, he takes my head in his hands and begins kissing me. His tongue is deep. I respond instantly. I can feel his erection pressing against my mound.

Never taking his eyes from me, Noah lathers the soap in his hand. Starting with my neck, he begins washing me. He then moves on to my shoulders and arms. I close my eyes when he reaches my breasts. With both hands, he rubs them gently in large circles. He pays special attention to the nipples and watches adoringly as they point. He leans down and sucks one breast while pinching the other nipple. I arch and lean back. Just when I need him to, he switches breasts, sucking the other and pinching the opposite. It feels good.

He takes more soap, lathering again. He leans in and kisses me. "Still dirty?" he asks.

"I am."

His grin is wide. He kneels down in front of me and begins rubbing up and down my thighs. He is teasing me by avoiding my center. I want him there, but when I move, trying to nudge his hand there, he pulls back. I squirm. He laughs.

He stands, takes more soap into his hands, and, with his mouth on mine, murmurs, "You really are dirty."

I only nod.

He turns me so that my back is to him. He starts on my shoulders and works his way down my arms. When he reaches my bottom, he lingers on my cheeks, one hand on each. As he rubs, he pulls them apart and slides his hand between, caressing there. I'm so aroused that my legs are tingling and threatening to give way.

With his right hand, he continues to rub up and down my crack. With his left hand, he spreads my folds, rubbing me. I can barely keep my balance. He's watching me, turned on. I'm lost, mewing softly. He begins to rub my clit with his thumb while his fingers pump in and out of me.

I am almost ready to come, and I begin bucking up and down. He works both hands. I am pushed to ecstasy. I arch and convulse, coming violently as he holds me in place. The water streams over me.

He removes his hands and pushes me against the wall. "My turn," he says, his lips grazing mine. I nod and spread my legs wide.

༄

The next Saturday, we go back to the pizza shop to meet with the girls about Noah buying the shop. When I left with Noah the week before, I handed the million-dollar check to Angela. Her eyes bulged, and her mouth gaped open. I told her that I would explain later.

"You've actually got a Knightly," she whispered.

I have to admit that I do.

When we pull up to the curb, all five girls have their faces pressed against the window. I laugh out loud. Once we're inside, they each greet Noah with a peck on the cheek. He acknowledges each of them by name. Every one of them blushes. Noah is kind and friendly yet businesslike and firm.

"He's kind of controlling," Mia whispers.

I want to tell her that she has no idea, but instead, I say, "He wants the best for us."

He speaks to each girl, inquiring about her goals and dreams. Maria and Teresa are interested in college. Gina wants to explore cosmetology school. Angela is thinking about nursing, and Mia shrugs and admits that she doesn't have much of a goal but is sweet on Vinnie Mannarino. Noah patiently encourages her to adjust her thinking.

Noah has set up five bank accounts, one for each of them, dividing the million dollars equally. He encourages my sisters to learn to budget and gives each of them a prepaid cell phone and his business card, explaining that he is there for them. It makes me want to throw my arms around him.

Parting makes us teary-eyed. My sisters and I hug and make wishes for the future.

Back in the car, I wipe my tears, realizing that things will never be the same again. It's a good thing, but it still hurts. The Rossi's Pizza sign blinks the word *Closed*. Noah reassuringly rests his hand on my thigh.

"Thank you," I say. "From my whole heart."

"That's what I'm trying for," he says with a wink.

Chapter 25

Things are happening fast.

Noah wasted no time in closing the shop. He thought that it would be less painful that way.

Most of the girls have relocated. Teresa and Maria are enrolled at NYU and share an apartment near campus. Gina and Mia have started cosmetology school and share an apartment as well. Angela is the only one who decided to stay in the old neighborhood.

As happy as I am, I feel a bit lost. It was comforting to know that the shop existed. Now that it doesn't, my new world is all I have.

Since coming back to New York, I've been restless. For whatever reason, I am now obsessed with the idea of finding my mother. Thoughts of who she is and where she might be consume me. Finding her seems more important than ever. I know that coming to terms with the past will help me move on.

I've tried to explain this to Noah. He claims to

understand but is not as receptive as I'd like him to be.

One night, unable to sleep, I sneak out of bed to watch the rain. It's storming. I sit in the dark on the floor of the great room, in front of the balcony window. Lightning flashes in the black sky.

Oddly, on nights like this, I feel closer to my mother—whoever she might be.

During the day, when the world is busy, I look out over the city and try to imagine where she is and what she might be doing. I know that the possibilities are endless. She could be anywhere, doing just about anything. This makes me feel lost.

However, on nights like this, when it's three o'clock and storming, I bet she's somewhere doing just what I am. She's having a restless night, watching the storm. Knowing that we are doing the same thing somehow makes me feel connected to her.

I'm lost in my thoughts, when I feel Noah's hands on my shoulders. He drops down beside me and pulls me into his arms. "Bad night?" he asks.

I nod.

"Your mother?"

"I just want to know who she is," I tell him. "I just think that I'll be better once I know."

He's silent and holds me tighter.

"Please find her," I whisper, knowing that this is unfair pressure. "Because when you find her, you'll find me."

Again, he is quiet. He offers only a kiss on my head.

After a while, I begin to drift off to sleep cradled in his arms.

"Find me," I murmur softly. "Please find me."

☙

I can't help myself. I squeal ecstatically. This alarms Noah and Mrs. Middleton, and they are instantly at my side in the bedroom, at the window, looking out over the park.

"Gabriella!" Noah exclaims. "What's wrong?"

"It snowed!" I declare, looking gleefully out over the white down below.

Noah sighs, a sound that is a mix of annoyance and relief. Mrs. Middleton smiles gently and then retreats from the bedroom.

"Isn't it beautiful?" I ask.

"Yes," he says unconvincingly.

I have my face pressed against the window. "It's rare to have so much snow in November!" I point out.

"You're leaving nose prints," he tells me.

I giggle. "I love snow!" I say. "Don't you?"

"Eh," he answers, and he starts out of the room.

I follow him into the kitchen, where he begins readying to leave for work. "How can you not love snow? Especially the first snowfall of the season?" I say.

He has put on his top coat and has his briefcase in hand. He's walking toward the door. I'm tripping over his heels. We are now in the foyer, where Mrs. Middleton is dusting.

"Please," I beg.

"Please what?" he asks, confused.

"Please stay home and play in the snow with me," I plead.

"Gabriella," he scolds. "I haven't played in the snow for twenty years!"

"Which is ridiculous!" I say. "Please play with me."

He turns to me and grins. "You are my playmate," he says before kissing me on the nose, "but no."

"Noah," I whine.

"Gabriella," he admonishes.

I give him my best pout. "There's got to be ten inches out there," I say. "Everything is closed. No one will be working!"

"I will be," he answers before entering the elevator.

"Not the best guy ever," I accuse sullenly.

He raises an eyebrow.

Admittedly, this is a bit unfair, but I really want my way. He leans in, kisses my forehead, and then disappears behind the doors.

"I can't believe that didn't work," I tell Mrs. Middleton sadly.

"Give it a minute," she says, continuing to dust.

I look at her, confused, and then grin when the elevator doors slide open to reveal a scowling Noah. I yelp and throw myself into his arms. "Best guy ever!" I squeal.

"You're spoiled, and that line is not always going to work," he warns.

I laugh and run to get dressed.

Twenty minutes later, we're walking through the

park hand in hand. The snow has coated the trees white. Everywhere we walk, we leave deep footprints.

I stop short, pulling on Noah's hand. He turns and faces me.

"We need to make a snowman," I tell him.

"I knew that was coming," he says with a smile.

"Please?"

"It just so happens that I make a great snowman," Noah announces, bending over and scooping up some snow.

I laugh. "Show me," I say.

※

"This is not your first snowman," I tell him forty minutes later as he puts the finishing touches on a smile made of pebbles. "Let's call him Bentley," I suggest.

Noah grins, obviously liking this idea. "Bentley it is," he agrees.

We step back and admire our creation.

"All but a carrot nose and scarf," Noah says.

I giggle, pulling a carrot and one of Noah's scarves out of my pocket.

Noah shakes his head. "I think I need to watch you more closely," he says playfully.

I hand him the carrot. As he places it, I wrap the scarf around Bentley's neck.

"Wait!" Noah protests suddenly when he sees exactly what I have brought. "Gabriella, that's an Armani scarf!"

I intercept his hand and stop him from retrieving it. "It looks better on him than on you," I tease.

"Gee, thanks," he mutters. I laugh.

"Nothing but the best for our baby," I say, kissing Bentley on the cheek. Noah rolls his eyes and pats the snowman on the head.

Arm in arm, we walk away. "Cold?" Noah asks.

"Just a bit," I admit.

"Let's warm up," he suggests.

After a bit of a walk, he leads me into Tavern on the Green, where we lunch on scallops and creamed spinach and watch more snow fall. Noah holds my hand and caresses my fingers.

I grin at him bashfully. "Thanks for taking the day off."

"I don't want to lose my best-guy-ever title," he says, smiling back at me.

"Sorry about that," I tell him sheepishly. "I guess I just want what I want sometimes."

"And what do you want, Gabriella?" he asks quietly.

I ponder the question and then tell him the truth. "Today I want exactly this," I say, looking into his sexy blue eyes.

He nods.

"What about you?" I ask. "What do you want?"

He looks straight into my eyes and simply says, "Same."

We are dining at the restaurant where we saw Grace Blattman for the first time.

"This place gives me the creeps," I tell Noah, wrapping myself in a hug.

"Why? We've only been here once ... Oh," he says, realizing what I mean. He looks at me seriously. "No woman is a threat to you, Gabriella."

"I'm not sure everyone knows that."

"Well, you should," he says. "But relax. I'm sure she's not going to show—" He almost finishes the sentence but stops dead as something draws his attention. I turn and see Grace sauntering across the dining room toward us.

"What are the chances of that?" he gripes.

"Just call me lucky," I mutter back.

We watch as she makes her way to our table.

"Why, we meet again, Noah," she croons, presenting herself. Then, facing me, she says, "And Gabriella, was it?"

"Still is," I say too softly for her to hear.

She turns to Noah. I think she might be a little drunk. She smells of alcohol.

"Unanswered e-mails and phone calls and texts, Noah?" she says confrontationally.

"I'm off the market, Grace," he says coolly.

Her mouth drops. I grin.

Suddenly, a water boy slides between Grace and Noah with a pitcher. I would not bother looking up if not for the overwhelming smell of marijuana that shows up when he does.

It is Philip from painting class.

He sees me. "Gabriella!" he exclaims.

I freeze.

"Just call *me* lucky," Noah mutters.

"And it was Mr. Bentley, right?" Philip says, acknowledging Noah halfheartedly.

"Still is," Noah answers.

"Hey, Gabriella, I got your number from Free Bird, and I texted you, but you never texted back," he slurs. He's high. "I thought we could hang out."

"I'm off the market," I say.

His face drops. Noah grins.

Grace and Philip stand beside each other at the table, waiting for more. Noah offers nothing, and neither do I. Finally, Grace walks away, and Philip follows.

I look at Noah. Noah looks at me. We smile at one another. I think we are both satisfied. Noah begins to rise from the table, even though we just got here.

"Where are we going?" I ask, rising to follow him.

"Anywhere else," Noah tells me. "This place gives me the creeps."

Chapter 26

Every day, when Noah arrives home, I can't help but look at him expectantly for some news about my mother. When he says nothing, neither do I. I try hard to be patient and to put it out of my mind, but the truth is, it preys on me. Since our first conversation about it, weeks have gone by without any word.

However, a month later, it all unexpectedly explodes.

One day Noah calls from work and asks me to find a phone number on his desk in his study. After I give it to him and hang up, I do exactly what I shouldn't: I snoop.

The way he answered me the last time I dared to ask him about the search is what pushes me.

"Some things are best left alone," he said at the time.

"Then you know something," I said accusingly.

"I didn't say that," he told me patiently. "Like I said before, these things take time, and you have to be careful what you wish for."

These weren't natural words for Noah. Something is up.

I decide that while I have my chance, I'll take a harmless look around. Mrs. Middleton has left early, and Noah is not due home for hours. Surely, there will be hell to pay for snooping, but I have to. I feel sure he has discovered something.

I start by carefully sifting through the papers on the desk. There is nothing of significance there.

Three out of the four drawers in the desk are unlocked. The largest one is locked. It is the same drawer that once contained a file folder on me. If there is something, I know that's where it is.

It takes me just short of thirty minutes, but amazingly enough, with nothing more than a hairpin in the lock, the drawer pops open. *So much for security.*

I take a deep breath and try to decide if I really want to do this. I decide that I do.

Carefully, I begin rifling through the files one at a time. At first, everything I find relates to business. But then I get to the file on me. It's much thicker than it was the first time I snooped. Back then, it only had a few pieces of paper and a couple of photos. Now it is quite thick. I open it carefully. On top are the random photos I found last time. Next, there are newspaper clippings from a New Jersey daily newspaper. Although they are difficult for me to see, they are not unfamiliar. They are all about me: the baby left in a basket on the church doorstep.

For a while, I was quite the human-interest story.

The articles span from when I was an infant until I was about ten, though the articles are pretty much the same story rewritten year after year. Thankfully, my mother put a stop to the yearly updates when she realized that they bothered me. They tell and retell the story of me being left by my birth mother and found by Father Cavanaugh. They explain how the Rossis raised me as one of their own and how I am living happily ever after. Each story has an updated photo of me sitting on Father Cavanaugh's lap, surrounded by my sisters and parents.

I glance through the articles quickly, not wanting to spend time on what I already know.

What I find next is confusing. There are police reports detailing my abandonment and discovery. I never knew these existed. I am not sure how they fit into the big picture. There are also copies of checks written from Father Cavanaugh to the local police chief. *Why would Father Cavanaugh have been paying the police?*

The last piece of paper I find is a copy of an e-mail. The recipient is Noah. The sender is a man named Daniel Harvard from a company called Harvard Investigators.

My mouth becomes dry, and I feel faint when I read the simple message: "Found her."

It is dated two days after I asked Noah for help. *Six weeks ago!*

I don't know how long I sit there in shock on the floor of the study, surrounded by the scattered papers.

Finally, I hear Noah come through the apartment door, but I make no effort to hide or clean up the mess. Moments later, he appears in the doorway.

"Gabriella!" he says, instantly furious. "What are you—" I think the look on my face stops him.

I shake my head and glare at him with tears of rage rolling down my face. "How could you?" is all I can manage at first.

He comes closer. "Gabriella—"

"No!" I shout. "How could you?" I throw the e-mail it at him. "You found her!" I scream. "You found her and said nothing! That's unforgiveable!"

He kneels down in an attempt to reason with me, but I am beyond reason. I raise my hands to strike him, but he holds my wrists. I fight him.

"You watched me cry!" I seethe.

He cringes. "I needed to find the right way," he says softly.

"No!" I yell. "You found her and didn't tell me. You were wrong!"

He nods. "Maybe," he concedes, but then he tells me that it's complicated.

"Why? What?" I cry. "What is she? A drug addict? A prostitute?"

He shakes his head. "Nothing like that."

"Then what?" I sob. "Then what?"

He looks me square in the eyes. His face is sad and sympathetic. I drop my hands. He relaxes his hold.

"Tell me," I whisper. "Please."

He nods, hesitating. I can tell that he wants to make

sure I am ready. The way that I never take my eyes off of him proves that I am.

"It's Angela," he finally says. "Your mother is Angela."

My head swims. I hear him but am confused. "My sister?" I ask.

"Yes," he confirms quietly. "Your sister Angela is your mother."

I feel faint but collect myself. Then he says something that makes me gasp: "And Father Cavanaugh is your father."

I reach for him. He reaches back. "Please tell me everything," I say.

For the next hour, Noah tells me everything he knows.

When Angela was fourteen, she helped out at the rectory two days a week after school. Father Cavanaugh took advantage of her. She hid her pregnancy for the entire nine months. She delivered alone in the bathroom in the middle of the night. Scared and helpless, she did the only thing she thought she could: she left me on the church doorstep, where she knew I would be safe. Father Cavanaugh found me. He put it all together but took me to the Rossis anyway, knowing they would take me in. The police found out the truth, but Father Cavanaugh bought them off. All of them corrupt, they let themselves look like heroes.

"So everyone knew?" I ask Noah.

"Not the Rossis," he says. "Angela never told anyone. They simply wanted you."

I lean my head against his chest. He strokes my hair. "Poor Angela," I gasp.

He nods. I pop up and face him. "Does she know that you know?"

"She does. I've met with her a few times. We were trying to decide what was best for you," he says.

I shake my head as more tears spill from my eyes. "Forget about me." I sigh. "My heart breaks for her."

"Mine too, baby," he says, holding me tightly. "Mine too."

᠖

I spend the next two days replaying my childhood in my mind, searching for clues. Now, looking back, it seems as if there were many. Angela's behavior always seemed much more maternal than that of a sister, but I always attributed it to our fourteen-year age difference. I now know that her feelings came from a deeper place. I think back and remember how she always seemed to consider my needs first and how she was always the one to take me to the park and shopping for school clothes. I think of the countless Halloween costumes she sewed by hand.

I can only imagine what keeping our secret must have been like for Angela. I think of the pain she must have felt every Sunday when Father Cavanaugh came for dinner. What must it have been like for her to have our mother fussing over him? How could she have felt when we lined up for pictures or took turns sitting on his lap? As I leaf through the pictures from our times together, it is easy to see now that Angela was the only one not smiling.

My feelings for Father Cavanaugh are nothing short of hatred. He did the unspeakable to Angela and then made fools of the rest of us. I now regret every smile I ever smiled at him, every kiss on the cheek, and every innocent hug.

"I'm so glad he's dead," I tell Noah. "I don't think I could control myself if I were to face him again."

"It helps with the closure," Noah says.

"And then there's Angela." I sigh.

Noah nods. "Probably the best mother I know," he says. "It's obvious that she wanted the best for you, and she did everything she could to see to it that you had that. Gabriella," he tells me firmly, "all I know is that you never spent a day in your life not being loved."

I know that he is right.

ௌ

Two days later, on Tuesday afternoon, Liam drives me to the Plaza for lunch. Noah has driven to New Jersey to pick up Angela. I love him for this.

I sit at the table alone, nervously watching the door. After just a few minutes, Noah and Angela appear. She is dressed in a floral dress and low pumps. I changed my clothes three times for her.

Noah escorts her to the table, kisses both of us on our cheeks, and slips away.

Then I have the lunch that I've been dreaming about for twenty-one years. I have lunch with my mother.

"Hi," I say.

"Hi," she says, smiling sadly. Her face looks worn. We're not used to this awkwardness.

"I'm sorry," she says.

"I'm not," I tell her. "I'm glad you're my mother."

Instantly, the stress in her face dissolves, and tears spill from her eyes. "Really?" she asks softly. "I didn't know what to do."

"What were you supposed to do?" I say. "You were so young. But what you did couldn't have worked out more perfectly. We never spent a day apart," I point out. "All this time, I thought you were far away, but you were right there with me. Every minute of every day, you never left me, and I was never lost."

"Oh, Gabby!" she sobs. "I was so afraid that you might hate me."

"Never," I insist. "Not for one second. You know I always loved you best." My own tears are falling now.

"That's all I ever wanted," she tells me. "That's all I ever wanted."

꽃

As the days pass, I slowly come to terms with this new reality. As much as I expected that the news of Angela being my mother would change everything, it actually changes little. My mother, the woman who raised me as her daughter, will always be my mother, and Angela remains my sister.

I was wanted, and I was loved. As lost as I sometimes

felt, I was never really lost at all. I was exactly where I belonged.

For the first time in my life, as I look forward, I'm not looking back.

☙

"Bedroom," the texts reads.

Dinner is going to be late, I think.

I hear the elevator door open and the sound of Noah dropping his keys onto the entry table. My heart flutters, and my sex tingles. Already I'm getting wet. It's like a Pavlovian experiment. I wonder how on earth he does this to me.

When he enters the bedroom, I'm standing in the middle of the room. I can tell by the look on his face that this will not be a typical night.

He approaches me and cups my face in his hands. He kisses me, his tongue invading my mouth. He holds me tightly, exploring. Then he releases me slightly, pulling back and studying my face. Noah pulls me in again and gives me a not-so-gentle bite. I gasp. He smiles faintly and caresses my cheek. He lifts my sundress up and over my head. I stand before him barefoot, wearing only my bra and panties. Bashful, I look down at my hands.

"Eyes," he orders softly.

I look up at him.

"Are you wet, baby?" he asks in a low voice.

I nod.

"Words," he tells me. He steps closer, pushing his chest against mine.

"Yes," I manage.

"Yes what?"

"Yes, I'm wet," I say.

"Who are you wet for?"

"I'm wet for you, Noah."

"That's my girl," he says with a grin.

He unclips my bra. My ample breasts spring free. He tosses the bra to the side. He slides my panties down, and I step out of them. He eyes me up and down approvingly.

He leans in, takes one breast into his mouth, and sucks. He's being quite harsh. When I go to pull back, he nips my nipple not so lightly. I yelp. He makes a satisfied sound and does roughly the same to the other breast. This time, I don't pull back. I whimper as he gives the tip a quick bite. The pain is brief, but I know the pleasure that ensues is what he's aiming for.

He reaches down and begins to finger me. He slides in one, then two, and then three fingers. I close my eyes as he explores. He's rougher than usual, and I wonder what I am in for.

"Do you trust me?" he asks, now sucking my neck.

I nod and then answer, "Yes."

"Would I ever hurt you?"

"No." I sigh, losing myself in his touch.

He takes my hand and leads me to the bed. "Do as you are told," he tells me firmly.

I almost nod but instead whisper, "Yes, Noah."

"On the bed," he tells me.

I obey and climb onto the bed.

"All fours," he instructs. I almost protest and become wary, but our eyes meet. Wordlessly, he tells me that no is not an option.

Trust, I remind myself.

I gulp when I hear him open the night table drawer. I know that he is reaching for the cuffs. Silently, he cuffs one hand and then the other to the bedpost. My face is resting on the bed. My bottom is high in the air. I think this will be it, until he leaves for a moment and returns with two red neckties.

We've never done this before. I begin to tremble.

"Easy, baby," he says soothingly.

He comes from behind and swiftly loops the ties around my knees and then ties them to my elbows. I am completely helpless. He stands behind me and surveys his work. Suddenly, he gives me a hard slap on my bottom. I gasp. I feel a touch of pain and then pleasure.

I can hear him undressing behind me. He positions himself and begins massaging my cheeks, spreading them as he goes. He stops massaging them and pulls them apart, exposing me. I try to move but am bound too tightly.

Suddenly, I feel a gentle, moist flicker on my bottom. I jump and wriggle. He laughs softly. "Every part of you is mine," he murmurs.

I can feel his breath on me. Again, I pull futilely on the restraints as his breath gives me chills. "Every part of you," he whispers in my ear.

Then, without hesitation, he rams his manhood deep into me. The sensation is wonderful.

"Yes, baby," he grunts. "Feel me."

He is rock hard. Mercilessly, he penetrates me again and again. At first, I cry out at the invasion. I know that this turns him on greatly. But my body quickly begins to accept him, and he glides in and out easily. I like the feeling. Closing my eyes, I enjoy feeling myself tight around him. He goes deep, pulls out almost entirely, and then penetrates again. He makes it last a long while. I'm moaning loudly. We come at almost the same time. I quiver and begin to collapse, but he holds my hips up firmly as he deposits his warm liquid into me. He groans gruffly and pulls out gently. After he catches his breath, I feel him massaging my cheeks again. Then he places a kiss on my bottom.

"Every part of you," he murmurs.

Chapter 27

"You're unfair," I tell him, frustrated, on the car ride home from dinner.

"Gabriella, stop!"

"I won't stop. I know I'm right," I say.

It's a regular night out, but we've had a horrible evening because Noah is distracted and has things on his mind.

"Why won't you open up to me? Why won't you ever trust me with how you feel?" I ask.

"It's business. It doesn't concern you," he says.

"I know, but you should still trust in me," I tell him.

"Let it go." He sighs.

Of course, I won't.

"You're unfair," I say. "You insist on knowing every single thing about me. Good Lord, Noah!" I exclaim. "You know when my period is due before I do! But you won't even let me know three things about you."

Once at home, we continue the fight silently. After a stop in his study to check e-mails and close down his computer for the night, Noah appears in the bedroom. I'm giving him the cold shoulder. We undress in silence. I'm still angry, and I can feel his eyes on me, but I purposely don't budge. I make no eye contact. I sit on the bed. He joins me.

"What three things do you want to know?" he asks.

Now I look at him. He's got my attention.

"You're serious?" I ask.

He sighs and nods.

Moments like this are so rare that I want to make this count. I doubt I'll get this opportunity again. I settle in facing him. I remain thoughtful for a moment.

"When's the last time you cried?" I ask him.

His face drops. I've surprised him. He's pensive for only a moment before he shrugs and says, "February 3, 1984."

I look at him, confused, and think for a moment that he might be kidding, but I can tell by the look on his face that he is not.

"I was ten," he says.

I take this in. There's something wrong about someone not crying for twenty years. A million questions fill my head. I open my mouth to ask more, but he stops me.

"Could we just leave that question alone?" he asks softly. I'm touched by the tone in his voice.

"Of course," I tell him. I realize that I've gone somewhere too sensitive, so I back off.

We're both quiet for a few moments, regrouping. We lie back. My head is on his chest. I peek up at him.

"Two more?" I ask.

He nods, but his face is serious again. He's not comfortable with this, but he's ready for the next question.

"Who are Mrs. Middleton and Liam to you?" I ask. I've been suspicious for a long time.

He shrugs too quickly. "Hired help."

"Noah, you have to be honest for this to be fair," I tell him. I know he's holding back.

He sighs and grins at me. I've caught him. He clears his throat. The anticipation is killing me.

"Okay," he says, smiling. "Mrs. Middleton was my first-grade teacher, and Liam was the kid who sat next to me in her class."

For a second, I am speechless. Then I squeal. "The picture!" I yell, referring to a photograph I picked up off of his desk one day. He only let me look at it briefly. I now realize he was afraid I would recognize them. He snatched it out of my hands.

"Oh my God, Noah!" I wail. "That's beautiful!"

He rolls his eyes.

"Oh my God! Tell me about it," I plead.

"There's not much to tell," he insists.

"But what were they like?" I ask.

"She was the teacher, and he was the kid who sat next to me."

"No, what were they *like*?"

"They were great," he says, his voice softening. "She was wonderful, just like she is now. Kind and caring and sweet. She taught me to read." He laughs.

I laugh at this thought too. "And him?" I ask.

"Liam was my buddy," he says, as if this should explain it all. "He was six like me, except he was always bigger and stronger than I was, and he was very, very funny." Noah grins. "We used to get in trouble, and Mrs. Middleton would make us sit on the naughty bench together until we promised to behave," he says, laughing.

"And then what happened?" I ask, laughing too.

"Nothing," he answers, chuckling. "We would promise to be good. She would let us up. We would do it again. Then back on the bench!"

"That's so great!" I laugh. "And how did all of this happen?" I ask, waving my arms around.

"Well, over the years, Liam and I stayed close, and Mrs. Middleton became like a second mother to me. Liam has worked for me from the start, and when Mrs. Middleton retired from teaching, she came on board."

I can't restrain myself any longer; I pop up and kiss him on the cheek. He laughs. I love the whole idea. Then I'm quiet and begin to think.

"And before you start worrying about them," he tells me, "just between me and you, I pay each of them more than I pay all five of my brothers combined."

I gasp. He's read my mind.

"They are far from employees," he assures me. "They don't need to work."

"That's awesome," I gush. "You're the best guy ever!"

He throws his head back and laughs. I fall back into the pillow, giggling.

"You do keep your circle small," I say.

He nods, agreeing. "I guess I do."

"Not many outsiders," I note. "Except me."

He leans over and kisses me.

"Third question," I announce.

"All done," he says while trying to distract me with nuzzles. I wiggle away.

"A deal's a deal," I say.

He groans and falls back into the pillow. "One more." He sighs.

I roll over onto my tummy and balance on my elbows. I look at him seriously and dare to ask the question that I've asked before but that he's never answered.

"Why me?" I ask softly.

He looks at me seriously and pushes my hair away from my eyes. "It's very simple, Gabriella," he says quietly. "You're the first woman who ever took my breath away. You took my breath away the first moment I saw you, and you've taken my breath away every day since then. You're my one and only. You have to be mine."

I look back at him and nod. It isn't the answer I was expecting, but it is the perfect one.

"That simple?" I ask him.

"That simple."

I nod. "Show me," I say, never having wanted him more. "Show me how I'm your one and only."

"Say please," he growls, crawling on top of me.

"Please," I murmur, gladly losing myself in his touch. "Pretty please."

After he makes slow and gentle love to me, we lie there in the dark and begin to drift off to sleep.

"The twenty-fifth," he says lazily.

"What about it?" I ask, confused.

"Your period is due on the twenty-fifth," he tells me confidently.

I shake my head and groan. He laughs. I give him a gentle punch.

※

We are at Noah's parents' house for his youngest niece's birthday. She has just turned a year old.

Between his parents, five brothers, sisters-in-law, and many nieces and nephews, we are kept busy with all the celebrating and find ourselves there often. It seems that we are always celebrating one of them. I think it's nice. Noah is indifferent. He does not have the highest tolerance for family functions, but we always attend. I like this about him. I like that he is fair. Still, he won't let me buy gifts. He prefers to give the same card with an equal amount of money for each of the kids on every occasion.

We stand in the kitchen, recording with our phones, laughing, and singing as his niece dives headfirst into the minicake set on the high chair tray before her. Everyone roars as she rubs icing in her hair.

Noah grimaces and then, as if he's unable to watch, walks out of the room and retreats to the quiet of the family room. I follow him.

"Unacceptable?" I joke, sitting down next to him on the couch.

"Please tell me that you agree." He sighs.

"A little," I say.

He puts his arm around me. I snuggle up.

"Cake, and then we run," he tells me.

I nod. He leans in for a kiss. I pull back when I see his twelve-year-old niece, Katie, appear in the doorway, holding two pieces of cake.

"Hi, Katie!" I say. Noah pulls back.

"My mom says to give these to you," she says uncomfortably as she hands them over.

"Thanks," I tell her.

She looks as if she might say something but instead turns to scurry out of the room. Her mother, Joyce, stops her at the door.

"Did you ask them?" she says.

"No," the girl murmurs.

"Well, do it!"

"Mom!"

"Katie! Katie has something she wants to ask you two," Joyce blurts out, grabbing poor Katie's shoulders and shoving her toward us.

"Mom!" Katie yelps, mortified.

"Katie is doing a science fair project for school, and she needs you two to participate," she explains.

"God, Mom!" Katie cries.

Joyce leaves the poor terrified girl alone and heads out of the room.

"Katie, it's all good," I tell her. "Uncle Noah and I would be happy to be a part of your study."

Noah makes a noise. I touch his leg.

"Really?" Katie squeaks, instantly perking up.

"Of course," I say.

"Let me get my stuff!" she says, and she darts off.

"Gabriella," Noah groans.

"Oh, Noah, she's your niece. It's for school. How harmful can it be?" I say.

He's about to tell me, when Katie returns with a journal, pen, and calculator. She's bouncy and excited. I smile at seeing her this way.

"Okay, okay," she says nervously, jumping about a bit. "You two sit there." She points to where we are sitting. "And I'll sit here, I guess," she says, taking a seat on the coffee table in front of us. "Ready?" she asks after clearing her throat. It's obvious that she's trying to put on a professional demeanor. "Okay. My name is Katherine Bentley. Thank you for being a part of my study. The name of my project is 'Hot Love: Are You a Match or a Miss?'"

I gasp and cover my mouth. Noah makes another noise, shifts in the seat, and shakes his head. Instantly, all I can think is that he's going to kill me.

"Wait, Katie," I say, trying not to sound as panicked as I am. "What's the name of your project again, honey?"

"It's called 'Hot Love: Are You a Match or a Miss?'" she chirps proudly.

My mind races. *Well, I can at least rule out having misheard her.*

Noah leans back in his seat and looks at me skeptically, as if he is genuinely interested in how I am going to get us out of this.

"Now, this is for school?" I clarify.

"Yep!"

"For a science fair?"

"Yep!"

"Okay, what do we do?" I ask.

"Just answer questions," she says. "My mom and dad did it, and so did Grandma and Grandpa."

"Okay, we'll do it," I say. Secretly, I want to know how Noah and I will score.

"Gabriella!" Noah shifts in the seat.

I touch his thigh and settle back into the couch next to him.

"Thanks," Katie says. "I was hoping you would, because I'm thinking you two might be better at love than the rest of them are."

I smile. Noah makes another sound.

"Go ahead, Katie," I tell her.

"Okay," she says, crossing her legs and tucking her hair behind her ears. She clears her throat in an effort to get back into her professional persona. "Some of the questions are for both of you, and some will be just for you, Gabriella, or you, Uncle Noah."

I nod.

"You answer the questions, and then I give you points for your answers," she tells us. "Okay, first question: How many times a week do you have sex?"

"Gabriella!" Noah thunders.

I jump. "Katie, honey!" I all but shriek. "That's a very personal question!"

"I know," she says, crinkling up her nose. "Actually, it wasn't allowed to be an actual question. I was just curious. Grandma and Grandpa wouldn't answer either, but Mom and Dad do it about three times a week when they're not fighting."

"Katie, that's way too personal." I'm starting to lose my good nature, and I'm afraid to look at Noah. "Just start over, sweetie," I tell her.

"Okay," she says. "For both of you: Do you believe in love at first sight?"

I'm relieved. This is an easier question.

"Yes," I answer surely. Noah, who is apparently still on question number one, is too angry to speak. He does not answer. I look at him. He glares at me. He tosses his hand in the air in an "I don't care" gesture. I turn back to Katie.

"That's a yes," I tell her.

"Great!" she says, marking in her notebook. "Question number two: When is the last time you fought?"

"What time is it?" Noah growls.

"Noah." I sigh.

"It's eight fifteen," Katie answers innocently, checking the clock on her phone.

I ignore them both. "Let me think," I say. "Last Tuesday, we had a tiny disagreement."

Actually, like all of our fights, it was pretty huge, but I want the points, so I leave this detail out. Katie counts on her fingers and then tabulates and marks in her book.

"Question number three: When was the last time you kissed?"

Instantly, I jump up and kiss Noah on the cheek. He is unmoved. Katie and I laugh and high-five.

"Uncle Noah was just about to give me a kiss when you walked in with the cake," I tell her.

"Really? Then I'll give you credit," she says with authority. "Question number four: Do you make each other laugh?"

"Oh, all of the time!" I answer honestly. Noah nods. Katie marks this down.

"Get ready," Noah mumbles.

I'm about to ask what for, when Katie says, "Question number five: Do you ever make each other cry?"

Noah saw this question coming. I did not. He shifts in his seat. We glance at each other. I don't know what to say; all I know is that I don't like the question.

He clears his throat. "Sometimes we make each other a little sad, and yes, we cry."

"Okay." She shrugs and puts our answer in the book. "Question number six: Have you ever said, 'I love you'?"

"Yes," I tell her as I reach for Noah's hand to thank him for answering the last question.

"Question seven: Do you ever say, 'I hate you'?"

"No, we don't do that," I tell her. She nods.

"Question eight: Who's the boss?"

"I am," Noah growls, making us both jump, his tone shocking both Katie and me. Katie looks at me for confirmation.

"Uncle Noah's the boss," I say. She marks this down.

"Girls listen to boys," Noah adds just to make sure we are all clear.

"This one's just for you, Gabriella," Katie tells me. "Does he make you feel pretty?"

"He makes me feel very pretty," I say confidently.

"Really?"

"Really."

"Cool." She giggles and marks the book. "This one is for each of you to answer separately," she explains, handing us each a scrap of paper and a pencil. "Write down your favorite memory together."

I think for a few moments and then mark the paper. Noah writes his answer instantly. We hand the slips to Katie. She reads them.

"Awesome." She giggles. "You both wrote, 'Seeing the stars.'"

Noah grins. I knew it was my favorite, but his? I look at him questioningly.

"Because it was yours," he says quietly. I love him for this.

"Last two questions!" Katie announces.

Noah nods that he's ready. I lean back and settle in under his arm.

"Gabriella, if Uncle Noah turned into a frog and the only way to turn him back was to kiss him, would you?"

"In a minute!" I answer quickly.

"Great." She smiles.

"Big points," Noah whispers in my ear.

"Uncle Noah, would you jump off of a cliff to save Gabriella?"

I look at Noah. He kind of grins. "Yes," he says. "I would jump off of a cliff to save Gabriella."

"I knew you guys were awesome." Katie sighs, marking the last entry. "I'll add them up, but I'm pretty sure you won!" She runs out of the room excitedly.

I turn and give Noah a kiss. "Thank you," I say.

"You're welcome," he answers, and he kisses me back.

"At least we won."

"I only play to win."

༄

We're riding home in the car. I'm thinking about Katie and her project.

"Noah?"

"Mmm?"

"Do you think it's okay that we make each other cry?" I ask him.

He reaches over and strokes my cheek. "I think it's just fine."

At first, I am confused by his answer and think he is putting me off, but after a moment, he explains.

"It's unavoidable," he tells me. "Where there is great love, there is great pain. We're deeply connected, Gabriella. When you allow someone to own your heart, sometimes they are the perfect caretaker, and sometimes they are less."

I take this all in. He's right; we do own each other's

hearts. I am quiet for a minute, but before the moment passes, I speak.

"Thank you for letting me own your heart, Noah. I'll try to take good care of it," I promise.

He takes my hand and kisses it. "And thank you for allowing me the honor of owning your heart," he says. "I shall cherish it always."

We drive in silence for a while.

"I'd kiss more than one frog for you," I say.

"And I'm getting pretty good at cliff jumping." He grins.

I think about this and realize that he is right. He is.

Chapter 28

We've been bickering all evening, mostly over little things. It all started when I told him there is a painting class at the university next semester that I want to take. He said he'd think about it. This set me off, and I smartly asked, "What's there to think about?"

He then told me that he's given the matter great thought and that the answer is no.

When will I ever learn?

Ever since then, I've taken it upon myself to be totally disagreeable. He remarks that apparently, I would rather spend quality time alone with my poor attitude and smart mouth in the apartment than paint.

Amazingly, we get through dinner. We are waiting for the valet to retrieve the car.

"Thanks for a lovely evening," I say sarcastically.

"There's only more when we get home," he says.

"Stop threatening me," I mutter.

"I never threaten, darling. Only promise," he says in a kind of a scary-serious way.

My heart flops, and I'm feeling a little regretful and worried that he might make good on this statement, when a man approaches.

"Noah Bentley! How the hell are you?" he asks, patting Noah on the back.

Noah greets him. His name is Alex.

"You know my wife, Carol," Alex says, reacquainting them. Noah kisses Carol on the cheek.

Their eyes fall to me. Noah realizes that he has not introduced me.

"Gabriella Rossi," he says simply.

They both greet me formally.

"Noah, do you have time for a drink?" Alex asks.

Noah toys with the idea and then agrees. We go back inside the restaurant to the lounge. We spend a total of about forty minutes with them. For the first twenty minutes, Alex and Noah talk business while Carol and I chat about nothing. For the next twenty, the four of us attempt neutral conversation.

"So out for a night on the town?" Alex asks.

I don't know what to say. Noah's mind is obviously somewhere else, and he says nothing. The question passes. More pleasantries are exchanged.

"How long have you two known each other?" Carol asks.

"Awhile," Noah answers, distracted, and then he continues to talk business with Alex.

Finally, Alex and Carol apologize for interrupting our date and say they will let us go to "get to know one another."

Noah doesn't correct them but accepts the apology, and we part. Back on the sidewalk, I'm furious. I'm fuming. I'm too angry for words, and Noah has no idea why.

"Stop," he says halfheartedly on way the home.

"I'm not doing anything," I tell him flatly. I've decided not to give him the satisfaction of letting him know that I care and choose instead to pretend that I don't and shut him out.

My lack of passion has him put off.

At the apartment, I get my own door and walk in front of him.

"Gabriella," he says as we enter the elevator, "what is it?"

"Nothing."

"Something," he says.

"Nothing at all," I say emphatically.

We enter the bedroom and undress, readying for bed. I climb in. Noah is only in his boxers when he climbs on top of the covers. He is genuinely confused.

"Get over whatever it is," he tells me.

"Already am," I say blandly.

He sighs. "Tell me," he says, exasperated. This type of exchange is rare for us. We fight passionately. Passive aggression is not our thing. "I'm ready to listen," he says.

I say nothing.

He attempts to move my hair from my eyes. I move away. He hates this. He studies me, apparently deciding to be patient. "Obviously, we are having a fight," he says, "but you're going to have to clue me in as to why."

I glare at him.

"Please," he says.

I give in and explode. "Tell me you don't know what you did! Tell me it wasn't intentional! All because I was fighting with you?" I say, seething. "That was mean, Noah!"

He flinches. He's honestly lost and shakes his head. He opens his mouth but has no words.

I can't restrain myself any longer. "You demoted me!" I scream.

His face drops. "I what?" he asks, perplexed.

"Miss Gabriella Rossi," I mimic. "Could you be any more formal? They thought I was your date. Not your girlfriend but your date! And you didn't correct them!"

His eyes grow wide, and then he closes them. Noah almost smiles but catches himself. "Wait! Not funny!" he quickly says. "Gabriella, I would never demote you." He says *demote* as if it's a dirty word. "You know you're mine."

"They didn't!" I rage

"Okay," he says, grimacing and apparently putting it all together. "My fault. Bad introduction. My responsibility."

I could burn holes through him with my eyes.

"Honey," he says softly, "I …" He starts to speak but seems to be at a loss again.

"Not a leg to stand on," I say.

He cringes. "Not this time," he admits, putting his hands up as if in defeat.

As with all of our fights, this one ends in sex. He holds me after and kisses the top of my head. "You know no one can demote the queen."

"Not even the king?" I ask.

"Not even the king."

"No matter how smart her mouth?"

"No matter how smart her mouth."

"No matter how poor her attitude?"

"No matter how poor her attitude," he says.

"Good to know," I say, cuddling up to him.

"Demote," he says, and he chuckles at the word. I punch him.

꽃

Noah clicks off the TV midshow. I look at him questioningly, although I'm sure I know what's coming. He looks back at me with eyes that are dark and sexy. He takes my hand and pulls me off of the couch, guiding me onto the floor in front of him.

"On your knees," he tells me. I obey.

He leans down, holding my head, and kisses me thoroughly. His tongue explores. I shiver a bit. Gently, he pulls my top off over my head. Just as delicately, he slides my panties off. I'm kneeling completely naked in front of him. He removes his cock from his sweats. He cups my breast in his hand and gently rubs the tip of his penis against the nipple. Almost instantly, it becomes erect. He then does the same thing to the other breast until it is just as pointed. He leans down and licks each until they become tender. He then takes my head and guides it between his legs.

"Suck me, baby," he says.

I nod, closing my eyes, and begin. Holding my head, he plays with my hair.

I bury my head deep between his legs and begin licking him methodically from his balls to his tip. Over and over, I do this until I've covered every inch of him. He groans. He is rock hard by now. His head is back, and his eyes are closed.

"Suck, baby," he whispers again. I continue to lick instead. He makes a noise and shifts on the couch. I'm driving him crazy. He's trying not to come. He wants to release in my mouth. I continue to lick.

"You're teasing," he croons. I nod and continue to lick him.

Apparently unable to take it anymore, he lets out a groan and, in one swift motion, flips me over onto all fours. Instantly, he is in me from behind. He rams me hard. I yelp. He's holding me by the hair to keep me in place. He plunges again and again. He's never been deeper. It has never been harder or better.

Finally, he groans loudly as he convulses and comes. I start to relax, but suddenly, he swats my bottom good and hard. I yelp. He turns me around and kisses me roughly, nipping at my lips. I gasp.

"That's what happens to little girls that tease," he tells me. I look back at him, soft and sexy.

"I'll have to remember to tease more often," I say.

For a second, he looks surprised, but then a small, satisfied smile crosses his face.

৩

We are headed for a formal evening out, a black-tie affair. Noah is dressed in a tuxedo, and I am in a red sequined gown.

Mrs. Middleton is seeing us to the door.

Noah growls unhappily. Mrs. Middleton and I turn to see what has precipitated this reaction. He holds his hand out right beneath my mouth. I am in trouble. I spit the gum I have been chewing into his hand. He immediately deposits it into Mrs. Middleton's hand.

He motions for me to walk in front of him. I know it is coming, but I still yelp, taken by surprise when he swats my bottom with his open hand.

"I will find out where you are getting it from," he says. "Then you'll both be in trouble."

Mrs. Middleton and I exchange nervous smiles. She is my supplier, with an endless stash tucked away in her purse for her grandkids and me.

৩

I never thought I'd see the day when Noah Bentley would obey anyone. In fact, I often wondered if there was anyone Noah listened to.

We are at Noah's parents' house. It's late in the evening. We've been celebrating yet another birthday. Noah, his parents, and I are in the kitchen. Everyone else is in the family room, watching the tail end of a football game. Noah's mother and I are making our way through a mountain of dinner dishes. She's washing, and I'm drying.

Noah and his father are sitting at the kitchen table, talking business.

"How are they doing?" Noah's father asks, nodding toward Noah's brothers in the other room.

"Mediocre," Noah responds with a shrug.

"Why no better?"

"Because they're morons," answers Noah flatly.

"Oh, Noah!" his mother scolds.

Noah's not one to mince words in the first place, but when he's tired, as he is now, he's even less tactful.

"Are they still on productivity?" his father asks.

Noah nods. "There's plenty of money to be made."

"Then why do they produce so little?"

"Because they're morons," Noah says flatly.

"Noah!" His mother's admonishment is sterner this time. "That's twice. Not again!"

"So why do they do nothing?" his father says, sounding exasperated.

"Because they're—"

"Noah!" His mother stops him short. "Mind me," she says sharply.

Noah stops. He lets out a small breath and looks down at his hands. His father grins. The kitchen is quiet. Then Noah Bentley says something I never dreamed he would. For all the world to hear, he says, "Yes, ma'am."

I stifle a giggle and dry another dish.

Chapter 29

"Maybe next time you'll listen to me," Noah says matter-of-factly.

We are at home in the bathroom. I am on my knees in front of the toilet, vomiting my brains out. He is behind me, holding my hair. I nod as best as I can and then throw up some more.

We were out to dinner with another couple. The man is a colleague of Noah's and seems relatively normal, but the lady is a little off her rocker. I am not sure if that's really how she is or if it was just the fifteen glasses of wine she had kicking in.

Just when the evening was supposed to end, she had the idea of ordering another drink for herself and for me. Noah squeezed my thigh as a warning, but the drinks were at the table in seconds. Each was a bluish-green color and had an umbrella hanging out of it. They looked harmless enough. I picked up my drink and took a swallow.

Noah leaned in to me and whispered, "You'll be

sorry." Then he added, "But if you insist, take sips, and only drink half of it."

I took none of his advice and gulped my way to the bottom of the glass.

I barely made it in time to the apartment and then to the bathroom. I am paying dearly for not listening to him, and he is not unhappy about this.

"Every rule I have," he says coolly, "is for your own good."

I manage a nod as I continue to heave while wishing for death.

※

"You are being a brat," Noah says.

"And you are being a bully!" I tell him.

We are in the bedroom, and I am modeling bathing suits for Noah's approval. I am standing on top of the bed, using it as my runway.

He has agreed to let me swim in the pool occasionally, but only when he or Liam can be there watching me.

Mrs. Middleton and I went shopping that morning and chose several suits. Unbeknownst to me at the time, Mrs. Middleton added a few of her own choices to the bag when I wasn't looking.

Now Noah and I are fighting.

I chose all bikinis. Mrs. Middleton threw in two tankinis with little skirts, one pink and one blue.

Noah instantly rejected all of my choices, but he approves of the two modest suits from Mrs. Middleton.

I am kind of mad at her for selling me out like this, but I bet she had her orders and probably knows Noah better than me.

"The pink or the blue?" Noah asks with a grin.

"Neither," I whine, jumping up and down on the bed like a spoiled two-year-old.

"More fighting then," he announces.

"You know we don't fight well," I say, exasperated.

"Why not?" Noah asks calmly with a smile.

"Because you don't fight fair!" I shout.

"How's that?" he asks, amused.

"Every time I disagree with you, you ..." I can't finish because I am so frustrated.

"I what, Gabriella? Tell me," he says. "I what?"

"You spank me!"

"Like I'm about to do now?" he says with a raised eyebrow.

I frown, defeated.

He throws his head back and laughs. "Pink or blue?"

"Both," I say angrily.

"That'll show me." He smirks.

I am trying hard to stay angry, but his smile is disarming, as always.

Suddenly, he rises from the chair and lunges for me. I hop back and try to make a break for it by jumping from the bed, but he is too quick, and I end up leaping right into his arms. He tosses me back onto the bed and begins tickling me. I laugh and squirm and wriggle beneath him.

"Tell me you didn't just call me a bully," he orders.

He tickles me until the suit is on the floor.

※

It is a Thursday night in mid-November. We have spent a relaxing evening together. Mrs. Middleton made a dinner of comfort foods: pot roast and mashed potatoes. The meal was perfect for the weather outside, which is steadily getting colder as the season heads into winter. We stay for nearly an hour in the great room. Both of us are on the couch but at opposite ends. Noah concentrates on the work he brought home from the office, while I read.

Occasionally, we look up, catch a glimpse of one another, and exchange smiles. I like to look at him when he's unaware and consumed by his work. How sexy he is still amazes me.

Tired of reading and almost ready for bed, I get up off of the couch and move to the carpet in front of the fireplace. Dressed only in an aqua teddy and panties, I have caught a slight chill, and I want to warm up.

It doesn't take long for Noah to put his paperwork down and join me. He has on black sweats and a white T-shirt, and he is barefoot. He sits down beside me and rubs my back. I am sitting with my arms around my knees, which are pulled up to my chest.

"Cold?" he asks.

I nod. "A little."

"I can take care of that kind of thing, you know," he says with a teasing grin.

"I know you can," I say playfully, "and have many times."

This makes him laugh out loud. Suddenly, his expression is serious. He looks at me as if he is trying to read my mind. Noah's moods change quickly, and sometimes it is difficult for me to keep up. Although I can read many of his moods, there is still much for me to discover, because he has many layers.

"Happy?" He asks it in such a genuine way that I can tell he really cares.

I think and then answer him honestly. "I am," I say softly.

He nods and gets up on his knees to be eye level with me. He takes my hands, puts them down at my sides, and then reaches out and holds my face in his hands, drawing me closer. I untuck my legs and turn to face him, kneeling too so that we are facing each other. He kisses me. The kiss is deep, long, and complete. When he kisses me this way, my entire body tingles.

Satisfied for the moment, he pulls back. Again, he pauses and looks at me as if I am a puzzle. I can't read his expression. I don't know that I have ever seen this one before.

"I'd give a penny for your thoughts," I say quietly, "but my boyfriend has all of the money."

"Ah," he teases, "he's one of those."

"Most definitely," I agree with a grin.

We're quiet for a moment.

"What *are* you thinking?" I ask softly, taking his hands. I kiss his fingers one at a time.

He closes his eyes, obviously enjoying my touch. Then his expression becomes serious again. He looks into my eyes. "Why me?" he asks. "I explained why you. Why me?"

He's vulnerable. He's never vulnerable.

"Simple," I say, just as he did. "That first day, you may have looked at me first, but I looked back. You're not the only one whose breath was taken away."

※

"What you be grated for, Uncle Noah?" shouts Stewart, Noah's four-year-old nephew, from the other end of the table.

It is Thanksgiving, and the children have been asked to name one thing they are grateful for.

"What am I *grateful* for?" asks Noah. "Let me think, Stewart."

Noah has asked for a little more time only because he trying not to be too disagreeable. He probably knows that if he says the first thing that comes to mind, Thanksgiving will be over.

"Holiday manners," I whisper.

"My ass," he whispers back.

"You be grated for three-headed red-eyed dinosaurs?" Stewart asks Noah before dissolving into a fit of laughter.

The children have each taken a turn answering, and so far, three-headed red-eyed dinosaurs have been the consensus. Honestly, the whole thing is getting kind of old. We started this game before we carved the turkey, and here we are, almost finished eating, still talking about three-headed red-eyed dinosaurs. Noah, of course, was annoyed from the get-go. I don't think it would have killed anybody to encourage the children to be grateful for something nice.

"Go with the dinosaurs," I tell Noah.

"Uncle Noah, I'm waiting!" Stewart persists, banging his spoon obnoxiously on his plate.

Noah makes a disgruntled noise. He's not ready to budge.

"Hey, Stewart," I say, trying to deflect the attention from Noah. "Do you want to know what I'm grateful for?"

"Okay." He shrugs.

"I'm grateful for four-headed purple-eyed dragons!" I announce.

The children erupt in laughter and conversation. We begin whispering to one another.

"I just bought you some time," I say. "Be nice."

"I don't want to be nice," he tells me. "I want to be home."

"Everyone wants to be home," I answer, "but it's Thanksgiving, and Thanksgiving is all about being with your family and being miserable."

"Well then, we're doing it perfectly." He looks around disdainfully. "What are you grateful for?"

"Lots of things," I tell him. "Too many to mention."

"We've got the time," he says, waving at the chaos before us.

"Okay," I say. "Your family, my family, Mrs.

Middleton, Liam, Paul, and Guppy. Dinner at Il Mulino and breakfast at IHOP. Watching the stars and the butterflies. New York and New Jersey. Me and you. Lots of things."

He takes my hand from my lap and kisses it.

"What about you?" I ask. "What are you grateful for?"

"Let me think," he says. "Got it! Sex," he answers emphatically.

"Noah!" I scold.

"You asked!"

"Think of something else," I say.

"I can't," he tells me. "That's what I'm grateful for." He laughs.

"You're not grateful for me?"

"Of course," he says. "I'm grateful for sex with you!"

"Noah!"

"Uncle Noah, time to decide," Stewart announces, interrupting us.

I frown at Noah. He smirks.

"Go with the dinosaurs," I whisper.

"But I'm grateful for sex," he whispers back.

I sigh before taking his hand firmly in mine and guiding it under the table. I put it between my legs. He shifts in his chair.

"I'll go with the dinosaurs," he tells Stewart.

৯

It is late in the evening. Noah has retreated to his study to tend to some work he brought home from the office.

Mrs. Middleton is busy in the kitchen with the dinner dishes, and I'm feeling lonely.

My sisters are scattered, and my heart aches for my parents. I eye the beautiful sunset over the New York skyline through the balcony window and decide to step out. After grabbing a throw blanket from the back of the couch, I carefully slide the door open and slip out without a sound. The furniture has been taken in for the winter, so the balcony is empty.

With no place to sit, I go to the far wall and snuggle under the blanket against the brick wall. I study the pinkish-purple sky. It's majestic. Looking at the sky makes me pensive. I think back to what all those years of Catholic school taught me.

I know what is here, but I wonder what is there.

I reach inside my blouse and pull out the cross that I wear around my neck on a chain. I pull it off over my head and dangle it before my eyes in the divine sunlight. The reflections bounce and dance. I hope they reflect all the way to heaven. I whisper a couple of prayers.

Suddenly, the balcony door slides open. It's Noah. Surely, he's going to scold me for being out here.

He frowns. "Gabriella, it's freezing out here!"

"Not so bad," I protest.

He eyes the dangling cross. He walks across the balcony and joins me. I adjust and share the blanket with him. He reaches out and caresses the cross with one finger.

"Pretty. A gift?"

"Thank you. Yes. From my mom," I say.

"Are you praying?" he asks.

I nod.

"For?"

"Just blessings, I guess. Do you pray?" I ask, rehanging the chain around my neck and tucking it back under my blouse.

"No," he answers matter-of-factly. "I don't."

"Not so big on God?"

"Nope."

"Jesus?"

"No."

"Angels? I like angels," I tell him. "I believe in them. We all get to be one."

He smiles.

"So no faith at all?"

"Not really," he admits, "but I bet you have enough for both of us." Then he scoops me up in his arms and carries me into the apartment.

Later that night, Noah cradles me in his arms as I replay our earlier conversation in my head. We are almost asleep.

"Noah?" I ask quietly in the darkness.

"Mmm?"

"If you don't believe in anything, then what comforts you?"

At first, he doesn't respond, and I assume he has fallen asleep. But just when I have given up, he answers me.

"You do."

The next evening, Noah comes home with a small package. He meets me in the bedroom and joins me on the bed. The wrapping is aqua. It's from Tiffany's. I pick it up and begin to unwrap it. I can't even guess. He grins at me. I grin back at him, and I gasp when I see what is inside.

It's a tiny golden angel.

"I thought it might fit on your chain," he says.

I'm touched. "But you don't believe in them."

He shrugs. "When you live with one, sometimes your mind can be changed."

Chapter 30

"So you're angry?" he asks from across the room.

"Yes, Noah," I say, turning to face him. "I'm angry. I should be set free every once in a while!"

We were out with his family for his parents' anniversary. His sisters-in-law were particularly wound up, but he forbade me to go near them. He insisted I sit next to him with his hand firmly on my thigh all evening. I felt like a toddler in time-out.

Noah is mostly undressed but still wearing his trousers. His body is incredibly tan and muscular. A perfect six-pack lies beneath a chest full of black hair. He crosses the room gracefully.

I am in front of the mirror, removing my jewelry, dressed only in my bra and panties.

"Show me," he says, now beside me. I have no idea what he means. I have never seen him exactly like this before. He is standing confrontationally close, and he has a dark, intriguing look in his eye. He undoes the clip of my bra with only one hand. My breasts spring free.

"Show me, Gabriella. Show me how angry you are," he says almost without emotion.

I stare at him, trying to read his face, but he shows nothing.

"Show me how angry you are," he repeats.

"Stop!" I say, my eyes filling with tears of anger. "Stop making fun of me!"

"I am not making fun of you," he says in a sultry voice.

Then, with a force that belies his ultracalm demeanor, he grabs me by the arm and tosses me onto the bed. I look at him in shock as he crawls onto the bed to meet me.

"Show me how angry you are," he whispers, beginning to nuzzle my neck. I wriggle beneath him, trying to break free. I am angry and begin to fight.

"That a girl. Fight. Show me," he says in a low and seductive voice.

We have never played rough before. But I think I want to. I like this. He licks my neck. I wriggle beneath him. He adjusts so that his full weight has me pinned and helpless.

"Show me how angry you are, Gabriella," he croons in my ear.

I'm incredibly turned on. This is a new experience. He's sucking hard on my neck. I groan. I feel pleasure and pain. He growls. Then he rams three fingers into me. I arch. He laughs. He nibbles my earlobe. For a split second, one of my hands breaks free, and I use it to push on his shoulder, which allows me to move just slightly. However, my advantage lasts for only a second, because he's able to readjust his position so that he is even more in control.

"Show me," he says again, his lips grazing mine.

I fight with all of my strength. He presses his lips to mine and manages to open my mouth, exploring with his tongue. He kisses me roughly. He growls with satisfaction and then moves down to my breasts.

He bites. I gasp. This greatly pleases him. He then bites the other breast. I cry out again. He still has me pinned with his hips but momentarily lets go of my hands to rip the panties from my body and undo his trousers. He kicks his pants off and is naked on top of me. With his legs, he spreads mine, and with one quick thrust, he is inside of me. I am soaked, ready and willing. I don't fight anymore. He is relentless and plunges in and out until he comes inside of me. He collapses on top of me. I lie still beneath him. Exhausted, I wait as his breathing becomes regular. When it does, he slowly removes himself from me.

He leans sideways, balancing on one elbow, and faces me impassively. "Still angry?" he asks with a raised eyebrow.

I glare at him.

He furrows his brow and says, "I guess we'll have that occasionally."

Then he simply gets off the bed and heads for the shower.

It's late in the evening in early December. We're out to dinner in a secluded corner booth.

"Can I have …" I scan the drink menu.

"You can have anything you want anytime you want it," he says, taking my hand and looking into my eyes. "Anything anytime, Gabriella. You know that, don't you?"

I blush. We've never been more in love. Things have never been better between us.

"You're the most beautiful woman in the world," he says, softly caressing my hands.

I am getting tingles. I see the look in his eyes, and I know what always comes next.

"We're not staying for dinner, are we?" I ask, smiling.

He takes my hand and guides it under the table onto his crotch. He's rock hard.

"A small change of plans," he says with a grin.

"Feels like a large change of plans to me," I whisper back.

Soon after, we are barely in the limo, and he's already inside of me. As always, I'm wet for him.

"That's my girl. Come for me, baby," he growls in my ear.

By the time we arrive home, I have.

Liam drops us at the building's entrance. Noah holds my hand as we take a few steps toward the door. Just as we enter, a slight movement in the alley draws my attention. In the faint light, I can see that it is Simon. He's back. In a split second, we make eye contact.

He looks horrible: filthy and gaunt, as if he hasn't eaten in weeks. I think he might recognize me, because he raises his hand, as he did last time, and opens his mouth to say something, but thankfully, no sound comes out. Noah does not notice.

In the elevator, Simon's face haunts me. It must show.

"You okay?" Noah asks.

"Fine!" I say, perking up instantly. "Just perfect." I smile.

"I'm going to shower," he tells me as we enter the apartment.

"Okay. I'm going to grab a snack," I say as casually as I can.

Before we part, he grabs my hand and pulls me close. "My one and only," he whispers in my ear. He raises my chin and kisses me softly and deeply.

I wait in the kitchen until I hear the bathroom door click shut.

I know it's a huge risk, but I'm sure I can pull it off. I dive into the refrigerator and pull out three apples and just enough ham, cheese, and bread for three sandwiches. I make the sandwiches quickly. It takes at most two minutes. I think I have enough time. Noah more often than not lingers in the shower. I'll be downstairs and back before he's even out.

I go back to the fridge, grab a bottle of water, and get a brown bag from the pantry to toss it all in. I prop open the apartment door with a vase and slide out. My heart beats wildly in the elevator.

I can't let Simon go hungry. I do my best to sneak through the lobby without being noticed and slip out the front door.

When I reach the alley, I don't see him at first.

"Simon," I whisper. "It's me. Gabriella."

I hear a rustling and follow it. He has moved farther down the alley. It's darker. He's away from the light. I take a few hurried steps and end up tripping right into him.

I crouch down next to him. "I've brought you some food," I tell him. "I don't know if you remember me. I'm from upstairs."

"Gabriella," he says, and he reaches toward me.

The smell of alcohol is stifling, but I take his hand. "I can't stay," I explain quickly, holding out the bag of food. He snatches it. He smells like urine.

"Gabriella," he says again.

"I'm sorry, Simon, but I've got to go." I turn and dart back down the alley. I've just about reached the light, when I run smack into Noah. Our eyes meet. I've seen him angry before but never like this.

֍

"Over the bed," he orders.

I am already crying. "No, Noah, please!"

"Over the bed," he repeats coldly.

"Noah," I sob, reaching out to touch him. He pulls away. This kills me. I flinch. "Noah, I—"

"Over the bed!" he yells, grabbing me by the arm and tossing me.

I give up and lie across the bed, burying my face in a throw pillow. I can hear him undo his belt. He raises my dress and lowers my panties. I hold on tightly to the fringed edges of the pillow. I brace myself and hold my breath, but what I expect does not come. When I look up, he is gone from the room. The belt lies by the side of the bed.

Moments later, I hear the shattering of glass. I know for sure that he has poured himself a drink, taken a sip, and then thrown the glass against the wall. It now lies in pieces on the floor.

For the first time ever, Noah doesn't come to bed, and he is gone before I wake.

The next few days are excruciating. Each begins with a silent breakfast before he goes to work. At noon, he calls and speaks to Mrs. Middleton but not to me. This hurts. He returns by six, and we share another silent meal. We watch a minimal amount of television and then go to bed.

There we are together but separate.

I feel as if I have done something irreparable.

Finally, on the fourth day, Mrs. Middleton finds me on the balcony at noon.

"He called," she says softly. "He said to be ready and downstairs to go to his parents' at six."

I only nod.

༈

For the most part, we drive in silence. Finally, I dare to speak.

"Another birthday?" I ask timidly.

"Yes. Clara, Brent's third," he tells me.

When we arrive, he gets my door, as always. *Forever the gentleman.* He cups my hand in his. I would give anything for laced fingers, but it's better than nothing.

"Ready?" he asks on the doorstep before we enter.

I nod. His face looks worn and tired.

༄

We sleepwalk through the evening. We stay close to one another, making it through dinner, the cake, and presents. We're just about to leave, when Noah excuses himself to speak to one of his brothers about a work project.

I remain in the family room with the moms and the kids. After a while, I sneak off to the restroom. On my way back to the family room, I pass Noah's father's library. I catch a glimpse of Mr. and Mrs. Bentley sitting together. They are speaking quietly. I try to slip by unnoticed, but they see me.

"Gabriella," his mother calls.

I stop, backtrack, and peer in.

"Join us," she says.

I smile and go in. Mr. Bentley pulls up a chair for me. I sit and join them. Mr. Bentley pours me a drink.

"How are things?" Mrs. Bentley asks.

"It's been a tough few days," I admit.

"That's a tough man you're dealing with," his father says.

I nod in agreement and take a swallow of my drink.

"This is generally a difficult week for Noah. It's Lucey's birthday," she explains.

I think back to the child's drawing in Noah's desk—the crayon-drawn stick figures holding hands, labeled as Noah and Lucey, surrounded by hearts.

I must look confused.

"Noah has never mentioned Lucey," Mrs. Bentley says. "Has he?"

"He hasn't. I found a drawing once, but he wouldn't explain it," I say.

Mr. Bentley shakes his head.

"Lucey was our daughter. Noah's sister," Mrs. Bentley explains, nodding toward a large family photograph on the wood-paneled wall.

It is a family photo of the Bentleys, taken many years ago. The boys were all young. I search for Noah and find him. He's adorable, about nine or ten years old.

I recognize everyone in the photo except the little girl positioned on the floor, surrounded by the boys. She is amazingly cute with a bright smile and black hair like Noah's. She appears to be about four or five years old. I can tell by the photo that she was cherished.

"Lucey was our little princess," Mr. Bentley says.

"Everyone's little princess but especially Noah's," adds Mrs. Bentley.

"Those two certainly were unique," Mr. Bentley says. "He adored her, and she idolized him."

"What happened to Lucey?" I ask, not wanting to intrude but desperately wanting to know.

The Bentleys gently reach for each other's hand.

"It was an accident," Mrs. Bentley says. "We were vacationing at the lake. Lucey was only five. It was our fault completely. We had just arrived, and we were busy unpacking the car. The boys were running around and playing on the dock after being cooped up during the long ride. We'd said that they could play but needed to keep a watchful eye on Lucey too. Tom and I each thought the other had her. As it turns out, the only one who was truly watching Lucey was Noah. He was so protective of her, and she always minded him—except that day."

Mrs. Bentley's voice trails off, and Mr. Bentley picks up the story.

"The rest of the boys ran off to explore, and Noah was left alone with Lucey. Again, it was completely our fault, but apparently, Lucey accidentally let go of the balloon she had been holding. It flew away but got caught in a nearby tree. Well, Lucey began to cry, and Noah made her promise to sit on the dock and wait while he retrieved the balloon. He was gone for only minutes, but it was long enough for her to fall into the water. By the time he got back with the balloon, she was gone. Noah never forgave himself." Mr. Bentley dabs at his eyes with a tissue. "It changed him forever. No matter how we explained that it wasn't his fault, he continued to believe that it was. He refuses to talk about it."

My eyes fill. I don't know what to say. My head swims as all of the pieces of Noah's complicated puzzle fall into place. I feel as if my eyes are suddenly open, and I can now begin to understand him. All the fear, all the control issues, and his "Girls listen to boys" motto make sense now. My heart hurts.

"Here's our favorite photo of her," says Mr. Bentley, taking a single photo of Lucey from the wall and handing it to me.

I study her innocent face and caress the frame. How excruciatingly painful it must have been for all of them but especially for Noah. I look up to find Noah standing in the doorway. He frowns when he sees the photo in my hand.

"Ready?" he simply says.

I nod and hand the picture back to the Bentleys.

We're silent most of the way home. Noah's face is unreadable.

"Noah, I'm sorry about Lucey," I finally manage. He swallows and stares at the road.

"How much did they tell you?" he asks after a moment.

"I think all of it," I say. "Noah, it wasn't your fault. You were ten."

He flinches as if I have hurt him, so I stop. Instead, I hold my hand out for him to take. He does and laces his fingers in mine. We drive the rest of the way home in silence.

Later, I'm in the bathroom, dressed in only a T-shirt and panties. Noah enters. He leans against the sink and pulls me in front of him. Our eyes meet. His beg for understanding; mine assure him that I do. He pulls me closer. I wrap my arms around him and quietly weep into his chest. As I do, I feel his tears fall onto the top of my head.

Chapter 31

We spend the next few weeks rebuilding, falling back into our normal routine of breakfast together. I spend my days painting in my studio and texting him. He works and calls me between meetings before rushing home at six. We have fancy dinners out and quiet evenings at home.

In some ways, we are the same as always, but actually, we have never been better.

We make love more than ever, and we talk more than ever too. Noah is getting better all the time at sharing his feelings with me. Instead of bickering, we actually talk. As always, Noah is interested in what concerns me and listens attentively.

One day, at my insistence, we visit Lucey's grave. Noah hasn't been here since the day of Lucey's funeral. When I see the pained look on his face and the way he kneels pitifully at her headstone, clearing away the overgrown grass with his hands, I am not sure I have done the right thing. But when we are in the car, driving away, he quietly whispers, "Thank you," and I know that I have.

※

One evening, after dinner, Noah explains that a guy he works with will be stopping by for a couple of minutes, and then he retreats to his study. This surprises me. He never invites anyone to the apartment, especially not employees.

I'm watching the news, when Mrs. Middleton appears.

"He'd like to see you in his study," she says with a small smile.

When I enter, Noah is sitting behind his desk, and a man dressed in a blue custodial uniform is sitting in the chair in front of him.

Noah smiles easily when he sees me. "Gabriella," he says, "I believe you know this gentleman, my coworker."

The man turns to face me. He smiles shyly and offers his hand. "Hello, Gabriella," he says. His face is slightly familiar, but I can't place who he is or where I know him from. I shoot Noah a confused glance. His lack of proper etiquette is odd. Noah grins but still gives no clue.

Then, suddenly, I look back at the stranger and realize that he is no stranger at all. This is confirmed when I spy the embroidered name patch on his breast pocket. It is Simon from the alley. He is sober and clean-shaven, dressed in a Bentley Industries uniform. What has happened is clear to me. I look at Noah and want to hug him, but instead, I hug Simon, who blushes.

"I just wanted to stop by to thank you both. You, Mr. Bentley, and you, Gabriella," he says bashfully.

"No need for thanks," Noah says. "Bentley Industries always needs a good man like you, Simon, and you're welcome here anytime."

The three of us stand there, grinning happily.

"Well, I guess I better get to work then," Simon tells us.

Noah and I see Simon out together.

The moment the elevator door closes, I throw myself into his arms. "Best guy ever!" I exclaim, smothering him with kisses.

He laughs. "Everyone deserves second chances."

"I believe that," I say confidently.

"I'm glad you do," he says. "I'd hate to think where I'd be if you didn't."

෯

I guess you could call it a girl thing, but I don't like her the moment I set eyes on her. She is new. Eduardo, the maître d', introduces her to us, telling us it is her first day. Her name is Missy. She is bleached blonde and dressed in a tight black waitress uniform. The top three buttons of her blouse are undone.

Instantly, she begins fluttering around Noah. She is way too attentive, bouncing to and from the table a million times. Her breasts are bigger than mine and bounce along with her.

So far, she must have said "Mr. Bentley" thirty times. She is in waitress overdrive, and she's a horrendous flirt. I hate flirts.

It is the wrong night to press my buttons. Noah has been away much of the week. I've been lonely, and my period is due.

"You okay?" Noah asks.

"Tired," I lie.

"We'll eat and run."

"Won't help," I say, pouting.

"Mr. Bentley! We have new special!" Missy is back, having only left the table a moment ago.

I roll my eyes. Noah catches this and looks confused. Missy begins babbling about cod.

I refuse to give her my attention. Noah's look of interest annoys me.

"Sounds excellent," Noah says when she finally comes up for air. He looks at me expectantly and raises his eyebrows. "Cod?"

"No!" I answer as if it's a ridiculous suggestion.

"Okay then." He is being remarkably patient.

I try to think of the opposite of cod. The only thing I can come up with is steak. "Filet," I mutter.

Noah orders for me and then orders himself the cod. I call him a traitor in my mind.

"Great choice, Mr. Bentley!" Missy gushes. She leaves to go put our order in.

"Gabriella, what is wrong?" he asks when we finally have a second alone.

"Nothing." I sigh.

"Then sit up and behave," he says, now obviously losing his patience.

"More bread?" Missy is back and perkier than ever.

I glare at her. Noah follows my eyes, beginning to catch on. He frowns at me as Missy chatters in his ear about brioche, pumpernickel, and rye. He thanks her before turning his attention to me. She disappears.

"Gabriella, she's a waitress," he says.

Before he can continue, we are interrupted by an elderly couple who are old friends of Noah's parents, the Andersons. As the three of them chatter on, I spy Missy flitting around and giggling with her coworkers. It's not my imagination; she is keeping one eye on Noah. The conversation between Noah and the Andersons ceases because Missy appears behind them with our salads. The Andersons excuse themselves with rushed good-byes.

"Extra dressing for you, Mr. Bentley," she bubbles. To me, she says nothing.

Noah thanks her and asks for more butter. She trots off.

When he sees the scowl on my face, he closes his eyes momentarily, as if he's gathering his last bit of patience. "Gabriella, she is a waitress," he says emphatically, enunciating every word.

"I was a waitress," I say.

"There's a difference." He opens his mouth as if to tell me why, but this time, Eduardo interrupts, checking on us. Pleasantries are exchanged. Eduardo leaves.

Noah clears his throat. "There is a difference," he says quietly. "You—"

"Here we go!" Missy is back with our meals. She proclaims Noah's meal to be extra special, while she lays mine in front of me without comment.

Noah makes a noise. Even he is frustrated by now. Next come the water boy and business associates for small talk. We give up and eat in silence.

Finally, we are finished.

Noah folds his hands in front of him and frowns at me. He almost speaks but spies Missy approaching from the corner of his eye and stops. She is back with the dessert menu.

"Oh, Mr. Bentley, let me show you these great desserts we have!"

I feel as if he is being more patient with her than he ever is with me. Noah looks at the menus she's holding in front of her chest. I know she is doing this on purpose. She waves the paper excitedly, so he has no choice but to look squarely at her boobs. Then I notice something. She has undone another button on her blouse. Her boobs are practically flopping onto the table.

"This is my favorite," she insists. She reaches over and puts one hand on Noah's back, leaning into him so that her left breast is pressing into his shoulder.

"Not happening," I say to myself.

I don't plan what happens next, but she finally has pushed me too far. My only regret is that I'm not a half second faster. Noah, who is in tune with all things me, sees me grab my wineglass and catches my hand midthrow. He deflects most of the wine before it has a chance to land on her. Actually, most of it lands on him.

The next minute is kind of a blur. All I know is that I am suddenly out of the restaurant, and Noah has plopped me not-at-all gently in the passenger seat of the Mercedes. He comes around and, with a slam of the door, is in the driver's seat.

"Good God, Gabriella! What was that?" he thunders.

I say nothing. He runs his hands through his hair and leans back against the headrest with a thud. "I know you didn't like her, but God," he fumes.

I sit there mute and unapologetic.

"Speak!"

I say nothing.

As he's a man who avoids public displays at all costs, this is no doubt mortifying for Noah. I, on the other hand, am just wishing that I had better aim.

He lets out a long, hard sigh. He turns and faces me. He looks gorgeous in the moonlight.

"You may not," he says, enunciating every syllable, "no matter what you are feeling, throw your beverage on the waitress!"

On another day, this would have probably been rather funny, but not today.

I look back at him impassively.

His eyes widen. "Tell me you understand this," he demands.

I stay silent. I couldn't be in more trouble anyway.

"Gabriella," he warns.

Again, I say nothing.

He bites his lip. He is not used to this kind of resolve from me. "Words," he growls.

Defiantly, I let another moment or two pass. Then I only offer one word: "Mine."

Our eyes lock. We stay that way for a moment before he gets it. His face softens the slightest bit, and a trace of a smile crosses it.

He looks into my eyes and says quietly, "Yes, darling, I am yours."

Then he starts the car and takes me home.

※

The next morning, when I enter the kitchen, I find Mrs. Middleton busy, as usual, and Noah on the phone, pacing around his half-eaten breakfast.

"No. No, Eduardo. Don't be silly. Everything is fine. No, no need for that. Everything is all right. Please put the meal on my tab, and you will see us next weekend. No, really. No harm done. Everything is fine. Thank you for your call. Take care." Obviously, they are talking about last evening and my confrontation with the waitress, Missy.

He ends the phone call and closes his eyes, grimacing. When he opens them, he gives me a threatening look. Then he rolls up the newspaper he has been holding and taps me on the head playfully. "Lucky for you, I'm late for a meeting."

I giggle and pop up to kiss him on the cheek. He growls and is gone from the kitchen.

"My parents' at six!" he calls over his shoulder.
"Another birthday?"
"Yep!" he yells, and he is gone.

⚜

"Happy birthday, Son," Noah's father says at the door. He pulls Noah in for a hug.

It's not just another birthday—it's Noah's birthday. I feel awful. I had no idea. I frown at him as we join the party, which is already in progress. He takes my hand and gives it a squeeze.

"No big deal," he whispers.

"It is to me," I mutter.

His mother has made his favorite childhood meal, lasagna, for dinner. I wonder if she'll share the recipe. The cake is double chocolate.

Noah is not comfortable being the center of attention, even among his family. He tries hard to hide his dislike for it all but does a poor job. I'm sympathetic since his family does not seem to notice or care—I'm not sure which it is. But I feel bad for him as he sits surrounded by balloons while everyone sings.

In lieu of presents, the children shower him with crayon drawings of everything from hearts and flowers to dinosaurs and frogs. He comments about each picture, pointing out his favorite part. I love watching him with the kids. He's good with them.

As soon as an acceptable amount of time has passed, he says we need to leave, blaming an early morning meeting. I don't think anyone believes him.

Finally, in the car, he leans back against the headrest. "Done for another year!" he exclaims, relieved.

I laugh. "That bad?"

"You have no idea."

"You could have told me, you know."

"No worries," he says, and he drives us home.

Once at home, we sit on the floor of the great room, in front of the fireplace. He's in black sweats and a T-shirt and is barefoot. I'm bathed and in his favorite pink teddy.

"Birthday drink," he says, handing me a glass of raspberry liqueur.

"I wish I had something to give you," I say.

He caresses my cheek, drawing me in for a kiss. "I know something you can give me," he says.

"What's that?" I ask with a grin.

"You," he says softly, pulling a tiny black box from the pocket of his sweats.

I gasp.

Then he gets down on one knee and says, "Will you marry me, Gabriella? You would make me the happiest man on earth."

I nod but find no words as tears fall from my eyes. I couldn't love him more.

"You haven't answered me yet," he reminds me softly as I rise up on my knees to kiss him.

"Yes," I murmur, closing my eyes and kissing him. "Yes!"

After making love, we are on the floor, snuggling in front of the fireplace.

"When?" I ask him. I'm thinking that he will surely say next year sometime.

"Saturday," he says.

I turn and look at him, confused. "What Saturday?" I'm sure I have misunderstood him.

"This Saturday, the eighteenth."

"Noah, that's four days from now! We cannot plan a wedding in four days!"

"You can, and you will," he says.

"I don't understand. What's so special about the eighteenth?" I stop when I realize the significance. I grin at him. The eighteenth is exactly six months from the day I moved in with him. It is the day when I was supposed to decide whether I would stay or go.

Suddenly, it all seems perfect.

"The eighteenth it is," I tell him, smiling. He grins back.

Chapter 32

I can barely sleep. The next morning, I'm giddy and can't sit still at breakfast.

Mrs. Middleton gushes over my ring. Noah, who is across from me at the island and dressed for work, pretends to read his newspaper.

"How are we going to plan a wedding if you go to work?" I ask.

"We are not planning a wedding," he says. "You are."

I open my mouth to protest that I don't have a clue where to start, when the doorbell rings. I'm puzzled. No one ever rings the doorbell and certainly not at this early hour.

"That's for you," Noah says, rising. I follow him to the door, where I hear a commotion inside. I press the button. The elevator door slides open to reveal my five sisters. They tumble out squealing and screaming in delight before throwing themselves at me and demanding to see my ring.

Hugs and kisses are exchanged. Noah waits for a

pause, but when there is none, he finally calls, "Ladies!" to get their attention.

All five of them instantly stand at attention. He has four credit cards and a cell phone in his hands. He begins to pass them out.

He hands Mia a list and the phone. "The guests," he explains. She nods. He hands Gina a credit card and says, "You're on flowers." He assigns Teresa to music, and Maria is on food. Then, handing the last credit card to Angela, he simply says, "Whatnot."

They cheer. I laugh.

"Have fun," he tells me, leaning in for a kiss.

I'm speechless.

He smiles and picks up a suitcase that he has placed by the door. "See you Saturday," he says, "at the church."

He's moving out, and the girls are moving in. I throw my arms around him and laugh. "Best guy ever!" I say.

"Best girl ever," he whispers back.

෨

The next three days are an endless slumber party. We plan, plan, and plan. Thank God for Mrs. Middleton, who actually knows how to plan a wedding. She organizes us. It's amazing what one can accomplish with a limitless credit card carrying the name of Noah Bentley.

By Friday night, we are exhausted but ready. We are lying around the great room, having pizza and talking.

"Tell us, Gabby," Teresa says. "What's Knightly really like?"

I contemplate how to answer. I think of Noah. God, how I miss him. We've been inseparable for six months. Being apart feels odd.

"Noah is amazing," I tell them. "He's nothing like I ever expected, but he's everything I'll always need."

৩

"I miss you," I whisper into the phone late that night. I'm lying in bed.

"How much?" he asks quietly.

"Very, very much."

"Very, very, very much?" he says sexily.

"Very, very, very much."

"Just this once," he says softly, "touch yourself."

"Noah!" I scold, embarrassed.

"Lie back, baby," he instructs quietly.

"Noah," I say, objecting again.

He ignores me. "Lie back, and slide your panties off," he says in a low and sultry voice.

As always, I find myself doing as he says.

"Now spread your legs. A little wider."

He knows me. I comply.

"Close your eyes," he says.

I do this.

"Now find your bud," he instructs.

I feel myself flush but do what he says.

"Now rub," he tells me. "Nice and soft at first."

I begin to moan.

"That's it, honey," he says. "Now harder—and faster."

I'm beginning to lose myself.

"How does that feel, sweetie?" he croons.

"Good," I manage, gasping.

"Harder and faster," he orders.

I obey.

"Come for me, baby," he growls. "Come for me."

I rub harder and buck upward, moaning loudly.

"That's my girl."

I come to the sound of his voice.

୭

The next day, at exactly five o'clock, I begin slowly walking down the aisle of St. Patrick's Church as "Wedding March" plays. The church is adorned with dozens of white roses. It looks like a dream, but I know that it is all real.

I spy Noah waiting for me. He is breathtaking in his black tuxedo. He smiles encouragingly. I smile back.

Liam is standing to Noah's left. He is the best man. All of Noah's brothers stand next to Liam. On the other side, Angela is my maid of honor. My sisters are dressed in red and have formed a line.

Finally, I reach Noah and giggle as I take my place at the altar. As the priest begins, every magical moment of the last six months plays in my head.

When it is his turn, Noah looks directly into my eyes and says, "I do."

My eyes fill with tears as I listen closely to the words

of the priest. When it is my turn, I've never felt surer of anything in my whole life. Without hesitation, I say, "I do."

Noah grins and winks playfully. Then, just loudly enough for me to hear, he whispers, "Good girl."

Christina Frank

Good Girl

Christina Frank is a wife and mother of three living in Pittsburgh, Pennsylvania. She's been writing from a very young age, and she knows she's done it right when she makes herself laugh or cry.

Printed in the United States
By Bookmasters